Everybody Knows

Everybody Knows

David Wesley Williams

JackLeg Press
www.jacklegpress.org

ISBN: 978-1-7375134-6-9

Library of Congress Control Number: 2022936385

Cover design: Jennifer Harris and Jay Snodgrass

Cover photo: Clayton B. Fraser for the Historic American Engineering Record

Author photo: Barbara Williams

"Memphis After the War" is used with permission of the author, Adam Wesley Williams.

This is a work of fiction. The characters are made up. The story never happened. There are some real places rendered (Memphis, Nashville, and the state of Tennessee, such as), true facts referenced (tributaries of the Mississippi River, Bible verses and blues lyrics, the history of capital punishment in the aforementioned Tennessee, et al.), and actual people represented (Davy Crockett, Memphis Minnie, Sputnik Monroe, the like), but all in service of a story that is wholly the product of the author's fictive nature and worried mind. It's a cautionary tale, set in the future. The truth, whatever it may be, awaits around the bend.

For my wife, Barb, and our son, Adam
To Memphis

Contents

God Moves on the Water

They ate, they drank, they married, they were given in marriage, until the day when Noah entered the ark, and the flood came and destroyed them all.

—Luke 17:27

I would go to the hill country
but they got me barred

—Charley Patton
"High Water Everywhere, Part 1"

1

She sat on the top step of the porch, watching the rain.

He stood in the doorway, watching her.

"It's not the end of the world," he said.

It was dusk on a Sunday, some ten years after the year the world didn't end. It was early that summer in a town called Lower Grace, in the west of Tennessee, in the great nation under God, and under water—or up in flames, all depending. No cranny of the country was safe, no crook or bend. The West was burning up. In the Midwest there were dust storms like something out of Deuteronomy. Elsewhere were tornadoes and hurricanes and epic electrical storms; government weather radar, just before it went down, recorded a single lightning bolt that stretched from Kennebunkport, Maine, to Paducah, Kentucky. There were sinkholes, spontaneous combustions, plagues of insects—winged fuckers the size of Piper Comanches.[1] Washington was beset by swamp creatures, no shit. ("Is it news when it was always inevitable?" a wag wrote in the final edition of *The Washington Post*.) No aliens, though; *Somebody beat us to it*, their absence seemed to suggest.

The rain was almost quaint, in comparison, if only there wasn't so goddamned much of it. It played mad rags on the roof of the little country house, and the wind moaned low like a chorus of mourners who had lost faith in hymns. Sounded like murder ballads out there now: "Henry Lee," aka "Love Henry," aka "Young Hunting," and another dark little number sometimes called "The Coldwater Girl," the women giving as good as they got:

From the bridge my love, I did shove
But not before I kissed him

---

[1]The plane Patsy Cline died in—a single-engine Piper PA-24 Comanche that went down in the West Tennessee woods on March 5, 1963. Inclement weather, inexperienced pilot, and the old lament: if only they'd stayed put.

It's been ten year, and nary a tear
I've yet to meet the one who's missed him

And then the one about the dreadful wind and rain, crying *Oh, the dreadful*, and the sky—Christ, the sky. It might have been a bolt of fabric from a factory where 1930s prison garb was made.

"I think the end of the world's been called on account of rain," she said.

They said no more for the longest time, her watching the rain and drinking what was left of the gin, and then switching to what there was of rum, and him watching for some hint or sign, from her or from above.

He still believed in heaven. She didn't even believe in Chattanooga.

2

This is a story of rain and more rain, high water and the search for higher ground—Beulah Land, or that bluff in Memphis. God is high up in heaven, watching, with silver flask and furrowed brow.

This is the blues, played on a single strand of broom wire, with the world about to end.

This happened, just not yet.

3

It had rained for weeks, first as a few plump drops and then as a steady drench. Then it almost stopped and the sun almost shone, but only almost. Then came the rain again. For a full week it fell. From great oaken buckets it sloshed.

And then the rain did stop, as if in its muddy tracks. For a full minute it did cease.

"Finally," he said. "I think it's run out of ways to fall."

She said, "Just wait," and watched with a kind of wearied bemusement as it rained a hail of bullets across the land. She might have been using her drink stirrer as a baton, the conductor of all this doom.

This lasted all of one day and the night that followed—not that day was distinguishable from night, these days.

Then it was one endless drop. It spanned town blocks and country miles and days of the week.

The rain became time, place, law, religion, and the arts.

The rain was myth and legend and tomorrow's headlines wrung from the morning rag out of Memphis.

The rain was all. There was only rain.

Then the wind joined in. Oh, the dreadful wind and rain.[2]

She sat watching it, and he stood watching her.

"You're going to catch your death out here," he said, "or else get religion."

"*Religion.*" She said the word like it was sure enough something you might catch, come at you in droplets you couldn't even see, make you dog-sick, can't breathe, can't breathe, like with that death virus, back in the year the world didn't end. Then she said, "You really think anything happens when we die, husband, but there's one less soul in the world, and what's one less soul, more or less?" She leaned back against the front-porch beam. She sighed. She was thinking. She said,

---

[2]From "Wind and Rain," a traditional murder ballad involving two sisters and one suitor; you do the math. A love song, then, leavened with death. Amid a stretch of foul weather, the story plays out: One sister drowns the other. When the latter washes ashore, a fiddler comes along and makes a fiddle from her bones, stringing it with her long, golden hair. And the only song the fiddle will play? The one about the dreadful wind and rain.

"Well, I guess there must have been a couple, three in there somewhere who made a difference."

The year the world didn't end had only made her more caustic; it seemed to her the only sane response to those times, first to the virus, and then to that killing of a Black man by a white cop, on video for all to see, a knee to the neck, can't breathe, can't breathe—it was the Year of Can't Breathe, in more flipping ways than one—and the protests that followed, and the riots, too, and the police with tear gas and rubber bullets (what, no fire hoses? no dogs?), and cities in flames. Still, the world didn't end. The country survived it all, and itself, some kind of way. It toddled along a few more years, making changes but coming no nearer the root causes than ever, mostly talking to itself about change until it was black in the face, telling itself everything was fine, we're fine, aren't we fine, sure we're fine, define fine—until God or global warming, or something, brought down twenty-three kinds of proper hell upon the place, fire to the West, dust to Middle America, and to the South, rain. So much rain. Rain in buckets and flumes.

For that, good people, is how floods are made.

"All right, then," she said. "I'll give you old Abe Lincoln, Cool Papa Bell, and bawdy Ma Rainey. Don't say I never gave you anything, Mr. Flood."

He smiled. He could not help himself. He was a believer, and not just in the usual sense. He believed in God *and* man, believed in the eternal grace of the One and the essential goodness of the other. He believed the Creator had a purpose, or else … why? (Any number of reasons, she'd tell him. Lost a bet. Went on a bender. Just ornery that way.) He believed in reason and purpose. He believed in deep blues and old verities. He believed words could change the world, art could animate a nation, and that man, with his stout heart and his opposable thumbs and his head hard as hickory, would not just endure but, as a great man[3] put it, prevail. He believed all this in his bones and soul, and he also believed in her. It wasn't just love, but love was the better part of it.

"Did you hear yourself?" he said. "You said one less soul, not one less person. There's hope for you yet, Mrs. Flood."

Still, though, there was no hint or sign that he could see, except the rum was gone and it was Tennessee whiskey now, chased with the lightest rain. Too soft to even call it falling, a veil upon the land.

But rain is rain, and so the land sank further into itself.

The land swallowed deep and the river body rose.

The riverbanks swelled and the river god crept closer.

HAZARDOUS WEATHER OUTLOOK.

NATIONAL WEATHER SERVICE, MEMPHIS, TN

11:01 AM CDT SUNDAY JUL 16

THIS HAZARDOUS WEATHER OUTLOOK IS FOR ALL OF WEST TENNESSEE … NORTH MISSISSIPPI … EAST ARKANSAS … MISSOURI BOOTHEEL.

DAY THIRTY-NINE … TODAY AND TONIGHT.

THUNDERSTORMS OF GOTHIC INTENSITY ACROSS THE MIDSOUTH.

GOOD PEOPLE ARE ADVISED TO HUNKER DOWN. DRINK UP, THE REST OF ALL Y'ALL.

---

[3]William Faulkner's Nobel Prize speech, given in Stockholm in 1950, which in less time than it took Chuck Berry to get through "My Ding-A-Ling," inexplicably his only No. 1 single on the Billboard Hot 100 charts, the Bard of Yoknapatawpha County captured and encapsulated what it means to be human, in all its folly and fortitude. Also, the only major address in the annals of oratory to use the word "dingdong."

He sat beside her on the top step of the porch. She had a fresh whiskey. She was barefoot, with toenails painted blue the shade of dark in the usual way.

He ran a finger along the barbed wire-shaped scar on her left knee, the scar the color of midnight against her skin the color of dusk. It was her lucky scar, she said. She said she'd gotten it falling from the sky during a dream. He said that didn't sound very lucky, and she said there were all kinds of luck. She said you could hang from luck. You could drown in it.

"Anyway, it happened," she'd said.

Or anyway, that's the story she told him that night, the night they met, on the bluff in Memphis. Three days later, they were married.

Three years next month, he thought now, *river god willing and the world don't end.*

4

He tried the crank radio, a pirate station out of Memphis. Static and guitar scratch, the straggling notes of a song about home. The DJ came on and said, "We got reports of flooding from Paris and Brownsville, from Bunk and Christfallen. They say Nashville's been swallowed up whole, drunk down, poor dear. Governor Flattery, he made it out, but only just. Said to be ensconced on the steamer *Clementine,* headed west here to Memphis Town, for to establish a new capitol, high up on our bluff. Well, well. Come on if you're coming, Guv."

The DJ laughed. It was a hell of a thing to hear, that laugh, like a hoot with reverb. He may have been half lit. He seemed to be enjoying all this tumult of the world finally ending.

"They say the governor's accompanied by his wife, six mistresses, spiritual adviser, personal physician, other assorted quacks, and a whole cadre of country singers. A whole cadre, they say!" He said it to rhyme with tawdry.

The DJ then said he had a dispatch from the governor himself, on gold-leaf parchment, delivered just minutes ago, by carrier crow. But he did not read it. Instead there was a crumpling noise, and then the sound of needle to shellac, like a ghost hissing.

"It's only music can save us now," he said. "Only music."

He played a song by the old, dead bluesman Jaybird Coleman[4] and another by a band of Memphis punks who called themselves the Porch Ghouls. The one performer was of a religious bent, or at least he was for the three minutes and eight seconds of that particular record, and the others had in gospel fervor what they lacked in God-fearing reverence. Both selections were river songs. The DJ said he had a blue million of them, and nothing but time, time.

The DJ played songs about the Mississippi and its many tributaries, such as the Hatchie and the Big Black and the Wolf. He spoke knowingly of these bodies of water. He said there was a section of the Wolf called the Ghost, and it flowed the color of golden ale and teemed with tipsy catfish. He said it was hard to find and nigh on impossible to leave. Again he laughed; more hoot, more reverb.

He said Hatchie was an Indian word for river, and so Hatchie River, as a name, was redundant but nonetheless pleasing on the tongue, and anyway, he added, there was precedent for such nomenclature, citing the *cancan*. He said the Hatchie River danced but not the *cancan*. He said the Hatchie was a slow dance set to a languid music, and then he

---

[4]Alabama bluesman Burl C. "Jaybird" Coleman, born in 1896, was a veteran of the U.S. Army and toured with the Rabbit Foot Minstrels. He cut such classic sides as "I'm Gonna Cross the River of Jordan Some O' These Days" and "Ah'm Sick and Tired of Tellin' You (to Wiggle That Thing)." It's said that his career was managed, for a time, by the Ku Klux Klan.

played another song, a slow one, languid, called "Steamboat Gwine 'Round De Bend," an instrumental for solo guitar and bedsprings.

The last chiming notes of the song drifted and disappeared, as a river might, around the bend. That slow vanish, time in liquid form. Then the DJ came on again. He said he'd gotten a request, "from upstairs." He did not say whether it had come by way of carrier dove, or rather if a spirit's voice, perhaps that of the Holy Ghost itself, had cooed in his ear; all the phone lines, at any rate, were down. Digital communication, too, was useless; it had been the first to go.

5

This is a Southern Gothic, mock-apocalyptic, shrunken-epic satire of politics, race, religion, sex, climate change, literature and the creative process, technology and the news cycle, country music, the blues, crime, capital punishment, and the proud American predilection for violence, set at flood stage.

This is written by a dying, old writer, who was created by God, who was created by the author, who will need all the nerve he can tap or muster to pull the thing off.

This is a true story, made up and written down. This is a fable, a folk song, a murder ballad in which the women give as good as they get. This is a prayer, a prophecy, a cry, a crank call to arms, a cautionary tale, and the worst weather report ever was.

File under *Picaresque.*

File under *Current Events,* subsection *Speculative.*

File under *Spirits,* between the bourbon and the rye.

6

The Honorable H. Walt Flattery III, fifty-first governor of Tennessee, settled into the chair as his cabinet members and aides stood by watching. This was on the top deck of the steamer *Clementine*, on the third day out of Nashville, fallen capital, in the time of the last great Southern flood. The great ship was making west for Memphis, last city standing, in an uncertain meander under a daguerreotype sky.

The governor, known to friends and voters alike as Trey, raised and lowered one nether cheek and then the other. He stretched his arms down the length of the arm rests, gripping the ends, his fingernails testing the strength of the wood. He thought of Christ on the cross and Casey at the bat, of holy moments and greatest hits. He thought of his own place in history, and something his best friend and chief of staff said, or maybe it was a Nashville weatherman: *In the future there will be no history. Hell, there won't even be a future.*

He thought perhaps he ought to carve his initials into the wood. Or rather, have them carved. Was there a sub-cabinet member under whose purview this would fall? Was there a state calligrapher? Maybe some old Pigeon Forge whittler had snuck aboard and could be pressed into service. Even the governor had to make do, when the world was ending and Memphis was the state's last hope.

Memphis. The Bluff City. *Fucking Memphis,* they all said. Scourge of the late state of Tennessee. A town where conventioneers drank beer straight from troughs on Beale Street and screwed woman not their wives in fleabag rooms paid for by the quarter-hour. A town where the locals gorged themselves on pig meat and built shrines to false idols, as the devil sat smiling on the wraparound porch of his great mansion on the bluff, pleased at what he'd wrought with so very little of his own labor. This is what they all said about Memphis. *Fucking Memphis.*

The governor relaxed his hands, let his arms go slack. He rocked back and forward and back again. He stomped his feet against the three-foot-high, white-painted, wooden platform on which the chair sat. And spirited stomping it was, for a seriously dressed man of presidential ambition, falling somewhere between a martial beat and a child's tantrum.

For the governor was a simple man but a complicated boy.

He thought nothing, not even the end of the world, could stop his destiny.

Hell, he thought there was still a country to be president of.

HAZARDOUS WEATHER OUTLOOK
NATIONAL WEATHER SERVICE, NASHVILLE, TN
11:01 AM CDT THURSDAY JUL 13[5]

THIS HAZARDOUS WEATHER OUTLOOK IS FOR ALL OF MIDDLE TENNESSEE AND WELL INTO THE WESTERN PART OF THE STATE ... PARTS OF MISSISSIPPI AND ARKANSAS. YOU TOO, KENTUCKY.

DAY THIRTY-SIX ... TODAY AND TONIGHT, TOMORROW AND THE NEXT.

THUNDERSTORMS OF BIBLICAL SCOPE ACROSS THE MIDSTATE REGION. SEEK SHELTER. TARRY NOT. HIE THEE TO HIGHER GROUND, YOU PIOUS FUCKERS.

The governor settled himself with a deep, contented sigh. He crossed and re-crossed his long legs, smiled faintly at the foreboding sky, and then reached for and was handed his

[5]The birthdate, in 1821, of Confederate general Nathan Bedford Forrest, the so-called Wizard of the Saddle—also of the Ku Klux Klan. Every July 13 is Nathan Bedford Forrest Day in Tennessee.

drink, a Boulevardier[6] in a whiskey glass borrowed from the Oak Bar of The Hermitage Hotel in Nashville.

He took a swig. He licked his lips. He said *Ahh.*

Now he gazed out from the chair, finding the vantage, elevated as it was, not altogether unlike that of a throne.

The governor had wanted a throne, if only just for the hell of it. But this was Old Smokey, the state's old, mothballed electric chair, instead. It had been among the treasures of Tennessee rescued by the governor's aides and staff from Nashville's museums, music temples, and government buildings in the final hours before fleeing the capital.

The steamer *Clementine* was filled, fairly to bursting, with historical splendors, artifacts, and oddities. From the state museum there was a musket belonging to Daniel Boone, a powder horn of Davy Crockett's, and a beaver-hair top hat of Andrew Jackson's, as well as a thirty-five hundred-year-old Egyptian mummy, donated to the state in 1859 and now draped in the coat from country great Hank Snow's "Golden Rocket" Nudie suit.

The suit coat was among a raft of items the governor's aides and staff liberated from the exhibition galleries and storage rooms of the Country Music Hall of Fame and Museum. They carted away instruments by the crates—guitars, mandolins, fiddles, harmonicas, accordions, autoharps, and a five-string banjo on which Uncle Dave Macon played the likes of "The Bible's True" and "Keep My Skillet Good and Greasy."

They gathered the hand-written lyric sheets and ashtrays, the hymnals and decanters, of famous country stars. Pistols and lariats and snakeskin boots. Toupees and pomade tins and coal-dust mascara in old plastic tubes. Cane fishing poles and a cow skull painted Tennessee Volunteers orange and a Sparks-Withington refrigerator, shot full of holes,

---

[6]The governor's favorite cocktail. The ingredients of a Boulevardier, as follows: Campari, sweet vermouth, bourbon, and airs.

purportedly by Hank Williams, after being sacked by the Grand Ole Opry.

And more … Jimmie Rodgers' typewriter, an Underwood #5. The steer horns off Webb Pierce's 1962 Pontiac Bonneville. Any number of bar napkins on which were written the choruses of classic country songs. There was even a rumor, unsubstantiated, of a Jack Daniel's Old No. 7 bottle containing Nathan Bedford Forrest's brain.

As to clothes, they carried what they could and wore more, in layers—Lester Flatt's string tie over one of Patsy Cline's cowgirl dresses, over the black pants Marty Robbins sported on the cover of his "Gunfighter Ballads and Trail Songs" LP. They wore ten-gallon hats, stacked ten high. They sang as they ran in the rain, blue yodels and back-holler rave-ups, beer-joint weepers and novelty numbers. You would not have thought it was God they were fleeing, by the fun they were having. You would have thought the world ended every third Thursday.

From the bars and saloons of nearby Lower Broadway, from Tootsie's Orchid Lounge and the Teardrop Room and Club Rooty-Toot, they commandeered beer and whiskey enough to float the steamer *Clementine*. And from the nearby Ryman Auditorium, "Mother Church of Country Music" and long-time home of the Grand Ole Opry, came church pews.

One of the last items taken from the city, and that which caused the greatest debate among the governor's aides and staff, was Old Smokey. It was part of a temporary exhibit at the capitol, on the history of criminal justice in the state. It was the prize of the exhibition, and a particular favorite of school children on field trips. They asked endless questions about it. They wanted to know how many prisoners had died in it, and did their hair stand up on end, did their ears puff smoke? Were sparks let off and could they be seen from space, from heaven? What did God think of state-sponsored murder by electric chair, and could He grant the condemned a stay, or was it only Governor Flattery? Did executed men pee their pants? Could you hear radio broadcasts coming from the gold fillings in their teeth? Had they ever executed a woman? A dog?

"We might have use for it," said the chief of staff, with a covetous eye and a practical tone. Or perhaps it was the eye that was practical and the tone covetous, for next he said: "Floods bring out lawlessness, you know, and Memphis, poor old shine, is that way in the best of weather."

The chief of staff was a short, stocky, mutt-faced man named Bate. He was the governor's oldest friend, dating to the dusty gentility of childhood in Belle Meade, outside of Nashville. Bate's father worked for Trey's father (handled things, the better way to say it) and when Bate's father was sent up for some vague malfeasance (took a fall for Trey's father, the better way to say it), young Bate moved in with the Flatterys. The boys became inseparable. They played baseball and egged houses, drank beer and chased girls together—all pursuits for which Trey, long and lithe even as a boy, had the superior skills. Trey was the star pitcher of every baseball team he played on, and Bate, for as many years as he could make the team, was the catcher. One stood on the mound as if it were Lookout Mountain, gazing down on the world like some young hung god in cotton; the other crouched behind the plate, got up in what were called the "tools of ignorance."

It was said about Trey that he could have been a star of the major leagues, if he had less ambition. It was said about Bate that he could crouch standing up. And yet: It's the catcher who decides what the pitcher throws next. For that, they had an elaborate series of signals worked out between them, though Bate mostly only called for the fastball. The signal for it, a stubby middle finger. The joke was so far inside that Trey wasn't in on it. He threw so many fastballs as a youth, when his body was still growing and forming, becoming itself, that by sophomore year of college his right arm was shot, a diner hash of muscle and tendon. He was finished as a baseball star. It only made him that much more heroic.

College was Vanderbilt, and there they excelled beyond their wildest—Bate, at foment and duplicity; Trey, at chasing and being chased by girls. Junior year, while Trey was busy banging the chancellor's daughter, a private-school sophomore and prep state champion at eight hundred meters, Bate privately led a two-day takeover of the psychology building without ever telling either side, student protesters or administration, the motive for the act; it was as much performance art as political act. It ended, on the morning of the third day, amid vague intimations of a suitcase bomb somewhere in Wilson Hall, when the chancellor, dressed, as instructed, in the costume of the VU mascot Mr. Commodore, delivered to the front stoop of the psychology building a city-ham-and-two-eggs breakfast platter from the Loveless Café. Practical joke, psychological ploy, political gambit? More or less. Diversionary cover for Trey and the chancellor's middle-distance daughter to fuck in peace? That, too. For Bate operated on many levels, was a master of both the short con and the long game; and Trey, like the devil, was a leg man. When they were graduated (Bate, with honors he pretended to dismiss; Trey, to raised eyebrows he returned with a wink), it was said that the governor ought to keep close watch on his office, and his marathon-running wife. (It was too late already on the latter count.)

But politics was long game, not short con, and so first it was business (timber, shipping, printing, music publishing), and only then, with fresh fortunes stacked atop family money, with power tucked in every crease and influence in every crevice, did Bate set Trey's eyes on the henhouse—that is to say, the governor's mansion. By now, the clout was all Bate's. Alas, he had neither the grace nor face of the front man, and so, still—still and always—it was handsome Trey Flattery in the fore and mutt-faced Bate in the shadows, the power behind the throne.

Or electric chair, as it were.

Trey and Bate. Bate and Trey.

It was said that one was the most powerful man in the state, and the other was governor. That when you voted for the one what you really got was the other. That one was handsome and mostly benign, ambitious, was all, and the other had compromising pictures of the devil in church, diddling some rosary beads.

One other thing about all that: It was entirely coincidental, and deliciously so, that the nickname given Trey in the bedroom should so perfectly fit the two-headed political animal the best friends became. More from the bedroom later. For now, let's just say: Bate and Switch.

7

"You there," Bate said now. "See that it's done."

He was speaking to Meems, the deputy director of communications. He would not have called him by his name had he even known it. There were cabinet officials Bate would refer to as *you there*.

"Sir?" said Meems, who was barely more than a boy, by the look of him.

"The chair, son. Bring the bloody goddamned chair."

Meems was aghast, and not a little spooked, at the sight of Old Smokey. But then, Meems was frequently aghast and often spooked. Politics had not been what he expected when he was hired on in the communications office, out of a little Bible college in East Tennessee. Meems had lived a sheltered life. A mama's boy and only child, his best friend growing up had been a one-eyed tree squirrel he named "I'll Fly Away,"[7] after his favorite gospel song.

---

[7]From the pen of songwriting great Albert E. Brumley ("Rank Strangers to Me," "Turn Your Radio On"), who was influenced in the writing of said number by a prison lament called "The Prisoner's

The boy Meems grew up believing, if it can be believed, in the essential goodness of man. He believed in prudence over expedience, sagacity over connivance. He believed that God's ways were not so mysterious, really, if your faith be hard and true and up to any test. So he reported for work that first day expecting to hear in the halls of the capitol something like the soft pluck of harp strings, the gentle beat of philosophical debate—"Athens of the South," and all—but it was more like a rude blast of horns, keeping time with the heavy clang of coin.

Schemers. Connivers. Money-changers on the capitol steps. It was all a little much for Meems, who quickly began to lose his faith in man. But, alas, not in God, to whom he prayed harder than ever. He prayed for courage. He prayed for pluck. He prayed for gumption. And God, in His goodness, or His love of the underdog, called for His golden eyedropper and did grant the boy a little of each—or anyway, Meems found them, in himself. And kept them to himself, mostly. For all outward signs suggested Meems was, as ever, the scared boy who arrived that first day out of Bitter End, in Carter County, in northeastern Tennessee. It's why he was kept on, and promoted, from intern to gopher, from gopher to minion, finally from minion to deputy director of communications. But if Meems was blossoming, the boy was wisely keeping it to himself.

Now, though, he spoke up. It took them all by surprise. The audience was his, then, if only because an audience will always gather to see how a fellow human might fall.

He cleared his throat. He took a deep breath. He told himself he was a school boy again, about to deliver an oral report on the subject at hand; it might have been the evolution

---

Song," which provides the wings/human flight idea. In Brumley's version, the singer dreams of having wings like a bird and flying from the prison that is the world on up to heaven. In "The Prisoner's Song," most famously performed by Vernon Dalhart, the singer envisions angel wings, but has a more earthly destination: back in the arms of his darlin'. Recidivism, that's called.

of farm implements in Tennessee, or the Alvin York story. A voracious learner, Meems knew the details of both of these subjects—and of the history of capital punishment in his state. He told it now. He began, steadily enough, though it took all of his physical strength.

Meems said Old Smokey had been built about 1915, using wood from the old state gallows. He told of all the state-sanctioned killing that followed over the next forty-five odd years, some hundred and twenty-five condemned souls put to their deaths. He told of wrongful executions, and here his voice began to falter.

The boy deputy paused now, to draw on his reserves of courage, pluck, and gumption. He breathed deeply. He thought of his mother in Bitter End, and God in heaven. He continued, again steadily enough. He told of how the killing stopped in 1960, but started up again in 2000. He told of Old Smokey being retired and replaced, in 1989, by a new chair, using wood from the old. He said this new chair was still available, for those sentenced before Jan. 1, 1999, but that the state now preferred to carry out executions by—

"Talk them to death now, do we?" said Chief of Staff Bate.

The boy deputy Meems went silent. He became, again and as always, invisible to the others. So they took no notice of the boy's blushing face, the hint there of a grin. For he had stood up, however briefly, to the most powerful man in the state. It was a start.

There was now some further discussion on the subject—the commissioner of correction, a tall, thin, and earnest man with the unfortunate name of Lynch, wondered whether the taking of the electric chair onto the steamer *Clementine* might constitute a more or less official return of Old Smokey to its former role and purpose. Was it, he wondered aloud, a policy statement? There was now, after all, a condemned man on death row, a convicted murderer named

Cheatham. He did not qualify for the chair but was insisting on it, if die he must. He was suing for the right.

Lynch considered lethal injection to be a more humane means for the state to murder its most heinous actors, until such time as there was a safe, effective pill they could take, or perhaps in the far future some sort of beam or ray could be shot into the condemned man's brain, with hardly any pain inflicted at all, just a little smarting. Not that Commissioner of Correction Lynch was squeamish, or soft on crime, or, in the parlance of man, "a pussy." He favored capital punishment and wanted more of it. He believed in its qualities of deterrence, and he also believed, yes, a little, in the culling effect. He was, in all ways, a *true believer*; he thought it a solemn thing, capital punishment, and abhorred any suggestion of spectacle. God and the good citizens of Tennessee were watching.

Lynch felt that for the Volunteer State populace to be fully comfortable with state-sanctioned murder, for the state to be seen by the rest of the union as a shining example, it must shed the act's most gruesome aspects. He secretly commissioned studies and surveys that told him what he suspected—that for all the public support of capital punishment, for all the thirst for blood and hunger for vengeance, there was a nagging good in man, a sort of secret shame, almost, that could not fully reconcile strapping a prisoner into a chair and shooting him full of seventeen hundred and fifty volts at seven amps. To say nothing of the risks, with such a contraption, and at such voltage and amperage, of unforeseen electrical mayhem. If you were killing a man, and you needed someone standing by with a fire extinguisher, something was afoul with the entire enterprise. The state's drug cocktail was little better, for there was a chance it would not work, quite, that it might leave the prisoner just shy of expired. Surely it was cruel and unusual punishment to have to kill a man twice just to get the job done once—or inefficient, at any rate.

Lynch wanted the citizenry to awake the morning after an execution knowing justice had been swift and compassionate, making the state worthy of God's blessing, the union's envy, and perhaps a Nobel Prize, if someday they gave one for that sort of thing. Condemned men and women—there were women on death row, too—might even prefer it to life in prison.

"Why, there might be volunteers!" he fairly exclaimed.

This last statement held some promise for others in the group, but as for the rest of what all Lynch was saying—what in hell was it, exactly, the man wanted?

It was this head-scratcher: more dying but less killing.

8

The party now looked to the senior counsel. He was a little, old, country lawyer named Bills, who had practiced his particular style of *awshucksterism* all the way to the U.S. Supreme Court. He was known for his rural genius and folksy mannerisms—a trick leg, a one-shoulder shrug. He favored, some would say perfected, that most Southern phrase, "I might could." He said it so often, and at such crucial moments, the joke was that he used it with the parson on his wedding day, when the parson asked, "Do you, Cecil Robert Bills, take this woman ..."

"Well," the senior counsel said now, "I might could argue Ol' Smoke there's just like the proverbial manger on a city hall lawn at Christmas. Historical object, is all. Display purposes only. An artistic representation, you might could say, of state history. It could be a carving of the state bird or Johnny Majors[8], but it's, just coincidentally, of course, Ol' Smoke."

---

[8]Football hero hailing from Lynchburg, a one-traffic light town in a dry county in the south-central section of Tennessee. Best known as the home of the Jack Daniel Distillery. About the town's name,

"Our manger, huh," said Bate, who always did enjoy how Bills could make the most inflammatory sentiment sound like a breakfast order at Cracker Barrel.

The senior counsel continued thus: "Why, we could park a 1934 DeSoto Airflow coupe on the front lawn of the governor's mansion and it wouldn't mean we advocate"—he stretched that last word a country mile, took it for a good, long Sunday ride—"that everybody"—he pronounced it *everbody*—"should go back to driving cars the size of New England whaling ships."

He paused, then added, "That, gentlemen, would be my legal advisement on the matter here before us."

Now he bowed his head ever so slightly, and then took a step back on his trick knee, rose and shrugged his right shoulder. Just watching him, you wanted to bust out a chorus of "Dixie." That's how he'd risen to the height of his noble profession, and so charmed SCOTUS, which had swallowed like Jack and Cokes his argument for states' rights. (Even the dissenting opinion stated, "Protestations to his dubious legal arguments aside, didn't you just want to hug the little fellow and take him home with you?")

"As to your personal views on the matter, Senior Counsel?" said Chief of Staff Bate, knowing the answer.

"Why, you know me, Mr. Bate. My personal views are limited to brand of whiskey and choice of fishing hole. As regards the law"—the word had four a's and three w's, coming out of his churn of a mouth—"why, I might could argue either side." Here a grin. "But I do tend to favor the state's view in such matters."

---

there are several theories. One has it that the place was named for a Judge Lynch, while the 1939 guide to Tennessee produced by the Federal Writers' Project of the Works Progress Administration submits: "Lynchburg was named for a frail little man, Tom Lynch, who was always chosen to wield the lash on men sentenced to be whipped. The tree used as a WHIPPING POST still stands in the center of town."

"The buttered side of the bread, Senior Counsel?"

"Why, *sho*. And you, Chief of Staff?"

Bate had strong opinions on this matter, as on most. In this, his views were quite the opposite of Commissioner of Correction Lynch's. He thought executions should be excruciating in their infliction of pain. He thought they should be public, too, and possibly televised, perhaps on a pay-per-view basis. Better yet, free, for the maximum possible audience. It wasn't so much an issue of deterrence as simple vengeance. The bread-and-circus aspect appealed, as well.

Bate believed capital punishment, in time, could become bigger for Tennessee than country music, and far less whiny. God's feelings did not come into it; he didn't think God's opinion mattered a fiddler's damn, if indeed the Old Coot existed. As for death row's next man up, Cheatham, well, if he wanted the chair, Bate had said, he should by hell have it. And a footstool, too. Put a cold bottle of Yazoo Sue in his hand, a cigarette between his lips, and have the state light it with those seventeen hundred and fifty volts at seven amps …

"Why, my view is the governor's view, of course," said Bate, stepping toward Bills and patting him on the back.

Bills leaned in and said, softly, but not so much so that the others couldn't hear, "Have you told him what it is?"

The debate ended in laughter. Then the governor's men carted off Old Smokey, along with armfuls of billy clubs, ball bats, and post-maul handles that had belonged to that legend of Volunteer State justice, Buford Pusser.

9

Now the sound of needle touching shellac, like a ghost's heart skipping a beat.

The DJ played "God's River," by the minstrel singer Emmett Miller,[9] from 1928 on the OKeh label, backed by the Dorsey brothers, and the great Eddie Lang on jazz guitar. It's a song about dying and going to heaven, via the waterway of the title. The so-called "Minstrel Man from Georgia" sang in that high, liquid voice of his, sounded like a bit of helium had gotten in the corn liquor, somehow. He did not break into a full yodel, as he was wont to do. It was a swaying number, with a limber beat and swooning horns, all owing, doubtless, to the singer's destination and his sureness in getting there; if he missed the boat, why, he'd simply paddle his old canoe up God's River, to heaven there. It was, in its way, something of a spiritual. But Mrs. Flood, she was not swayed.

"God's River, my crack," she said, with a laugh that might have turned horses' heads in a meadow. "Shit Creek's where you'd find that black-faced peckerwood."

Cora Flood looked at her husband, John, to see what he might have to say on the matter. He was a university folklorist and an ethnomusicologist, and so could listen to the aforementioned Mr. Miller as a singer, a sound, a voice: as an influence on Hank Williams, Jimmie Rodgers, Merle Haggard, the genre known as Western Swing. *So, a lot of white shit,* his wife would say about all that. Beautiful, startling music, it was, though, full of wit and sway. Like a wink you could hear. Like

---

[9]Jazz and blues critic Lit Mitchell, in his so-called seminal study of river songs for the short-lived quarterly *Beat Down*, posited that "God's River" was in fact God's own favorite of this sub-genre and that He loved to imitate the Minstrel Man from Georgia; and further, that He, too, sometimes blacked up for the amusement of the citizens and denizens of Gloryland. This last bit caused a minor stir that *Beat Down* blamed on an editing error and Mr. Mitchell's drinking.

cartoon whiskey. And yet, and yet: he blacked up, did Emmett Miller. He fronted a band called the Georgia Crackers, fuck's sake. It was a lot for an enlightened white man with a Black wife to reconcile, even if he was an ethnomusicologist and she was, protestations aside, an avowed fan of Mr. Miller's music.

"It was 1928—" he tried.

She raised the back of her hand. "You wanna go back there real goddamned fast?" she said.

He thought she was about to smile but the light was poor and so he did not chance it.

The song ended and the DJ said, "That goes out to all y'all poor, stranded things out there not lucky enough to die and go to heaven like the late Mr. Miller. Be a good day for it, dying. But ain't for us to say when. If we didn't die ten years ago, we may never. Still, though, this rain, huh? So stay high and dry, good people. May the wind be at your back, but not too much wind, mind you, and may the only drop to touch you be from a bottle of the black stuff. Auld Irish blessing!"

"DJ's drunk again," he said.

She said, "Drunk still."

"Still," he said, "words to live by."

"Die by," she said.

There was no topping her, and so he sidled up, took his own swipe of the sour mash.

Packing list for an evacuation (his):

Flashlight.

Crank radio received as a public radio pledge-drive gift.

Shoebox of books containing Twain's *Adventures of Huckleberry Finn*; Faulkner's *The Reivers*; Welty's *A Wide Net and Other Stories*; a 1939 guide to Tennessee produced by the Federal Writers' Project of the Works Progress Administration;

Melville's *Moby-Dick*; the old Flood family Bible with its white faux-leather cover.

Notebooks containing research for his academic work in progress, a critical study tentatively titled, *Sanctuary & Desire: Blues, Spirituals, and the Sound of Searching in the American South.*

A collection of 78 rpm records including Charley Patton, Cannon's Jug Stompers, Charley Jordan, Daddy Stovepipe and Mississippi Sara, Blind Willie Dunn & His Gin Bottle Four, Bogus Ben Covington, Emmett Miller, and the only known extant copy of "See You in the Flood" by the Mississippi Sheiks,[10] recorded in December 1930 at the Edwards Hotel in Jackson, Mississippi, but never released.

"This is a soggy river town," she said.

"Most river towns are," he said, "if it's any kind of river at all."

This seemed to cheer her some, for him to be the bearer of such news. She wagged her drink stirrer at him; it was a wand now. She sipped the whiskey. She poured him a glass and leaned in. She knocked him a kiss. Her kiss had a kick like a hot rhythm section, and he did so love the old songs, the Hokum Boys or Blue Moaners, maybe a little of Lovie Austin's Blues Serenaders with bawdy Ma Rainey on the vocals, singing, "Honey, where you been so long?" She kissed him like that sometimes, like she was just fresh back from long gone and glad to see him; hell, glad to see anybody.

---

[10]The Mississippi Sheiks, built around the vast talents of the Chatmon family, arguably could be called America's greatest band ever. Bob Dylan's a fan. Muddy Waters said he'd walk ten miles to see them play. They had it all—wit, swing, and chops to spare; their lyrics were shot through with dark wisdom and wry asides, social and religious commentary; one of the latter, concerning hypocritical men of God, rhymed *preachin' king* with *shake that thing*.

He ran his finger some more along that barbed-wire scar and then he considered her legs at great length. He admired their shape and sheen in the blue dark; he hoped for a lightning bolt, illumination, for better to see her skin, that scar, the full dusk of her. The power was out, or else he'd have turned on the porch light.

"Well, well, well," she said.

He considered her toes, kissed and even counted them.

"All there, Mr. Flood?" she said.

Now the sky spat and the wind sighed; they seemed to be having a conversation about the end of it all.

He ran a finger the length of her shin, up and down, up and down. He settled on up. He bypassed that barbed-wire scar, lest he cut himself.

Said the sky to the wind, "Think it'll ever stop raining?"

He stopped at the hem of her dress and then he didn't stop. "Ahem," she said, and sipped whiskey through a hairline crack of smile. He ran a hand up under that blue-flowered dress, between the soft tatters of fabric and the cold sheen of dark skin. He mapped the territory, teased out new trails. He lingered and stalled and then found himself on the edge of forest.

"You lose your way, great white explorer?" she said.

It was her favorite party dress, blue-flowered and drink-stained with a couple, three lucky cigarette holes. She had worn it that night, the night they met, on the bluff in Memphis, as a three-piece band played the electrocuted blues and the Saturday-evening sun bruised the sky good and purple. He thought they could use a bluff about now.

Said the wind to the sky, "Don't think so, no."

She turned on him, threw a leg over, and so now they rolled on the porch of the small country house as husband and wife, trying to save their marriage as the great sky fell and the river god rose to meet it.

"All there, Mrs. Flood," he said.

10

Correlation and causality in the life and times of H. Walt "Trey" Flattery III, governor of Tennessee: he came from money. Nothing truly bad had ever happened to him. He was fifty-two years old. He was six-feet, one-inch, slim and gleaming. He had grace and bearing, and with his looks could have been cast as a Southern governor in a Hollywood movie set in any era from antebellum to present day—he wasn't elected so much as typecast. He seemed always to be looking at the horizon—the literal and symbolic future—even when it was really the cut of some woman's calves as she walked by.

You would not have called him intelligent, but he wasn't stupid; it was more that his intellect was never fully developed. He had neither the time nor need for it, growing up. It would have gotten in the way. Held him back. Made him think entirely too much. Trey Flattery didn't merely coast through life; he floated. He was ambitious but in a way the charmed often are; his ambitions were due him, they were birthrights. He was born winning, and never had to try very hard with women, for example, though he sometimes did, for fun. He had few secrets but this was one: he respected women, preferred their company to that of men, and thought them superior to men in most ways that mattered. He thought them not just smarter, but wiser as well, but that they let men go about being governors and chief executives and industrialists and leading lights of change, because men needed something to do between wars and football seasons. And men, brought up on competition, gravitated to such roles and activities. Women were brought up on thoughts and discourse—things less apt to muss their hair. Or maybe it just kept the men out of the women's way for a blessed second. Trey didn't give it a lot of thought, really. It was somehow, at once, an enlightened *and* chauvinistic way of looking at the world, at women and men, and it helped explain why the governor, if more enlightened and less chauvinistic, could have been a good man and a great leader, but instead settled for being a successful one. At any rate, women loved him. He was elected with seventy-two percent of the female vote, though he was on his third marriage, and it was an open secret in Nashville that he had two mistresses (both aboard the steamer *Clementine*). Even his failed marriages failed to constitute something "truly bad" in his life; the partings were amicable, even amiable, and the odd old-time's-sake assignation was not out of the question.

And men? They tended to see in him those qualities they wished most for themselves—he was slick in an offhand way, bit of a scoundrel but good-natured about it, and, it was said, often enough to be an unofficial campaign slogan, that he "got more tail than the Tennessee Titans." That last was never said by Trey himself. He didn't brag, and got a kick out of those few things he did poorly—he shot for sport, but not well; he was a surprisingly stiff dancer, for all his grace. He couldn't swim—something only Bate knew. As for Trey the political animal: he was a glib speaker and a deft debater, for he didn't get caught up in policy depths and wonkish nuance. He never really *said* anything you could hammer a nail through. He looked at the horizon and spoke vaguely of a future, just down the road, where there would be better times, fruitful times, times of plenty. The poor would still be with us, of course, but the sex would be out of this fucking world.

He had a little religion, not much. He had a lot of faith—in his own good fortune. He was raised Protestant, but as governor he attended, or anyway his double attended, a non-denominational church the size of a basketball arena, and with all the trappings of one: live music, giant video screens, pyrotechnics, T-shirt cannons, and the gospel of more as delivered by a pastor who was a former Hot Country singer twice nominated for "best stubble" at the CMA Awards.

In the end, most everything, then, came easy to Trey Flattery. And for that which didn't, there was Bate, always Bate.

Back on the top deck of the steamer *Clementine*: "It's not *not* uncomfortable," the governor said of Old Smokey. "Solid workmanship, the best of materials. Quality all the way. Top notch!"

The governor knocked again on the wood. He said, "Is it an oak, by chance, Mr. Blankenship?"

"White oak, sir," said Blankenship, the state historian. He spoke with the stuffy air of authority, for Blankenship was a serious man—the most serious man, it was said by some, in all of state government. The only serious man, said some others—said it like seriousness in a man was like rickets in a child; how could he truly expect to rise and thrive in a man's world, with such a condition?

"White oak, you say. Is that the state tree, by chance?"

"It is not, Governor," said the state historian, stuffily, authoritatively, and unable to sound any other way. He had been serious as a toddler. Now just past thirty, he looked ten years older, and his hairline older still.

"That would be the tulip poplar," he said.

"Is it sure enough?" the governor said, in a gently chiding way. He wondered if the state historian used that same tone of voice in intimate moments with his wife, if the two of them had such moments. She was on board—he'd seen her earlier, getting sick over the side of the boat, aft on the cabin deck. She had locks upon locks of red hair, and they were getting the worst of the sickness. She seemed tall, even bent over the side of the boat. Pale, long legs, she'd have. Goosebumped from the cold rain. *Ahh.* He had not gotten a look at her face, and so was intrigued; what sort of face would have ever looked twice at the state historian? Not a beautiful one, surely. Still, it might be a pretty face, or a handsome one, and anyway there were those red tresses; surely they would not have been squandered on less than at least a handsome face. And surely her eyes were green, to go with that red. The state historian did not seem to the governor to be the sort of man to keep a red-headed, green-eyed woman satisfied. He seemed fusty and bloodless. Was fusty the word? Was fusty *a* word? It sounded like cartoon cussing. Anyway, he thought, she would be altogether too fiery for the poor man, immolation a very real threat. He would find reason to see her, accidentally meet her, someday soon, after she'd gotten her sea legs—and washed her hair.

Ah, but the state historian. Such a silly man, to be so serious, the governor thought. He did, though, know a great many things. He seemed to know every little thing as regarded Tennessee. The governor liked to quiz him, as one would a particularly bright child. The state historian realized as much, and resented it. But he could not help himself, ruled as he was by duty, his own stuffiness, which was really stiffness, and his love of, his religious-level belief in, facts.

"What's the state fruit, Mr. Blankenship?"

"Tomato, sir."

"Wild animal?"

"Raccoon."

"Drink?"

"Milk."

They could have gone on this way, for the state of Tennessee has an official butterfly (Zebra Swallowtail), two official fish (smallmouth bass and channel cat), and three official flowers (Iris, Passion Flower, and Tennessee Coneflower). It has an official amphibian (Tennessee Cave Salamander), official reptile (Eastern Box Turtle), and official rifle (a .50-caliber Barrett—a sniper rifle.)

The governor didn't know whether he was jealous of the state historian, of all people, or admiring of him. Or, more likely, the state historian didn't figure into it, at all; women's husbands rarely did, where Trey Flattery was concerned.

He took a drink of his Boulevardier. He crossed and recrossed his legs, thought of red hair, green eyes, long legs of pale. He gave Old Smokey a rat-a-tat knock with his knuckles. He so liked doing that.

"How many men have died in this chair, Mr. Blankenship?"

The state historian could have given names, ages, racial breakdown, occupations—one had been a Bible salesman, another a one-armed short-order cook; two had talked with a lisp; no less than six had at one point in their lives worked as carnies. Yet another had the same name as Tennessee's fiftieth governor. But the state historian could take only so much of being treated like a precocious child or trained dog, and so ...

"All of them," he said.

(That was the state historian for you: even in the rare show of flippancy, the facts all in order.)

The governor and the chief of staff laughed and clinked their cocktail glasses and looked out beyond the bow of the great ship.

And a fine vessel it was, the *Clementine*, a four-decker with a red, stern-mounted paddlewheel, and twin cross-compound steam engines with two thousand indicated horsepower. It was as long as a football field, to the inch, with a beam of sixty feet, six inches, the same as from pitcher's mound to home plate on a baseball diamond. These were no coincidences, for the great steamboat, built in California, was the baby of an old Scot from Dumbarton, named Douglas, with a fascination for his adoptive country. He imagined that the gridiron hero Red Grange, the "Galloping Ghost," with his Scottish-Irish heritage, might someday sleep in the ship's finest stateroom, and that perhaps the musical star Jimmie Rodgers, "The Singing Brakeman," in whose blue yodels the shipbuilder heard faint echoes of his own people's laments, might stroll the decks, playing his guitar and singing his songs of rovers, gals, and gamblers, muddy water, homesick hoboes, and Memphis street corners, to the backing of the ship's twenty-eight note, three-octave calliope. Alas, the ship was all too grand for rabble;

it was presidents and titans of industry, cotton barons and whiskey heiresses, who rode the *Clementine* in those early, glory days.

The first, or main deck, held the cramped quarters now occupied by the crew and the lesser of the country singers who had been brought along for the journey west. The second, or cabin deck, included staterooms and a library. The third, originally the Texas but re-dubbed the Tennessee, was the pleasure deck, with a dining room, a gambling hall, and two lounges, one large with a dancefloor and stage for musical and other performances, and the other small and intimate, for serious drinking. It was said that you could get everything but saved on the Tennessee deck of the *Clementine*.

The top, or sun deck, included the largest and most elegant staterooms and suites. The governor held his daily briefing outside, on the top deck. The weather was chancy at best but the governor considered it a show of the Volunteer State's stalwart nature and best stuff; or maybe it had been Bate's idea, the governor could not remember. Anyway, the rain had mostly stopped and sometimes there were even hints of rumors, unfounded as they were, of sunshine.

11

The Floods, Cora and John, lay on the porch, after. They were nearly spent and nigh on sated. She reached for the bottle of sour mash. Kentucky bourbon was her preference—sacrament, she called it—but she liked the label on this Tennessee whiskey, black the color of her scar and on it the face of some silver-bearded ancient with eyes wild like Moses on a bender. "A pint of Old Testament, my man!" she'd tell the counter man at the package store in Lower Grace, and the counter man—born again, or claimed he was—would look at her with his best scold and say, "God'll get you for that, Cora Flood." Then he'd look away, lest she—or God—see his smile.

She took the next-to-last sip, and offered the last to her husband. John watched Cora drink—it was, he thought, a little like a sacrament, the way she drank, eyes closed and head thrown back, like teasing heaven—and then took the last sip. She leaned in. She kissed his lips for a taste of those last traces.

"You're a piece of work, you are," he said.

She said, "And here, I thought I was just a piece."

From an early draft of *Sanctuary & Desire: Blues, Spirituals, and the Sound of Searching in the American South: A Critical Study of Race and Identity*, by John Flood:

> *I was sitting outside a little country shack in Holmes County, Mississippi, interviewing Billy "Brain" Thomas, the drummer for the regionally famous juke joint band the Tchula Three. He was somewhere north of eighty, a sweet old man who would turn irascible in a second. I never could tell when it was an act, or if it all was. He knew all the greats of his generation, had played or socialized with most of them, but mostly he just wanted to talk about how the Tchula Three were tight as Muddy's best bands. I asked him about Muddy but he just said, "Shit," and looked at his shoe as if he'd just stepped in a pile of it. Then he laughed real big and said, "Nah, man. Muddy was a prince. Muddy was a good man. It was Muddy almost got us that tour with Mick and them."*
>
> *I felt in that moment like his straight man and I felt like a wind-up, hand-tooled, small-batch white boy set at the feet of a real-live blues legend and I guess maybe I felt, too, a little like a bleeding-heart messenger sent to the Mississippi Delta with*

a case of Four Roses in lieu of reparations, for what last living bluesmen I could find. But mostly, ever since I'd heard the crudely recorded old club recordings, first on reel-to-reel and then on cassette, of the Tchula Three, I was a believer. Billy was the drummer in the band. He'd been called Brain since he was a kid because he'd beat like hell on whatever he'd see with whatever he could find, a hammer or broomstick or his bare hands. Brain it, Billy, they'd say. Brain, they'd call him, in time. A skinny boy and then a skinny man, but arms of steel. People said it wouldn't do to put him in prison, he'd just bust out. They thought he might become a boxer, the best out of Mississippi since Archie Moore, the Old Mongoose. But then Billy met Gus Hollows, who played guitar like Billy beat drums. Together, they weren't just loud and violent, though they sure as hell were that. They came to see that noise could be toyed with, trained, harnessed, and that two noises together weren't just double the noise but twice the power. They came to see that noise was music and music, well, music was sex. They took on a bass player, named Roy "Yea Tall" Graves, who had no real power or grace with the instrument but a decent sense of rhythm and way with a lyrical turn of the old dirty blues ("Lay your burdens down, baby / put 'em on the floor there with your dress"). They all could sing but Yea Tall usually took the lead; there was a playful menace in his voice that was as much a trademark of the band as anything. Some say that's where Mick got it—that playful menace. But it would have had to be second-hand, maybe through Muddy (but not the Howlin' Wolf, whose menace was not playful), for the Tchula Three played every juke in Mississippi and were hired for lots of ritzy white-folk parties, played shacks and antebellum mansions, and governors' residences in two states, but they had never set foot inside a recording studio. They were loud, but not so much as to carry all the way across the pond.

"You almost toured with the Rolling Stones? Seriously? The Tchula Three?" I said.

It was just the two of us, outside of the little country shack. The photographer I was traveling with was inside the shack, sleeping off some of Billy's homemade whiskey. The Four Roses (I really had brought him a case) had been no match for Billy, and he'd brought out his own stuff. I just sipped but my photographer, he dove right in.

"Nah, shit, white boy. Schedules, you know. They was playing Europe, stadiums and shit. Hell, we had a regular Saturday-night gig at this little juke in Marks. Or maybe it was Belzoni. This little hole called The Dive. Or maybe it was a dive called The Hole. We played 'em all."

He was looking off in the distance when he said it, but there wasn't anything there, just flat, bare field as far as you could see. It was like you could see all the way to Memphis if you wanted. Then he turned to me. I knew why. He wanted to know if I'd call bullshit on him. He wanted to know what kind of white boy I was.

I guess maybe I did, too, because then I asked him what he thought about cultural appropriation.

He looked at me funny.

He said, "The fuck?"

It was about this time the photographer wondered out of the house. He still seemed pretty much cobwebbed, but happy to have had the experience—another story to tell. He collected experiences, was the thing about Walls. We met in grad school, up East. He was old-money Memphis. His grandfather was a cotton merchant. He knew Billy, was how we were here. He'd hired the Tchula Three for frat parties during his Ole Miss undergrad days.

Billy looked over at him, said, "White boy here just asked me what I thought about—wazzit?"

"Cultural appropriation," I said.

Walls laughed real big. He was built lanky and had that look that old-money people had no matter how much of it they'd pissed away. I remembered something an economics professor at school told me. Or maybe it was a philosophy prof. A rich person can never get so poor that he hits all the way bottom; there's too many other poor bastards down there already to break his fall.

"He means does it piss you off Elvis got more pussy than Blind Willie McTell?"

Billy "Brain" Thomas thought about that. He stroked his chin and took a pull from an unmarked bottle. He looked off again at the flat countryside. I thought he was about to turn irascible on me but he didn't. It was more incredulous.

"Fuck makes you think Elvis got more pussy than Blind Willie, white boy?"

Packing list for an evacuation (hers):

.58 caliber, single-shot, flintlock dueling pistol, French-made.

Black silk dress with slit and fringes, worn just once, to a jazz funeral for the mistress of Louisiana's junior senator.

Copy of Morrison's *Jazz*, Baldwin's *Jimmy's Blues*, Faulkner's *Sanctuary*, Melville's *The Confidence-Man: His*

Masquerade, Twain's uncompleted *The Mysterious Stranger*, and a collection of Hurston's writings for the Federal Writers' Project of the Works Progress Association, *Go Gator and Muddy the Water*.

Collection of 78 rpm records including Bessie Smith's "Kitchen Man," Memphis Minnie's "Ice Man (Come On Up)," Lucille Bogan's "Shave 'Em Dry," and Chemutoi Ketienya and Kipsigis Girls' "Chemirocha III."[11]

And then some more of that rolling around. They rolled across the porch, as dead languages rose and spoke, as the blues went electric, as rain fell backwards or seemed to do so.

Porch sex like some new religion or musical form.

And yet again. More and then some, as the rain played sambas and the wind reels, and the sound of it like something out of Kenyan myth, or a Meridian, Mississippi,[12] Saturday night.

Later, much later. (Had they slept, after? Had they died and risen again?)

They sat on the porch and watched the rain some more. It was a billowing sheet now, spread over the weary, spent body of land. Land was fast becoming memory; there was little

---

[11]A spooky little marvel, from Kenya's Rift Valley. It's 1950. The singers are singing about a stranger called Chemirocha—that is, the American country star Jimmie Rodgers, aka "The Blue Yodeler" and "The Singing Brakeman," whose records were brought to East Africa by missionaries. Yodels as religious experience? Why not?

[12]Hometown of Jimmie Rodgers, as well as former Major League baseball pitcher Oil Can Boyd, and rapper Big K.R.I.T.. Former Temptations lead singer David Ruffin was born in nearby Whynot.

more of it than the rise on which the small house sat, and beyond it only half-trees with limbs like arms trying like hell to swim their way out of the great muck.

He tried but couldn't remember it not raining, and then he did: the night they met, that night in Memphis, the bluff there. It didn't rain that night. It didn't rain that whole summer. There was only hot breath and sweat, smoke and neon. They danced as that blues band played "Rambling on My Mind" and then "I Feel Like Going Home," and she shouted, "Make up your damn mind, you," then took the stage herself and sang "I Can't Be Satisfied." The way she sang it, dirge-slow, you'd have thought satisfaction had drowned that very day.

She'd get that way. Moods would strike her down and evil would gather 'round, a flock at her feet.

Her better devils, she called them.

But by night's end, that night, anyway, she was leading a joyful clamor. Horn players materialized and jugs were passed; satisfaction walked on water, that night in Memphis.

The stories they told about her—that she killed a woman, at a house-rent party in Memphis, late of a Saturday. Killed her with a railroad spike, some said, though not how. No, said others, it was poison, or pistol shot, kitchen knife, guitar string, a spell she cast—there were as many stories as there were tellers.

They agreed about as much on the why, though the smart money had it that this slain woman had been, briefly, Cora's lover, but the woman had gone running back on threat of death from the husband, who was, just to naturally compound things, Cora's former lover. "That's the why," they'd say, and someone would always ask, "Then why kill her and not him?" And was told, always, "Don't you see? She found a way to do away with the both of them and only had to kill the one.

She's dead and he's up a pole for the killing, ain't he? Ain't it like Cora to do twice the harm with half the work?"

He'd heard the stories, versions of them, after he married her. He only said, and then only to himself, "Then why didn't the police come for her? You can't just commit murder without consequence, even in Memphis. Why was she walking free and free to marry and no more haunted than she is?"

And then, not even saying it to himself, not even thinking it, really, but knowing, somehow: *It's not like she'd deny it. She doesn't lie. It's her one virtue, even if she wields it like a vice. She's incapable of telling a lie. It's why I don't ask.*

Anyway, it was a town for tales, Memphis. As for truth, well, it was murdered nightly and back the next morning, a little woozy, was all.

The truth? You could get that however you wanted, in Memphis, like you could get your pork shoulder chopped or pulled, your ribs wet or dry.

Anyway, she took his name. Because she liked it better than her own, she said, though he suspected it was for cover. Still, though: which would you rather, Flood or Buggs?

When he suggested they move to the country, she said, "I reckon a woman with a new name could do with a fresh start altogether. Pack the bottles, Mr. Flood."

How they met and married, how that all happened: his work brought him to Memphis. He came, with a humanities grant from the National Endowment for the Arts, to look for ghosts—and found a live one. He was a folklorist and ethnomusicologist, a university professor, from Up North, which is to say Kentucky.

He collected old stories and songs, saw primitive art and deep meaning in found items, in NuGrape bottle caps and broken plow handles and hand-lettered signs that spoke of Jesus, sorghum, tamales, $2 covers.

Splinters of crosses.

Vials of dirt.

A cotton sack said to have been dropped by Muddy Waters the day he walked off Stovall Plantation—the Shroud of Clarksdale.

That night in Memphis, the night they met: Saturday on the South Bluff. The air thick with the smell of summer heat and pig meat. Beer sold from a trailer and stronger stuff from behind a tree, buck a shot. That blues band in a tin-roofed gazebo, playing songs about homemade sin and juice-head women.

He saw her from across the way, the big river to her back, talking to some woman's man, swaying as she did, telling some long-legged tale in that short blue dress. And laughing. Lord, that laugh—a cackle, really, that carried across the way and struck him so hard his knees buckled. He wondered if she could sing. Then later she did, and that was it. All of her sang. Her hips, eyes.

So that night in Memphis, after the band and the dancing, when it was just the two of them on the bluff and the moon in the sky and the devil off somewhere, and God, too, the both of them, the devil and God, both soused and near to sleep—that night, the first they met, he asked her to marry him. He didn't know what got into him. He was possessed, like.

"Marry me, then," she said. "See if I care."

Later, in some fit or funk, she'd accuse him of collecting *her*, a gone, Black woman of song. He'd say, "But I love you. I have all along. You must have loved me, too. I don't guess even somebody as contrary as you would marry a man she didn't love, just for spite or something to do. You must've. Or else why—" and she'd just shrug and say, "Who was I, white boy, to deny you the first wild thing you'd done in your life?"

She was the second, actually. He didn't talk so much about the first, just hints and haws and then a change of subject. For that was long ago and did not end well.

12

Leo Chance and Cig Murphy were a couple of Nashville songwriters. They were down on the cabin deck, in a quiet space they had found, doing what Nashville songwriters do. They were smoking cigarettes and sipping whiskey and talking about life, women, secret chords, and how the Nashville music industry would be the death of them, if the flood didn't get them first. In this way they might get around to writing a song together. It was usually how it all worked out. They had the start of one. They'd been working on it since the steamer *Clementine* left out of sodden Nashville. It was slow working, songwriting. It was like building anything else, they supposed.

They had a chorus. It was a song for a woman to sing. The woman in the song was pining for her no-good man who was gone. She wanted him to come on back home, so she could kick his ass back out the door. Women would love it for its empowering lyrics and men would only half-listen and presume it to be a song about rough sex; it would probably be a Nashville smash, when some Music City producer got through with it. The producer would turn some knobs and slather on the slick. The songwriters would rue the record but cash the checks.

Leo Chance and Cig Murphy's quiet space had been the ship's chapel, but in their daily visits, upon which they never failed to find it empty, they filled it with enough bottles and smoke and guitar chords that it became a sort of lounge. They called it the Tavernacle. They didn't figure God would damn them for this blasphemy. They already were Nashville songwriters; they had sold their souls for hit country records by hack singers they detested. God would surely see they had suffered enough.

"You figure we're the only two songwriters on board, Leo?" Cig said. "I ain't seen any others."

Leo picked the chords of the chorus of their country song on his 1953 Hurtmaster archtop acoustic.

"Two of everything, I reckon," he said.

He ran through the chorus a second time, but less as a stroll this time, more as a strut. He seemed to have an idea, or anyway a notion. The sway of the steamboat seemed to be suggestive of a certain rhythm; something in its slow, westward crawl toward Memphis, Home of the Blues, called to him, siren-like.

"Like with the ark, huh?"

Cig sat at the chapel's white piano. He let his fingers fan across the keys and then set about to play lightly behind the guitar chords. He seemed to feel it, too.

"What I thought, yeah," Leo said. "You notice how both the governor's mistresses are on board."

"The supermodel and the singer." It was the latter they had in mind for their song. She'd had a string of Top 10 country songs, though they didn't sound particularly country to Cig or Leo. People liked her for some reason. She sounded like all the rest, only more so. Maybe it was that. Or the fact that she was a former Miss Alabama, or was it South Carolina? Cig never could remember.

"You think she'll like it?" Cig said.

"The singer? Our song? Oh, I doubt it," Leo said.

"Was she Miss Alabama or Miss South Carolina? I never can remember."

"Think it was North Carolina."

"What was her talent, you reckon?"

"Heard it was the Georgia Crawl."[13]

---

[13]A sexual reference from the blues—imagine that. The great bluesman Blind Willie McTell sings about how he loves it when his

"Wouldn't that put her from the Peach State?"

"Woman had talents that transcended state lines, was how I heard it told," Leo said. "Now she's the governor of Tennessee's No. 2 mistress, and a country star fixing to sing one of our songs, if we can write it poorly enough."

Leo played the chorus again. He grew playful with it. The chords strayed off on their own, they doubled back. Cig vamped a little on the white chapel piano, upon which sat a bottle of Old Pogue bourbon. He favored Kentucky whiskey to Tennessee whiskey, being loyal to his native state. He took a drink with his left hand while his right kept playing.

"Kentucky whiskey for sipping," he said, raising his glass, "and Tennessee whiskey for pickling brains." For he'd heard that story going around about Forrest's gray matter and that bottle of Jack.

There was a hint of soul in the playing of the one, a rumor of funk in the other; the song began to slink about the room, shed clothes, make eyes, feel itself up. It was becoming less and less Nashville and more and more Memphis. Leo took a sip of his whiskey and a drag of his cigarette and said, as an aside, "Nearer my devil to thee," then fell back into the beat of the thing.

Cig sang the chorus. Notwithstanding it was a song for a woman to sing, his voice served it well enough. It was warm with a gentle kick, Cig's voice. It was peppery and well-aged, gave off hints of Bluegrass State bourbon, both in tone and actual fact. He'd made a few records of his own. They'd drawn praise from serious reviewers, and sold about as well as you'd expect from records by someone named Cig Murphy.

---

woman does the Georgia Crawl, in "Broke Down Engine Blues," on Columbia Records. Labelmate Bob Dylan, a major McTell fan, would later cover "Broke Down Engine Blues," write a song called "Blind Willie McTell," *and* evoke the Georgia Crawl in a song from his 1979 born-again LP "Slow Train Coming." In it, Dylan sings of a God-fearing woman who walks in the spirit of the Lord but can, still and all, do the Georgia Crawl.

He sang as Leo picked. He sang,

Where is he, where is he
That lowdown man of mine?
Where is he, where is he
That low down man of mine?
Lost track of my whiskey
Now I'm sipping on borrowed wine

"Damn, Cig," Leo said when they'd run through it a couple of times. "We got a song here. It won't sell worth a damn in Nashville, and the governor's No. 2 mistress ain't gonna touch it, but I bet we can find us a Memphis gal likes it—and us—just fine."

"You ever had a Memphis gal, Leo?"

"Been had by two or three."

"Ain't we all, Leo? Ain't we all?"

Thus was the songwriters' afternoon spent. Glasses were filled and glasses were clinked, and songs were written and sung, and songwriters got themselves properly soused on drink and song, on life and its possibilities, on the promise of a place called Memphis, where music was not so much an industry but something to be played, without dictate or stricture. A song in Memphis could be ornery, earthy, shameful, or shameless. Why, Cig said he knew a Memphis songwriter who claimed he'd gotten the word *snatchbreath* in a song, and they'd played it on local radio. It was just the once, in the small hours of the night, on a low-wattage station at the left end of the dial, and buried in the seventh verse, rhymed with *catch yer death*, but they'd by-God played it. Leo laughed at that and said the dirtiest word he'd ever heard, and heard it from an old gal who sang in a Western Swing band, was *cuntfeathers*, and that maybe he'd write a song around it, call it the "Cuntfeather Blues," say, and he'd be able to get it on local radio, in Memphis, or maybe find some band to sing it from the rooftop of The Peabody hotel while all the swells danced and the ducks strutted. Cig said a man could sure enough dream.

13

They sat on the porch and drank. It was moonshine now, her dead uncle's handiwork. They passed the bottle, back and forth, back and forth, her taking swigs and him sips, until there was nothing left, only a drop, and she said her uncle told her that was a devil's tear, that last drop, and never to drink it, the devil's tear.

"I always figured that was the only thing could make the devil cry—sight of a near-empty bottle," Cora said. "But my uncle, he said it all had to do with bad luck, you know."

"Yeah," John said, sounding more like her by the sip, "I'd sure hate to break this winning streak we've got ourselves on."

She laughed one of those laughs of hers, not the cackle but another: husky with a deep bottom, a gallows laugh, a gutbucket number almost like the blues she sang the night they met, that night in Memphis, on the bluff there. It was as close as she came to singing, these days.

"My granddaddy, one time he died," she said. "I mean to say, one time he died and came back and told about it. That's what he said. Now, I don't really know if he died, but he was gone a good while. I mean *away*, you know. There but not there. I was beside his bed, a girl, watching him, his dead eyes, his not breathing. Then he was back, and he had some stories to tell. He told me them. He said he'd seen angels of the flesh and silver-winged hounds and he'd seen the night sky peel away like old whorehouse wallpaper to reveal God on His golden throne, surrounded by a burgundy-robed choir singing "Sinner You Better Get Ready" and "Get Right Church."

"He just told me, not the others. He waited for the others to leave the room. He said they'd think he'd gone full mad, lost what scraps were left of his mind. But me, he liked. Said I had a little of the devil in my eyes. That made me interesting to him, I think. Or anyhow, I was a good audience.

I was ten, something like that. I was a girl. Devil in my eyes—I'd been told it before, and I'd be told it again. I was told it all through my growing up, but all the rest, my mama, aunts, my sisters, this one boy I liked, they said it like just a little of the devil, a drop, a tear, was enough to taint whatever it touched. Like I had just a little of the devil in me, and just in my eyes, but I was lousy with him, still and all. Spoiled and ruined. *Spoilt* and *ruint*—how they said it.

"Fine, I was evil, then. So I scared my sisters, which I liked doing, and I scared that one boy I liked. That bothered me at first, but I warmed to it. He would have robbed banks for me, that boy. Hell—*churches*. But my mother and aunts, they prayed for me, pitied me. I could hear them talking, late at night, wondering could I be saved? Like saying, would the devil let loose of this girl? Can we prise her free? And me, five, eight, ten, twelve years old, and hearing this shit."

He just waited until she started up again. He wanted to ask how wild she'd been, but he just looked at her. She knew, though. She could read him like his face was the morning rag out of Memphis, or a page of Twain.

"I was some bad," she said. "Only a little. Sometimes a little more. I was more contrary than anything. I was just working up to really bad, I reckon. I didn't mind what I was told. Ever. Just for sport, you know. I didn't care when they said they'd whip me, and I didn't, either. They whipped me until *they* were sore, and begged would I say the word so they could stop. I said *more*. I said more and then some. I wasn't sorry. Hell damn no. Fuck *naw*."

He sat listening. He shifted just slightly closer, as if she might literally rub off. He thought: *More. Tell me more. Tell me more and then some. Tell me all and everything. Ask me to rob banks for you. Hell, churches.*

"And I'd disappear at odd hours," she said. "I'd slip out at night, go nowhere but down to the creek. I'd sleep there. They'd ask where I'd gone and I'd say Hot Springs, or out to the juke, or Memphis, looking for a man. They weren't lies—I was there, in my head. Memphis was my favorite place to want to be. Heaven sounded like a sentence handed down, and hell was just some place they made up to scare us all. But Memphis.[14] Shit, Memphis was real. City upon the hill, like in the Good Book, only not like that at all. That white stuff wasn't salt and the light was pure blue neon. Dreamed of that place. I mean, dreamed hard and woke up spent.

"And then liquor came into it. Figured out if I poured out some of a bottle of my uncle's hooch, they'd think I drank it. I hated to pour it out—that was the only sin I saw in it. And then I didn't pour it out. I was twelve, something like that, when I started drinking. I'd been smoking a year already. I lit up in church, one day. I shouted 'Holy Hell' when it ought to have been 'Hallelujah.' That's about the time they quit taking me to church, you know."

"They pushed you to all that, wife," he said, "your mama and aunts and the rest."

"They didn't have to push hard, husband."

"Well," he said.

"And anyway, now it's me, all me, full-grown, sitting here. A ruint Black woman in the rain at the end of the world."

He stood to go inside, to gather their things. It was time. There was a rusty, old party barge out back of the house, left by the previous owner. She said she wished it were a steamer, white with a big, red paddlewheel and draped lights on the bow, couples dancing on the deck to a little combo playing the "Beale Street Mess Around." She said she'd drink too much and put the make on Mark Twain. She sighed. She said, "But I'll settle for a rusted, old party barge and just a devil's tear to drink, and you, my man, my husband, to put the make on."

---

[14]Ah, Memphis as the Southern capital of sin—a familiar theme in literature, song, and life. Faulkner sent many a citizen of Yoknapatawpha County up road to the Bluff City for drink and jellyroll, and Welty referred Memphis as "the old Delta synonym for pleasure, trouble, and shame."

“Hate to see you have to settle,” he said, smiling.

14

Five days out of sodden Nashville, Music City, abandoned capital of Tennessee, and still as many from Memphis, Home of the Blues, City on the Bluff. Such was the slow meander west. The captain’s navigational skills were beginning to be questioned, but he would appear each night for dinner, steady of hand. Which is to say he did not spill a drop.

The captain was a tall, burly man with a bramble of a beard the color of the clouds in Turner’s “Dutch Boats in a Gale.” He drank bourbon from his native Kentucky. It was suspected among some on the voyage that he was nosing the steamer *Clementine* toward the commonwealth, where it was said the floodwaters ran amber with the smoky nectar.

Captain Bull Chandler was an imposing sight but amiable enough. He smiled with his eyes when someone at the table he’d joined for the night issued some witty rejoinder. He rarely spoke except to say, “Well said.” He kept his opinions to himself, except on matters of country music—he thought it died hard with Hank Williams, in the back seat of that robin’s egg-blue Cadillac on New Year’s Eve, 1952. He liked an after-dinner smoke, alone, aft on the Tennessee deck; the cigarette would half-disappear into that bramble of a beard. From a distance, it looked like someone was burning crops.

The sky darkened in all directions. It spit rain for a day, as if trying to decide. Then came a bully of a storm that lasted all of one afternoon; it lashed about the decks in a great fit of temper.

Then the rain stopped and the sky turned ashen, as if it had seen some spectral version of itself. It would not have been surprising for the sky to split open next, and a dragoon of dragons to come through, breathing fire and umbrage.

But came the next day, sunny side up, and it was widely seen as a sign. But of what? Better times, said Governor Trey Flattery. He believed it, the great charmed fool.

Four o'clock. Time for the daily cabinet meeting.

"Well, then. Seats everyone," the governor said as his aides and cabinet members fanned out across the pews lately liberated from the Mother Church of Country Music. "Shall we begin with a prayer, or the weather report?"

This was the governor's daily joke. His cabinet meetings were becoming more and more like happy hour. A bluegrass band with pop leanings was scheduled to perform later; it was an actual agenda item, just before a report on the preliminary findings of the Department of Correction's Joint Task Force for More Dying but Less Killing.

"Threat assessment, I should think, Governor," said Chief of Staff Bate. He was the only person standing; there's always one, at a puppet show. He nodded now to a man of military bearing on the second row. "I'll let Adjutant General Spears explain," he said.

"Ah, Adjutant General," the Governor said. "Always good to hear from you. You're looking very military, as always. Just so! Top notch! Tell me, then: do we have threats?"

"Yes, sir," the adjutant general said, and then no more.

"Well then." This seemed promising, if vague. "Care to expound?"

Adolphus Spears was solid and stolid and every inch a man of military bearing. He was not normally given to consternation, or equivocation, but these were, so to speak, uncharted waters, even for him.

"Um. Pirates, Governor."

"Pirates?"

"Well, call themselves pirates. Do pirate things."

"And what sorts of pirate things do they do? Murder and pillage, I should say. All manner of barbarous activity, no doubt. Have we made contact with them? Told them to simmer down and all that? Have we brought them to heel, Adjutant General?"

He was enjoying himself enormously.

"They have made contact with us, Governor."

He inched forward in the electric chair. He seemed about to clap. "And, Adjutant General? And?"

"They've made threats on your life, Governor. Tie you to the mast. Make you walk the plank. Things of that nature."

"Have they, sure enough!"

The governor came up out of his chair, as if relishing a fight to the death with a real, live pirate. But Bate sent him back into the chair with a stern look of the sort a parent would give a mischievous child who was starting to remove articles of clothing in public. Thus was the governor chided and chastened and brought to heel, with all the cabinet and wait staff watching. He slumped back in Old Smokey. He was about to pout, perhaps throw a tantrum. Then he thought—*that Bate, he's fooling, is all.* This had the hallmarks of Bate's doing. He would have conjured pirates, to make the journey seem all the more fraught, to make the governor appear all the more heroic, in the end. He would have crafted the "intelligence," and then slipped it, through a web of intermediaries, to the adjutant general, who would have been on high alert for such; a military man always has a sweet tooth for the very worst. Yes, this would be just the thing for Bate to do, the governor thought. The man was a master of sham, misdirection, manipulation, and political theater.

Now he'd turn surreptitiously and …

Wait for it, the governor thought, *the wink. Here it comes. Wait, wait.*

But the Chief of Staff Bate did not turn. He did not wink. He instead looked gravely about the ship, as if pirates were, alas and avast, the least of their worries.

"Is there something else, Dickie?" He had not called him Dickie, in public, since short-pants days.

"We have a more serious threat, Governor," Bate said, slowly turning to face his best friend since childhood. "We have intelligence that there is, stowed away on board this very ship, a—"

"Yes, Dickie?"

The steamer *Clementine* might have tipped suddenly to the southwest, as all on the top deck leaned in Bate's direction to hear what he said next.

"A newspaper reporter," he said.

Then the wink; surreptitious, it was.

15

He turned to go inside and she turned to watch the rain. It was pure noisy spite now. There was no reasoning with it; it would not respond to batons or wands. It did not fall from the sky but rather seemed to be flung from it.

And she sang, for the first time in ages. She sang snatches of Charley Patton's "High Water Everywhere, Parts 1 and 2." She sang, "Lord, the whole round country, man, is overflowed."

And she sang Memphis Minnie's "When the Levee Breaks," holding onto the words, clinging to them, as if they were driftwood.

From inside the house he heard it, or heard something—a sound like music, singing. He turned and listened but then went back to his gathering. Couldn't be, he thought. She doesn't, anymore. Or anyway, won't. Must be the wind.

When he reappeared in the doorway with a peach crate of their things, she was there to greet him.

"Well."

"Did you bring your old family Bible?"

He just looked at her.

"Because a Bible, they say, is handy in hard times, and particularly in a flood."

Still he just looked at her.

She stood, took the crate from him and set it to the side of them. She kissed his neck, draped her arms over his shoulders. "What you do is, husband, you put that Bible on the ground where you're standing." She kissed his lips. She said, "And then you stand on it." She pulled back and smiled. "See, a Bible's a good inch thick, what with all those books inside it, all those plagues and prophets, and their scoldings, all those tall tales and God sightings, and the revelations, *oh*, and the lamentations, *oh*, and the miracles, *oh*, and Jesus Christ Himself, and Queen Esther, too, and thou shall not this and thou shall not that, either, don't even think about it, get your hand from there, and the proverbs and the psalms and the odd parable, and some actual true shit, too, even, I guess."

She kissed the top of his head, the tip of his nose, her lips in a slow dart about his head.

"So, like I was saying, you stand on that Bible, a good inch thick. It won't save you, like you're taught it will," and kissed his lips, "but it'll buy you ten whole minutes from the rising water while you think of something better."

She stepped away, looked down at her bare feet and toes all there.

"That's what little I believe, husband," she said. "Lucky for me you believe enough for the both of us, huh?"

But it was as if he hadn't heard a word of it. He was grinning, still, eyes shut since she kissed him. But when he came to—it was like coming to, like he'd been knocked out, blissfully dead, there for a moment—the grin had been washed away as if by the rain or blown off by the wind.

16

"Trey. I need to tell you something."

"What was the meaning of that?"

"Meaning of what?"

"You know."

The cabinet meeting had broken up. It was the after-party now, down on the Tennessee deck. The lead singer for the bluegrass band with pop leanings had fallen in with Commissioner of Correction Lynch and Adjutant General Spears as they walked, saying he'd been thinking about the state's execution problem and had a solution: deep frying! Lynch looked distraught and Spears mildly intrigued.

Trey and Bate stood alone on the bow, looking out at all that nothingness. It was all just one great, gray smudge.

"Meaning of what?" Bate said again, his smile nothing less than serpentine. "The part of the meeting where I made you look like a child who'd lost his favorite squeaky toy overboard?"

The governor was at a loss to answer this, exactly. "All right. What did you need to tell me?"

"It's about Cheatham, the uppity—"

"We can't call them that anymore."

"Uppity?"

"Not even that."

"Time was when you could call a spade a—"

"Now you're just fucking with me, Dickie. Because you can say and do whatever damn thing you want, because you're back in the shadows, and me, I have to stand out front and smile and look dashing and say things people want to hear."

"You don't seem to mind the spoils. 'More tail than the Tennessee Titans'—we were actually thinking of putting it on your campaign signs. But the Titans objected. Trademark infringement, they said, though I suspect professional jealousy. But anyway, yes, Trey, I am."

"Am, what?"

"Fucking with you."

"Well, you've had your fun. Now what about Cheatham? I know all I need to know about him. Claims he's innocent, wants me to grant him a stay, like they all do. But if he's got to die, he wants the chair. I know all about Cheatham. Lethal injection isn't good enough for the—"

"You've sat in the chair, Trey. Would lethal injection be good enough for you?"

"This isn't about me, Dickie."

"Everything's about you, Trey. You're the governor, and maybe someday you'll be president, if there's a country left to lord over."

The governor brightened at the thought. "You think it'll come back, Dickie? The country, I mean?"

A decade before, in the year the world didn't end, in the Year of Can't Breathe, there were makeshift hospitals set up in city parks and sports arenas and abandoned shopping malls; ice rinks and refrigerated truck trailers that once held boneless chicken breasts and snow peas and cardboard pizzas became morgues. The virus turned great cities into ghost towns. Businesses shuttered, some for good. Only so-called essential businesses stayed opened, manned by essential workers, known more colloquially as poor bastards. People went about, when they went about at all, in masks and gloves, slathered in hand sanitizer, when they could find it. Gallows humor thrived: "How serious can it be if the liquor stores are still open." "Why you damn fool, that's how you know it *is* serious." The price of gas plummeted, of course, but there was no use for it, nowhere to go. *Go where, to buy some toilet paper? It's all sold out? Are you shitting me?* Doctors and nurses worked around the clock, without proper protective equipment, exposing themselves to the virus. They were hailed as heroes, what with the pro athletes sidelined and all. The president's response was about what you'd expect. He went through the five stages of dumbfuckery, on live TV: lies, damn lies, denial, braggadocio, and blame. He never went out of character. It was always somebody else's fault, never his. He could only be one thing, a bully windbag hate machine. Actually, that's three things, but he was duly elected, so who did America have to blame but itself, really? It isn't like the fucker misrepresented himself, ever.

And then, just when the country was starting to reopen—against the best scientific guidance, mind you—a Black man had the life squeezed out of him by a white cop, a knee to the neck, and the Black man saying *I can't breathe, I can't breathe*. Other cops stood and watched. A crowd gathered. A cell phone captured it all. Something had come along to knock the virus from the top of the charts, and it was a golden oldie.

America seethed and America burned, but then, in time, America—already a country in existential crisis *before* the virus and the protests, what with climate change, gun violence, economic and health inequality, and the shitty state of popular music—went back to watching football.

"Back from *what*?" Bate said. "I seem to recall your investments did just fine ten years ago, what with the stock market humming along and the sky raining bailouts for your billionaire friends whose corporations poor-mouthed it while they furloughed their workers. You were fine then. I guess you'll be fine this time, too."

"You think so?"

"The country looks to men like you, in times like these." He meant pied pipers, but the governor just took the compliment at face value, Flattery be his name.

"We'll be on the world stage, Dickie. Think of it."

"You'll be on the stage. I'll be in the wings."

"What's that phrase, Dickie?" He just wanted him to say it. He wanted to see if he had that little amount of control left, if ever he had it.

"Power behind the throne, Trey?"

"Behind every great man, I was thinking, Dickie."

"There you go thinking again, Trey. I warned you about it." Bate laughed, and then: "But as I was saying—Cheatham."

"Yes, all right. What about him?"

"Something's going to happen."

"Something other than him getting what's coming to him? I don't guess I'll be giving him that stay."

"You already didn't. I had the word come down, your say-so. Official word."

"Oh, really?"

"You were busy with—I don't know, Trey. What? Or who? Anyway, you have spoken, without having to. No stay for Cheatham, poor old shine."

"So what's going to happen? Tell me? Is he going to get what's coming to him or not?"

"That's a complicated question but the answer is yes, I suppose. But not in the way you mean."

"Can you be more specific, Dickie?"

"I can't, no."

"How should I—" He hated to ask but knew of no other way. "How should I react?"

"With grave concern for your person," Bate said. "But I shouldn't worry, really."

"Should *I*?"

"Good one, Trey."

"Good what?"

He patted the governor on the head and was gone.

The governor stayed on the bow for the longest time, looking out at all that nothing for something, though he did not know what.

17

Cunning, connivance, and outright treachery in the life of Richard Franklin Bate, Chief of Staff for the Governor of Tennessee: he came from nothing. His people had been scoundrels, mercenaries, gun molls, drummers, palookas; they may well have been pirates, if you traced the line back far enough. He was fifty-two years old, with that mutt face and a body to match. He was self-aware but not self-conscious. He put no truck in appearances—rumpled clothes thrown on a misshapen body, a shave if it was Monday, and off to screw the world. His looks did him no good with women but women could be bought. Prostitutes tended to enjoy him, actually, once they got past the first naked sight of the man. Built like the best of the Yankee gods, he'd say to them—Babe Ruth's weight and Yogi Berra's height. Sometimes it was Hollywood greats—Sydney Greenstreet and Peter Lorre. But he needn't have changed the line; it was always a different prostitute. It wasn't about the sex, anyway; that was *perfucktory*—his word for it. He could talk with them, scheme with them. He could tell them stories from childhood he hadn't realized he remembered. It was the closest he came to confiding, as an adult—honor among whores and mongers. As a child, he'd had Trey. Those two, thick as thickets. But the relationship changed as they aged, friendship to partnership to professional entity to political beast—Trey's looks, charm, and inherent harmlessness; Bate's base instincts, plotting, and zeal for the kill. They became like one of those country music brother acts, with perfect harmony and a string of hits, but hardly a civil word said between them offstage. And yet they still called themselves best friends, a term as strong as brother. No, stronger. They'd become best friends by choice, and they were in this together; it was the one way they'd get there. Blood was thick but thickets were thicker.

He had a near-genius IQ, but it was his cunning that made him dangerous; it was cunning that made him Bate. Cunning Bate, the man with the plan, and the clean hands. And yet he once killed a man. He was no more than a boy, really. This was in college, at Vanderbilt, junior year. It wasn't entirely his fault: the boy in question was a fellow schemer, scion of an old-money family in Little Rock, beaten by Bate at his own game. He'd come at Bate with an Arkansas Toothpick, a leather-handled stiletto-dagger with a twelve-inch blade, when it was clear he couldn't outwit him. He didn't know the first thing about violence, though—his scheming had never before come to that. The knife had been his daddy's and his granddaddy's, and now it was Bate's. He could have stopped the incident shy of bloodshed. Bate, that is. The boy's neck, though, felt good in his hands. The sound the boy made—a slow hiss that gave way to a resigned sigh, followed by a heavy throb of silence, like after an orchestra has played something by Mahler. Bate studied the boy's face, that pale, perfect skin, cheekbones that might have been carved from a century-old sweet gum by something larger than that Arkansas Toothpick, and eyes that even Bate had to admit were not simply blue, but azure. It was an experience, at any rate. And then, knowing how it felt to take a life, Bate had no need to take another. He could hire it out, if such need arose, like calling a plumber or electrician, ordering a pizza.

Bate collected experiences. He had tried, besides murder: gambling, morphine, contra dance, and the company of men. He was a student of motivation, desire, and desire's black-sheep relation, *want*. In the end, Bate could understand practically everything about the human race but the grip of religion, and the appeal of the steel guitar. For Richard Franklin Bate could not stand to hear a whine of any sort. It made living in Nashville difficult, when someone deigned to play some actual country music, but it was the state capital, after all. Or had been, at any rate, until the rains came.

18

Then the rain did stop. Finally. The rain had run out of ways to fall.

And so now the sun shone on all the rain had wrought.

The sun shone like some vengeful god, mean streaks on the memory of land.

There was little left of the rise on which the small house sat, and those trees were up to their middle fingers in muck.

"We'd best go," she said.

"Yes," he said.

They loaded the old, rusted party barge with supplies and belongings as would fit. They climbed aboard and shoved off.

They began to row.

It was that or pray.

Spirits Talking

I got six men
They leave me too tired to speak
But I get one day to rest
I call that a pretty good week

—Lil Cripes & Her Mean Time Five
"You Got to Want Me Blues"

The picture shows and pool rooms
They are an awful curse
Moonshiners, clubs, and dancers
The world grows worse and worse

—Blind Alfred Reed
"I Mean to Live for Jesus"

1

The old, dying writer had a thick head of white hair. Black streaks ran through it with a sort of cold logic, as if etched by a mathematician who had taken up art to get through winter. His brows were dark but for the dusting of first frost across the lower edges. His eyes were darker still; they were icy. He had a mustache that was more white than dark, as if first frost had brought with it snow that was rare for these parts. The mustache turned up at the ends; it looked like it might fly away, in some migratory fit, and flee that ancient face.

But now beneath the mustache there appeared the faint smile of possibilities.

"Just you look at him," said the old, dying writer's ghost of a wife. "The liar in winter."

He sat in an old, iron chair beside an old, iron table on which sat the morning newspaper out of Memphis, and a fifth of Three Queens bourbon. This was on the porch of the old house where the old writer lived with her ghost. He was dying but not yet. She was dead but not gone. This was in the hill country of North Mississippi, safe for now from the flood. (God forbid you lived in the Delta.) It was a white house with columns, a primitive Greek Revival—mansion, you might have called it, if you didn't live there. This was in a small town called Burden. He was the town's favorite son; son of a bitch, some said. He was a writer—a famous one, or rather a famously unread one. He was writing one last story. Well, he was ruminating on it. He had some ideas. He was not quite there. He sighed. He raised his glass and rocked it slowly, studying the brown murk.

So there would be a river. Always there were rivers, coursing through his stories. A river could take you home. A river could tug you under. A river didn't grow old and gray and wither to nothing, like a man. So, yes, a river. From there, all else flowed. Blessings and curses. Pride, venom. Tears, blood, secrets, and dreams. Stories.

He marveled that God could have begun from scratch, without a river to inspire Him.

She was standing in the doorway, dead to this world but no less Missus to the Mister. He sensed her, and then heard her—or heard the sound she made, anyway, flecking away the paint with her fingernails. Then she stopped, and sighed, and started again with the flecking.

"You don't rest easy, Missus," he said.

"I don't rest hardly at all, Mister."

"I thought that's all it was, was rest. Rest and juleps and breezes in off the ocean." He still liked to bait her.

"I didn't die and go to the gulf, Mister." She still liked being baited.

"I just figured, well, heaven, you know. Oceans."

"Damn heaven."

"Never was one for oceans, myself." The old writer again raised his glass and again rocked it slowly before taking a drink, as if it were all part of some ritual ceremony, or maybe he just liked stretching every act out that little bit extra, dying as he was but not yet.

"I think I may have seen a creek," she said.

"Well, now, that's something."

"You could have called it a stream. But it was just a creek. A piddling thing you couldn't paddle down."

"I prefer a river," he said, "to almost anything."

"Damn the river and damn you, too."

"Duly noted, Missus."

They both laughed. It had been ages.

Theirs had been less a marriage than an honest misunderstanding; he thought he'd married a muse and she a carpenter. He'd built the porch onto the front of the old mansion—it was old, already, when they bought it, more with her money than his—and a sewing room onto the side. He was good with his hands. It came easy, natural, and so meant nothing to him. His stories—his hobby, she had thought—were his work. He labored over them, bled for them, physically exhausted himself making them just so. They were his world, his home; he disappeared into them, vanished, climbed those trees in the country of his mind, and there lived out his days and his nights.

She'd read his early stories, thought them remarkable though she could not have said why. She encouraged him. She'd ring an arm around his neck, bend down that little bit to kiss him, and peck him one. He preferred kisses that lingered but not while he was writing. So he smiled at the peck—if it could even be called a peck; more a cold grazing of the cheek, really.

But then she'd glance at a word or phrase, or one would spring from the page, and she'd say something like, "Holy hell, Mister." *That* he liked as much as kisses that lingered; no—more. He'd married an intelligent woman, though not a particularly passionate one. Or perhaps passionate but not for him. Had he thought of that? No, he had not. But better, he thought, to have hitched yourself to intelligence than passion, a torch for life rather than a match set to a July the Fourth firework that would light the sky but only for a moment. Life was long and dark in stretches, it was lonely out there; a torch was heat and light, a torch showed the way, or anyway, would assure the cliffs and chasms were well lit.

A peck, then, and some small praise—it's like I'm keeping chickens, *she* used to think, except it's just this one: a trained rooster who struts while he types. Would someone pay as much as a dollar to see such a trick? A quarter more to read what it had written? Still, she thought, it was good for a man to have a hobby that didn't get anyone unnecessarily maimed or pregnant. Her second cousin's third husband hunted wild boar on an island in the Mississippi with nothing but a bow. They did not call the boar wild without cause; one tore through the second cousin's third husband's only gut like it was the Tupelo phonebook. Hell of a thing to have happen on Easter Sunday morning, but there you go; more ham for the rest. And her grandfather, he had a weakness for western swing tunes and cowgirl calves, and he had a second family, it came to light, out in Oklahoma. So, yes, a hobby was good, and he might even make two dimes at it. Or anyway, he wouldn't lose too much; paper was cheap and he'd have sooner parted with her, she thought, than with that thirty-year-old typewriter he clattered away on, that old Hermes Baby, hunched over the thing like some crone at her knitting.

He needed little in the way of tools beyond that hard head of his. And she'd know where he was, holed up in that room he called his office, with his books all around, and a small desk with a bottle of Three Queens bourbon in the drawer, which he called his toolbox, and the quietude—oh, he went on about the quietude, wrote odes to it, called it his religion—and an east-facing window that overlooked a grove and the tool shed that blocked the view of the graves of war dead in the town cemetery beyond, and four walls for to beat that hard head against, poor walls. He even wrote on the walls, like Burden's own Count No-Count—plots and outlines and good goddamns. But it was his office, after all, they were his walls. They could be papered over, at some later date. She had expected to outlive him by a comfortable distance. So she encouraged him with that peck and some praise.

And then she'd do the one thing that endeared her to him more than anything: she left him alone. She retired to her sewing room, built with his hands, with a wide, nearly floor-to-ceiling window that faced the woods to the west. Deer would stand on the edge of the woods, as if to be sketched, or crooned to. She didn't sing—she was the nervous type, needed silence to settle her—but maybe she'd take up drawing. She certainly had no interest in sewing, though she could not have loved that room any more if she had. It was there she drank.

Now she stepped out of the doorway, a ghost with a drink in its hand. (To some she had been a statuesque beauty and to others just tall.) Yellow hair gone white, in a long, tight braid down the length of her back like some spinal ghost X-ray. (To some she had been curvy and to others it was just scoliosis.) Skin that would have been called pale, had she been from poor stock, but instead shone porcelain.

She was the oldest of five sisters whose father owned most of Chisca County, in Tennessee, and had a hand in some concerns down in Memphis, and whose mother had been a patroness of the arts who would at times turn their home into a retreat, a colony of sorts, she called Taloowa. There were painters and potters, artisans of all types, protest singers and other budding anarchists; some writers, even, and one time, for kicks, a hundred-year-old Chickasaw storyteller and trick-shot artist named Bird on Down. He claimed it was his ancestral home, and the mother, unflappable in anything up to a seven-point-five earthquake, said, "Well, it's ours now, but you're welcome to stay a spell. Just no trick shooting in the main house."

The father would return from one of his "business" trips—down to Memphis, or to "the coast," it might have been Pascagoula or Marseille, he never said and no one asked—and would hardly recognize his daughters, for the latest spells they had fallen under (surrealism, anarcho-transhumanism, beat poetry, folk rock); all except the oldest daughter, who took a caustic view of creative types and mostly stayed in her room and pined—for what, she did not know. She hadn't realized the man she would marry was one—a creative type, that is, a writer. Shabbily dressed as he was, with a slumping stature and no airs whatsoever, she thought he'd come to patch the hole in the dining room, a trick-shot exhibition gone drunkenly awry.

He, though, was intrigued. She seemed to him a mystery, as if she were safekeeping some secret from all these pretentious types who flitted and lolled about the grounds, who pontificated and pronounced, but did not, near as he could tell, get a goddamned lick of work done. He was different, the writer. The work to him was sacred. The work was all there was. The stories did not write themselves, and an artists' colony was naught but a den of thieves, out to steal his time. It was only the ancient Chickasaw trick-shot artist with whom he felt any kinship—creation was performance, a physical act: a hole in the wall a small price to pay for some new way through.

She would watch him from the window where she pined. He seemed to her a repudiation of everything she'd grown up with. It wasn't so much what he was but what he wasn't. And while he was not handsome, exactly, she thought he might achieve a sort of dignity with age; she'd seen it happen with dogs. There was no pomp to him. He didn't need an audience; he didn't appear to *need* anything. And he *was* good with his hands—he really did go ahead and patch that hole in the wall, while all the rest stood around discussing whether the hole was in fact a work of art and patching it an act of desecration.

Her father returned from the coast one afternoon in a foul mood, to find his eldest daughter, the sensible one, in love with this writer of stories. The father outraged, of course. A writer, of all damned things a man could become in life.

"Stories, huh?"

"Yes, sir."

"Made-up little things."

He wanted to say that stories, made-up little things, were man's greatest achievement; that the human mind's ability to imagine whole worlds and then make others see them, conjure them, through nothing more than a series of scratch marks on a page, was something even God, in all His wisdom and knowing and *blah, blah*, had not seen coming. Instead he held his powder.

"It's like that, yes," the writer said. "I write made-up little stories."

"One step below pissing your name in the snow, young man."

The writer wore no mustache then, so had no place to hide his smile.

"I could be a newspaperman instead, sir." He remembered a story the daughter told him, how her father, displeased to see his good name flouted under a front-page headline in *The Chisca County Courier*, had bought the whole operation to shut it down.

The father gave a caustic laugh. "A noble profession—drunkenness."

"That's your studied opinion of the fourth estate?"

"You have some contrary experience to share with an old man?"

"Come to think, no." He was warming to the old son of a bitch, even if there was no future in it.

Later that night, the father sent word the writer was to meet him in a certain meadow at dawn. There the father offered the writer a sum of money to make himself scarce.

"You think I can be bought?"

"You misunderstand, young man. I don't want to buy you. I did that once with a newspaper and still have not found use for all those barrels of ink and rolls of newsprint. They won't let me just pour out the ink, told me it's toxic. The mayor said that. I said, 'Hell, man. We both of us knew that all along.' " The father shook his head and then raised a scowl to the writer. "No. I want to donate a sum of money to charity with the wish that a disease be cured."

"I'm a disease to be cured?"

"You misunderstand again, I'm afraid."

"It's early, sir. I'm a writer. We're night people. Bear with and please explain."

"The disease is my daughter's future unhappiness."

"Am I to understand, sir, that you see me as some sort of germ or virus?"

"More germ, I should say."

Still the writer smiled. He could not help himself. He thought he'd been called out here to be shot.

The writer left the old man there in the meadow at dawn with his money.

They were wed within a week, the poor writer and the rich man's eldest daughter, eloping to Memphis, where they stayed in a Midtown bungalow of a friend of the writer, a professional gambler who was off to Hot Springs to play the horses. "You know professional gamblers?" she said. He said, "Well, I know the one." They drank the gambler's bourbon and they played his records, old R&B and jump blues, mostly, and she said it was like getting drunk twice, drinking and listening to those songs both at the same time. The marriage was consummated to Louis Jordan and His Tympany Five's "Caldonia." It became "their song," though they never heard it again, after they left the bungalow. Theirs would be a quiet home. It had to be; his writing, her nerves.

He looked up now, tried to bring her into focus. He looked for those flecks of paint under the nails she'd always bite down to nothing. He wondered if she'd let them grow so she could take up paint flecking, trading one nervous habit for another.

He was telling her about the river, the one in this last story of his. And rain, too, he said. Rain for days. Like in that blues song by Charley Patton, he said. *Lord sent the sunshine / Devil he send the rain.*

She went on flecking and then stopped for a drink, and then: "Well, Mister, you may be near to dying but sounds like you aim to take the whole world with you."

"It's all I'm god of, Missus. These stories."

"God. I notice you didn't say boss man or overseer. So it's god, is it?"

"I'm all those things to them. I'm warden and counsel and hanging judge. I'm everything but a jury of their peers. I'm the mayor and the governor and the president, except I'm more the dictator because they can't vote me out. But I'm a benign ruler. I don't meddle much. I'm there, but not to save them. They're on their own, that way. But I'm there. I'm bootblack to them and bartender. I'm father confessor and priest behind the veil."

"Are you husband to them, too?"

"I wasn't the worst one ever. I never raised a hand."

"Have them put that on your tombstone, when you finally do die."

He turned to look but she'd gone.

There would be a woman, too, in the story. The old writer was famous, or infamous, for his depiction of women. Entire books were written on the subject, in search of consensus that never came. Some said he wrote like he'd never met one, much less crawled into one's head to observe its vast machinations. Others swore he'd been one, in some past life. He didn't say, either way. It wasn't for him to explain. It was all in the stories.

This woman wouldn't suffer a man so well. She would be wise—to the wiles of men and the whims of God, the kick of busthead liquor. And though the wisdom would be something like a curse, she would be strong. She would stand. (God help her—but the writer would not.)

He could picture her, now before him, in the dusk of that North Mississippi day. Tall, dark, and altogether a handful. Skin the color of ...

He raised the glass and rocked it slowly, studying the brown murk.

No, not the drink. The dusk.

He remembered something one of his characters said one time. She was a poor, skinny, pale-skinned girl who longed to be something else, anything else—a gun moll, first girl chief of the Chickasaws, but most days it was a big-legged, brown-skinned blues mama. She would leave her poor side of town and walk through the wealthy part of town, long strides on skinny legs, and her long, straight, almost-white hair flying wild as weeds behind her—walked, she did, like walking was singing and she was fronting Bill Harvey's Orchestra on old Beale Street in Memphis.

A rich boy, her age but ages younger, innocent as pie, would watch the show come to town. He spied her first from his upstairs bedroom window and then through the slender windows, the sidelights, that ran up and down alongside the front door. Then the boy watched the girl from the swing of the wraparound porch, peering out over a book.

They met that day and were together every minute all through the rest of summer. The girl was a spell he was under that summer, this girl who longed to be a big-legged, brown-skinned blues mama, the second coming of Memphis Minnie or maybe Bessie Smith. They would play a game where they were other people in other times. They would disappear into these days of make-believe. Some days they were bank robbers, sitting on the hood of a rusted-out DeSoto, and other days explorers on the banks of the Mississippi, but really the Sunflower, and this one day—this was lots of days, actually—she really was the big-legged, brown-skinned blues mama she so wanted to be, and he was polite white society that judged her. She said nobody had it harder in history than the brown-skinned woman. She said the brown-skinned woman walked down a dusty road carrying hope in a leaky bucket, but kept on walking, because up ahead she thought she saw more hope than a leaky bucket could possibly spill. She saw a shining lake or a river deep. She heard a gospel choir singing "Sweeter as the Years Go By." But down deep the brown-skinned woman knew it was only a mirage, that the shining lake or river deep was nothing but spilled whiskey, and that gospel choir was nothing short of trickery in man clothes, with a line of talk on a silver tongue that sang the barrelhouse blues.

He'd take her love, she said, and then he'd take his leave but not before he'd leave a little of himself, and then it would be down the road again, the brown-skinned woman walking, walking, trudging ever on, with a leaky bucket in one hand and a little baby child on the opposite hip.

"It ain't easy being a poor, pale, skinny white girl," she said, "but it's ice cream and sweet repose next to what it might could be."

The boy said, "Well, if she knows that man's full of trickery and his tongue's silver, why's she let him—you know."

"*My, oh,* but how polite white society judges her," she said.

Which was another thing about the girl's days of make-believe. Sometimes you didn't know whether you were playing a part or baring your soul. You didn't know what had come up from the ground and what was already there inside you, waiting for the moment to give it voice.

"I don't mean to judge," the boy said.

"You can't help but," the girl said. "You're a son of money and don't know, can't know, how heavy a bucket can be even when it's leaking. You're polite society's darling yellow-haired boy and even if you've fallen for a poor, plain-faced, pale-skinned girl you don't know what it's like to want. I don't mean to judge, either. But boy, you don't *wanna* know."

The old writer thought of that old story now, from his middle period, when he had turned reflective, looked to the past to explain the present. He had no memory of writing the thing, but remembered every word. It felt as real as living. Writing was that way, sometimes. Sometimes, once in a very great while, they wrote themselves.

It had not been published, just sent out and wholesale dismissed. Most rejections said *we regret we are unable to use your story at this time*, and he wondered, as he always did, why the gatekeepers of the literary world could not say what they meant, why they said *unable to use* when they meant *don't like, don't get, despise*. Use? Hell, it was a story, not a goddamned garden implement.

His wife read the story. He brought it to her one morning in bed, like breakfast, on a serving tray with coffee. He left the room and waited. He waited on the front porch, and in time she stood in the doorway behind him, still in her morning robe, with a cup of coffee in one hand and the story in the other.

"Well?"

"I'm not sure about the characters—"

"It's all characters. That's all it is. You might as well attack my use of vowels and consonants."

She ignored him and carried on: "—a white girl who wants to be, who is it, exactly, some latter-day Memphis Minnie or Bessie Smith or who was that other one? Ma Something? And a Delta boy of privilege whose defining characteristic—whose very soul and being—is his innocence?"

"I'm not writing a story about every girl and every boy. I'm writing about one of each. One particular. One in a hundred thousand, maybe. The hundred thousand mostly bore me. It's the one I'm interested in."

"But your audience, they're the hundred thousand, aren't they? I've told you—your problem, one of them, is you've got contempt for the people who just might read your stories."

"Oh, it's worse than contempt."

"Anyway, this girl—what's she see in the blues? What's she see in the boy? I'm beginning to see why they say—"

"Say what?"

"—that you don't know females. I'm beginning to think you married the first one you actually met."

"I'm not trying to explain them all, just this one."

"And the boy."

"What of him, exactly?"

"He's what, fifteen and scared of girls?"

"He's sure as hell scared of this one. I am, too, a little." He about said *was*.

This woman, the one in his latest last story, would be one in a blue million. She would be fierce and fearless. She would fell you with a look. God would blink, the devil himself shudder.

She wouldn't need a man, but he'd give her one, just for the hell of it.

He'd even be a good man, her man. He'd have reached adulthood and still with some of that innocence of a boy. This was fiction, after all. Anything could happen.

There would be a bad man, too. City-skyline size, raised on pig iron, canned heat, a murder ballad walking. Name of—well, it would come to him. Something that just sounded guilty.

She was back now from wherever. A ghost with a fresh drink. Where *does* she put it, he wondered?

He heard that flecking of paint, a sigh, a sip, and then: "What's it about?" she asked, a mite patronizing. What she meant was, "Does anything happen?"

He once wrote four hundred pages about a man trying to decide whether to drink his bourbon neat or on the rocks (one critic called it "his most trenchant statement yet on American ambivalence and the moral quandary behind Manifest Destiny"), so her query didn't come from anywhere strange. (How a man drinks his bourbon tells you everything, he would have said, if he would have deigned to explain himself. How a woman drinks it tells you even more.)[15]

"It's about everything," he said, "more or less."

His standard dodge, though it was true. His stories *were* about everything. They were about God and man, man and woman, the beast within both, the battle for the very soul of something or other, so on and so forth. The weather tended toward the extreme, the sky bawling and the river climbing its banks, claiming the land as its own—like God with His plagues, or the devil guest-editing the Farmer's Almanac. They were populated, his stories, with damn fools, horse thieves, blues queens, pistol-packing ingénues, mongers of many things, unreliable narrators, omniscient drunkards, outright sons of bitches, cigarette girls, gun molls, wing walkers, sandhogs in the sea, one time a dog that talked.

"Everything," she said.

"More or less."

---

[15]The old writer did deign, once, to explain his approach to writing. This was in an "Art of Fiction" interview with *The Paris Review*, in which he was asked if there were certain ingredients which every story should include. "Ingredients?" he responded. "You mean like coriander?" He continued, more seriously (or not) with a stem-winder of a list, here much abridged: "Psalms and blue yodels. A hearse with steer horns. A woman named Sis. Or Ida. A pistol, pearl-handled. Pack of smokes. Hooch enough to float a hearse. The Big River, on a bender. The second coming of Bessie Smith, dripping diamonds, gin, and high-yellow chorus girls. Coriander, to taste."

"You know, Mister, if you took out a little more and put in a little less, the gentle reader might be more apt to give it a go."

He sneered. "Nobody likes a muse who gets above her raising."

She gave it back in kind. "Said the talking dog."

He remembered a drowning, years ago, up in Memphis—a famous singer who had gone into the river, to swim. He'd worn his boots in.

"Time was," he said, "when God took better care of damn fools."

"What's that about God?" she said.

"That damn fool, up in Memphis—"

"You'll need to narrow it down for me."

"You remember. A famous singer, they said. I never heard him, but. He wore his boots into the river to swim."

"Maybe he meant to walk, was why he wore his boots." She was standing in the doorway, again or still. It was the same day or another. The days had a sameness now. "You know how you artists are, think they can do any fool thing pops into their heads."

"It would be a long walk, all the way across to Arkansas," he said. "But a pleasant one, I should think."

"Yes, you of all people know how artists are. Why, remember that one time, you—"

It happened sometimes. They'd start out talking about the same thing and then they'd be in two different conversations entirely. It may have been how they'd stayed married all these years and still could be in the same house together, even with the old woman being ten years dead, a ghost now.

"I reckon it's only the first step you have to fret over," he said. "I mean to say, if you've got the courage—liquid or otherwise—to chance it. I reckon if you can take one step without sinking, why, you're on your way. It'd be nothing to take a hundred more. A thousand, even. Steps, hell—outright strides, break into a lope or trot. You might stop to dance, even, if you were to come across an unattached lady out there on the water. Some siren, say."

He was always going on about sirens, she thought. A muse wasn't enough for him, never was. Not even a muse with money, who kept ribbon in that infernal typewriter and roof over that damned hard head, while he wrote those books few bought and fewer read, except the occasional critic who said he was something of a genius. He was something, all right.

"Siren, you say," she said, and thought: Where would he have been without me? What ditch? What alley? What did a siren ever give him but the West Hell clap?

She smiled. But he's here, she thought. He's home. There's that. She liked having him here, if only to abuse him. In lieu of love—she liked to say. He called one of his stories that. She couldn't remember what the story was about, and then she did.

"A black bear, indeed!" she said. "And you, with nothing more than a butter knife in your hand. You'd drunk up all the courage there was in two counties, that night."

"Hell," he said. "I reckon if you can take that first step and stay upright, it wouldn't just be the Arkansas shore that's in play. Why, walk up and down it. The whole length of the great thing. Big Muddy! Walk up to Minnesoty, down to the Gulf o' Mexico."

"Well, it was a good story you got out of it, that thing with you and the bear," she said. "Tussle, I think you called it."

"And on through the Yucatan Channel, toward the Caribbean Sea. La Désirade Passage—saw it on a map one time, just sounded like a place to go, to be, even if I am more of a river man, myself. La Désirade Passage. The desired one—what it means in French, I should think. I reckon I'd walk that far, at least, to be desired. But anyway, it would be a nice walk, no matter what was at the end of it. Surely you'd come across some unattached ladies, in all that way."

"Tussle," she said again. "What men go looking for after they've lost the battle with the old beldam back home. Try your luck with a nine-foot thing with fur and claws. Tussle with a bear—why, of course." A shake of her head. "I don't know that it was worth almost dying over. But in the end it was only the butter knife that was lost. So I guess it's like you said before. God does look out for damn fools. Or anyway, time was when He did, when there was a more manageable number of them."

"I never tried it, mind you," he said. "Walking across the river, I mean. Sacrilege and the currents, you know, and of course the long walk back."

"God forbid you'd lift a foot to come home, to see your poor, long-suffering wife."

This was happened sometimes, too. Those separate conversations would circle back and meet, like how in a small town you can't help but bump into former friends, old flames, creditors, or the restless dead.

"I could hear you suffering, Missus," he said, "from up in Memphis."

"*Pssh*. You couldn't hear me, for all those sirens."

"You ought to take it on the road, your show," he said, and then: "Well, anyhow, I'm here now."

"Because you're too old for damn foolery."

He sighed. He sipped. He looked over in her general direction. "The deceased she speaks a bitter truth."

"Don't remind me."

"I'm only just saying."

She sipped. She sighed. "You'll miss me when you're gone, Mister."

"You mean to say I'm not going to heaven, Missus," he said, "or that I won't find you there?"

"I mean there's a special place reserved for you." She couldn't hide her pleasure in saying this, even if she only three-quarters meant it.

He shared in her pleasure. "I hope it's not like Batesville. I got crossways there once with a casketmaker's daughter."

"Batesville? No, it's well south of there."

They laughed. They drank. They might have danced but he was too old, she was too dead, and the radio had forgotten the words of "Caldonia."

"My days aren't long, Missus," he said now, in the manner of pronouncement. "Just time for— "

"I know, Mister. Just one more story. It's not just old wives who have tales, huh?"

"I believe the adage refers to the age of the wives' tales, not the wives themselves. Anyway, I mean it this time. I mean to."

"All wives are old, on account of their having husbands," she said. "Any anyway, you meant it last time and you'll mean it next time. You'll live forever and go to God's own funeral."

He tried for the bottle of bourbon, but no. He was too old and stiff; he sensed death in his bones the way some do rain.

"Some days I feel like I went to His baptism, I'm so old."

She turned to go inside. "Oh, shall we gather …" Her words trailed off, but he heard them just fine.

The day passed and another came in its wake and the old writer had not died over the course of the long, dark night. He took it as a sign. Or anyway, he drank to it—bourbon, and lo it was neat—and then he set about to writing that latest last story of his.

2

They rowed until they collapsed and then let the currents take them. They lay on their backs and listened to the river swish like choir robes at a funeral; they swayed to that burgundy sound. They floated, a one-boat procession across the river of land. It looked about like land you could walk across, that river of land being the color of mud, dusk, and her skin.

She closed her eyes and began to hum. He closed his and listened. She became, for him, that choir. The deep thud of her voice, the thrum of her hum.

It was "I Got to Cross the River of Jordan" and "Creep Along, Moses" and "Glory, Glory, Hallelujah."

"They're beautiful, those songs," John Flood said.

Cora said, "Furry Lewis sang about glory, but he sang about jellyroll, too. They all did, those old blues singers. They sang about crossing the River Jordan, but they sang about getting all up in your wife's drawers, too. They sang about the Memphis strut and that Tennessee crawl. Sang about jive and knives. Sang those dirty blues and then turned around and cut a gospel record—piss off God and the devil, both. But shit, who am I, telling this to you, professor white boy?"

"They were torn," he said. "Conflicted."

He had written scholarly papers on the subject and now was trying for a book—old blues singers who sang smut on Saturday and every other night, and then shouted praises, come Sunday and some other mornings.

"The hell," she said. "Those ol' boys were just selling records. And ladies of the church, they got needs, too."

He looked at her and smiled. She took a swig of her dead uncle's shine. She said, "You don't know the half of what goes on up under those choir robes, husband."

3

She sat, legs curled beneath her, on a chaise, reading a book. It was outside, on the Tennessee deck, the pleasure deck, and so the loudest, but she'd found a quiet spot near the bow. Her name was Dolores, but her husband, the state historian, called her Lo. She had her red hair up. She had blue-green eyes, and a strong, plain face that got called handsome. She wore a loose, white, cotton dress, a summery thing at odds with the weather, which was gray-skied and starting to cool; there was a suggestion of rain. With little time before fleeing Nashville, she had gathered enough reading material for an Old World cruise but had neglected to pack a sweater.

She barely heard his steps from behind, and so she knew. What man on board the steamer *Clementine* could be said to float? Certainly not her husband, the state historian; he walked in a sort of pitched-forward half-hurtle, always as if in a mad rush to look up some lost fact in the stacks, to distill from it some truth that might explain man's current predicament or next grand folly. He had his head in a book now, down in their cabin, reading "Bear Hunting in Tennessee,"[16] selections from Davy Crockett's autobiography excerpted in a musty, old, cloth-covered compendium called *The Literature of the South*. The book included the words of Faulkner, Welty, Wolfe, and Warren, but the state historian believed the current state of the state had antecedents in the actions of a soldier and statesman, frontiersman and folk hero, who had become, two centuries later, a cartoon myth, two state parks, a county, and a Cold War-era nuclear weapon system. His wife, who preferred the truths of fiction to the vagaries of fact, smiled and kissed his head,

---

[16] Wherein the author and adventurer explains bear hibernation at some length, and much puzzlement: "They have not a particle of food with them, but they just lie and suck the bottom of their paw all the time. I have killed many of them in their trees, which enables me to speak positively on this subject."

whispered, "I love you, you silly, serious man," and took her own book out on the deck.

She kept reading as he watched. For twenty more pages she read—a long time to float, even for him. Then she shut the book and looked up and there he was, a glass of white wine in his hand. There he had been, for the final third of Molly's closing soliloquy in Joyce's *Ulysses.*

"Yes," she said.

"I hadn't asked yet," said Trey Flattery.

"No, that's how the book ends. That's her last word. Molly's."

"Well, damn it, woman," he said, smiling the smile that never failed him, not with women or the electorate, not even, some suspected, with God or the devil. "Now you've ruined it for me."

4

Now there came a newsboy on a skiff, waving the bulldog edition out of Memphis, shouting headlines.

"Cheatham to die! Governor done turned down his appeal! Cheatham to die! Baddest man in three states!"

"What about the flood?"

"Old news, ma."

"I ain't your ma, boy."

"I ain't your boy then. Sure as shit ain't his," said the newsboy, nodding at John.

She gave him the back of her hand and sneered. He shrugged and grinned.

"What's all that about Cheatham?" she said.

"Oh, baddest man in three states."

"I heard all that. What's he supposed to have done?"

"Bulldog edition run you a nickel."

"Play ball with me, boy."

"All right, ma. He was in the state pen, death row, account of a murder he ain't never done. Falsely tried and wrongly convicted's what Cheatham said."

"What they all say."

"He blames a woman."

"They tend to."

The newsboy jutted his chin, preening like, then shrugged.

"I ain't saying either way, ma," he said. "I ain't God or Judge Harsh. Just a newsboy on a skiff at the end of the world."

"When's he supposed to die?"

"Soon as they get the 'lectricity back on." He surprised himself at his quick wit; he thought he might get some, at this rate.

"So it's the chair, huh?"

"Still fighting over that. State want to give the needle, you know. But Cheatham says if he gotta go, he wants the chair." He began to sing now, all warbly and high, like some dive-bar diva in her cups, "On top of Ol' Smokey ..."

"Cheatham." She said it slowly, precisely, as if the word were a fish hook she was removing from flesh.

"Yeah, see, ma. It's like that, ain't it? Just *sound* guilty. Cheat 'um," the newsboy said. "Knew it, too. Stood up at his trial, said it's all on account of his name. Ha! And him, with a record long as my nevermind. But a man got to try. So he did. He tried. Damn sure did. Said if his name was Work or Church or Goodpasture, like that, you know, they'd-a never made him for it. He said it was a woman did it. Said she killed her and then framed him. Said a woman killed his woman, all because—"

"Because what, boy?"

"It's awful sore did," he said. "What the paper says."

"Sore did?"

"Awful so, they say."

"Sordid?"

"I reckon, ma. I ain't French or nothing."

“Well, what’s it say?”

He saw she was losing patience, so he did, too.

“Got it all in the bulldog edition,” he said. “Got funnies in there, too. Show me some coin or something else, big mama. I’ll show you my—”

She looked at her husband, to see what he was making of it all. But he was asleep, or acting it.

“Well, that’s all real tragic there, boy,” she said. “But what about this flood? What’s that Memphis rag of yours say about that?”

The newsboy unfolded the newspaper and held it at arm’s length from his face. He scanned it up and down.

“Cheatham to die!” he shouted. “Baddest man in three states!”

Now the newsboy drifted his skiff close and held the newspaper out for her to grab. She reached and he pulled it back. Skinny thing, the newsboy. All elbows, eyes, teeth, gall. Hadn’t ever gotten crossways with an actual grown woman until now and assumed they were just larger versions of girls.

“It’s like I said. You show me yours, big mama, and—” He threw back his head to laugh, and when he looked again it was down the barrel of .58 caliber, single-shot, flintlock dueling pistol, French-made. He’d seen guns before but not one quite like this, or from quite this angle.

“The hell’s that, ma?”

“That’s mine,” she said. “You still wanna show me yours?”

“Nevermind,” he said, handing over the newspaper.

“Your nevermind seems kind of a puny, all the sudden, boy.”

“You ain’t got to be that way, ma.”

She took the newspaper and shook it. From the folds of pages fell a 1917 Standing Liberty Quarter. He wouldn’t have been more surprised if it were a white dove come fluttering from. She flipped him the coin. It seemed to hang in the heavy air an unnatural length of time before it landed in his palm, heads up, and there in her glory the goddess Liberty with one breast bare and other concealed by a shield. She had a bit of a haughty look, it seemed to the boy, though he would not have used that word; he wasn't French or nothing.

"Why, I never," said the newsboy, breaking into a smile.

"You oughta try it sometime," said Cora Flood.

5

Back on the steamer *Clementine*, on the forecastle, which had become a sort of floating schoolroom for the sons and daughters of the government officials and country stars on board, the children were getting restless. That was just like children, the little snotnoses.

Their teacher was a banjo player in a latter-day string band out of Kentucky called Tom T. Y'all. He was a born performer, and, being a banjo player in a latter-day string band, did not require much of a crowd, or any encouragement really at all, to do his thing. He had played before indifferent drunks and lowing cattle. He had seen his own dear mother walk out, before the first chorus, and one time, in front of something shy of a smattering in a dive bar in Crowville, Alabama, a patron up and died, three songs into the band's set, on a barstool said to have been Hank Williams' favorite whenever he came through town. Other times, the band attracted actual crowds, lured under the guise, apparently, of seeing a Hot Country band with one of those nod-to-the-past names, and the crowds, misled so, would turn on Tom T. Y'all with hoots, hisses, full cans of tall-boy beers. On these nights, the band members toyed with changing their musical style to metal and their moniker to Fuck Y'all. They had long discussions about it. But they stayed true to the old-time songs they covered and the new old-timey ones they wrote; the banjo player, a strayed MFA student from Sewanee, the University of the South, was the lyricist.

So the banjo player could take indifference. He could even take ridicule; he could draw on his reserves of artistic integrity, dodge those incoming tall-boy cans, and carry on with the likes of "Keep My Skillet Good and Greasy," "Brain Cloudy Blues," and "The Next-to-Last Train Song."[17]

He could take it all and everything—but children? *Christ.*

"Any y'all little snotnoses know who invented country music?"

"My daddy!"

"Your mama!"

"God!"

"Colt Remington!"

"Dodge Ford!"

The banjo player ordered the young offenders thrown overboard.

This was his first teaching gig. He had been conscripted by some junior members of the governor's staff when he was overheard in the lounges of the pleasure deck using words like "anastrophe" and "periphrasis." The junior members of the governor's staff did not know the meaning of these words—something out of the medical sciences, they reckoned—but the banjo player seemed to be using them with a certain command, notwithstanding he was half lit and trying to impress the lieutenant governor's daughter. The governor's men cornered him afterward, said for him to come with them.

---

[17]The last song was a band original, with lyrics by the banjo player. A treatise on honesty, personal reckoning, and what remains of best intentions after a month on the road playing dive bars and living out of a van, it opens: "The truth is a slow train, and we're all just hobos, really."

He thought he might get himself keelhauled, whatever that was, for trying to put the make on the lieutenant governor's daughter, who turned out to prefer girls, and post-shoegaze indie rock, whatever that was. But the governor's men told him he was the new teacher in residence, and to work up a *crick-lum*.

And so:

String Band Theory.
Introduction to Patsy Cline.
Quantitative Analysis in Cheating Songs.
Random Vibrations: Uncle Dave Macon Died for His Own Sins; You're Strictly on Your Own.
Cognitive Bluegrass.
Imitation, Quotation, Appropriation, and Genre: Country's Black Roots and the White Man's Thieving, Conniving Ways.

The banjo player's name was Bascom Holcomb Miller, though most called him Bud. He was named for Bascom Lamar Lunsford, the lawyer, college professor, newspaper publisher, and old-time singer known as the Minstrel of the Appalachians, and for Roscoe Holcomb, the Kentucky coal miner, construction worker, farmer, and singer who inspired the term "high, lonesome sound." He used to introduce himself by the full name in the bars of Lower Broadway in Nashville, and for a time on stage of the Teardrop Room during Tom T. Y'all's brief residency there, but it was rare he came across a drunken soul, much less a pretty girl, for whom old Bascom or Roscoe rang so much as a note, so Bud it was. Bud Miller—a banjo player named after two cans of beer who could use words like "anastrophe" and "periphrasis" in a sentence while half lit.

It was a skill—got him out of a DUI check-point stop one late night/early morning out on Donelson Pike, didn't it?—

but he was increasingly thinking, as the old song goes, that the world was not his home. Or anyway, Nashville sure as hell wasn't. The country music there sounded like it was shot out of a pop gun. Hell of a thing to raise a child on.

He had been one, of course—a child, a real snotnose, even. But that was long ago and ended all of a sudden, on a summer day back home in Heel Lick, in Kentucky, down near the Tennessee line. It was the day his grandfather on his mother's side showed him the secret chord on the old man's Martin D-28 guitar. It was nothing but a C major, but the old man said it would bring the boy fame, heartache, women, and all the free corn he could drink. He said that single chord, played on whatever was at hand, would take the boy around the world twice and halfway back again. He said it would stop God in His tracks to listen. He said the devil would offer gold-plated this and diamond-studded that and all the string he could pull. The old man went on in this way for some time, as prelude to instruction, and the boy listened as he always did to the old man, with a sort of rapt attention he never could quite summon in church. Then, finally, he said, "What's string?" It was the old man's old guitar that answered. It was that secret chord, and others as well, a chorus of them, and couplets which the old man sang, but in a higher, lighter voice than that which he spoke, as if some bird were inside him and now stirring, fluttering to life. The words had wings. The notes were blue skies and the chords were white clouds, and it would never rain again, and then it did, the sky was awash, and the boy drenched by it, as if the world had turned upside down and rivers were sky and sky was land, and the old man was some ancient prelate of song. The boy may not have become a man, in that moment, on that day, but he damned sure became a musician.

Bascom Holcomb "Bud" Miller told the snotnoses all about the complicated history of country music. He told about how the banjo's origins could be traced to Africa, where it was made with a gourd and goat skin. He told about DeFord Bailey, the Black harmonica player who was an early star of the Grand Ole Opry, and was beloved and respected, though he was sometimes known as the Opry's "mascot," and was later fired from the Opry because of what was made out to be a publishing dispute. He said racism got called lots of things in those days, and in these.

He said country music was Southern music, but you didn't have to be from the South to play it. He said Hank Snow was Canadian, and Jerry Jeff Walker was born Ronald Clyde Crosby in Oneonta, New York. He said Southern music was immigrant music—English, Irish, Scottish and more. He said there was Black music in it, too, come all the way from Africa, against its will, on slave ships. He said he wouldn't give two bits or a damn for music that wasn't some kind of mongrel mix of influences.

He said white or Black didn't matter to the music, really. He said music really is what justice is supposed to be. He said you only had to have the chops and creativity to get your song across, he said it was the song, not the singer.

He said Southern Black men, and women, too, tended to sing and play the deepest blues, it's true, but if all you had to be was poor, dark-skinned, and oppressed by that fucker Jim Crow, why was there only one Robert Johnson, and one Mississippi John Hurt, and Good Lord yes, one Bessie Smith? Because of chops, he said. He said it all came down to chops, in the end.

He said there were little green men in outer space, no taller than salt shakers, who could play the old Appalachian reel " 'Neck O' the Woods" like they were born in Horse Cave or Butcher's Hollow, in old Kentuck. He said he once heard a Russian trawler captain sing a version of "Even the Lone Star State Gets Lonesome" that brought an entire Scottish village to tears—or maybe it was the scotch that did it.

He told about the Big Bang of Modern Country Music, when in 1927 a northern record man named Ralph Peer came to Bristol, set up a makeshift studio, and recorded the likes of the Carter Family and Jimmie Rodgers—a grand moment in the history of man, it's true, he said, notwithstanding that Uncle Dave Macon had cut records in New York City three years before. New York City! He said if Jimmie Rodgers was the Father of Country Music, like they all said, then Dave Macon was its Crazy Uncle. But he said Uncle Dave, the "Dixie Dewdrop," didn't invent country music either. He said country music had always been around, that it was older than dirt and the devil.

What about God, some snotnose wanted to know.

The banjo player said there was no God, that Hank Williams was as good as it got and we should be thankful.

What about Intelligent Design?

He said Intelligent Design was that yellow Nudie jumpsuit Dolly Parton wore on the back cover of her "Best of," Volume 2, record, and Elvis in gold lamé.

6

The Floods drifted for an hour or more. They passed abandoned outposts and the rusted husks of wrecked ships and what once was the town of Bunk. Or was it Christfallen?

They saw the granite head of some Civil War general. He wore his hat, and a scowl. The floodwaters were up to his stiff upper lip.

"Kin of yours?" said Cora to John.

Then a mile of nothing but water and sky. The water was the color of soot and the sky of ash.

They passed a half-sunken pier on which perched a row of turkey buzzards, serious as judges about to send a man to his death.

They passed a series of hand-painted wooden signs poking up from the water on long poles. The signs were white with red letters and written with an unsteady hand:

Hell, Mary
Mother of all floods
Pray for us swimmers

They drifted on. Past nothing and more of the same.

7

Governor Trey Flattery leaned on the rail, his back to the red-tressed wife of the state historian, gazing out at all that gray nothingness. He sipped his wine and said, "I was married in a tux that color."

She had unfolded her legs and stretched them down the length of the chaise. The book was on her lap, her hands clasped over it. She looked up at him. He seemed to glow as well as float; he hardly seemed real, and she wondered, idly, if what was left of the state was being overseen by an apparition.

"Was that the first time or the second or the third, Governor?"

He liked a little resistance. He smiled into his glass. Were her eyes green or blue? Both at once? It seemed so. Was there a name for that shade? He bet the state historian didn't know the answer to that one.

"The first," he said. "The second, we were on a beach, on an island I'm just slightly ashamed to admit I owned at the time. So it was something tropical, to match the island. I wore white, I suppose, and her as well. No, no. I remember. She wore blue—a shade of blue. I remember we all had great fun trying to come up with the exact shade, the name for it. It was Bate, of all people, who did. Azure, he said. He was sure of it. That man will surprise, once in a great while."

Azure—was that the shade of blue in her eyes? No, it was darker than azure. It began to sound like a silly word, the more he said it in his mind. Azure—it sounded like the name of some pretentious Nashville restaurant with fifteen-dollar martinis that tourists lapped up, hoping for a possible glimpse of Colt Remington or Dodge Ford at the bar, and sure they'd be able to tell the difference. Or a stripper's name. Azure.

"And the third?"

"What's that?"

"Your third wedding, Governor. The one that finally took—or anyway, so far, so good."

He smiled. What was it about her? Her impudence? It wasn't her looks, exactly. She squinched her eyes and wore no makeup and hadn't gotten one of those shots to puff up her lips. She was no Miss South Carolina. Or was it North Carolina? Still, though, those eyes were made all the more mysterious by her squinching, and the natural, as-is, all-original-parts, nature of her nature made the souped-up, tricked-out woman of his world seem sort of silly now, like a fifteen-dollar martini, or the word *azure*.

"Honestly, I don't remember. We didn't make a fuss. I'm sure I was presentable and she was lovely. The state supreme court judge who hitched us, I feel sure he wore black—was wearing black already."

He looked to sit but there was no other chair and she did not move her legs to make room on the chaise. He'd been leaning for ten minutes, and floating for twenty more before that, but she intrigued him, the red-tressed, mystery-eyed wife of the stuffy state historian. Maybe he'd have wheels put on Old Smokey. Wheels and a motor, too. He could challenge other Southern governors and presidential hopefuls to races. They'd have a circuit, of sorts, like NASCAR. He'd win. Women would swoon. But would this one?

"Well, I'm sure they all must pale—weddings, I mean—after you've been married on a tropical island," she said. "But why ashamed of owning it? It was yours, the island.

You bought it. I'm sure the money was fairly got. Or at least, strictly speaking, legal."

Most women didn't resist nearly enough, he thought. They were entirely too eager. (The country singer, Mistress No. 2, had brought pink handcuffs on their first "date.") This one, though, was outright insolent. The sharp mouth on her, the skinny lips, a strong jaw, that face that was not quite pretty but could be called, yes, he supposed, in a pinch, or a flood, handsome. Those red tresses, though. They were the real damn thing, even if they were so long only because she couldn't be bothered to have them sheared.

Dolores. Lo. Fiery bride of the fusty state historian.

"Nobody should own an island," he said now, gathering himself, for to begin his offensive. He turned full around to face her. He leaned back against the rail. "It's like owning a forest or an ocean, the sky, clouds. It's just too much, I don't know, hubris for one man to be showing." He about shrugged but did not, quite. He had never used the word *hubris* in a sentence and was glad to be leaning for it.

"But it gets worse," he continued. "I sold the island and bought a mountain." He turned and looked again at the sky, as if he might be about to put in an offer on it. "God must look down and shake His old head at me."

"And still," she said, "only just slightly ashamed."

"What can I say? I'm a deeply flawed man. I don't deny it. But I'm self-aware, at least." He seemed to think about this. He frowned—but not really. "That makes it worse, somehow, I think." There was a hint of pride in his voice, and they both caught it, like something in the wind, which was just beginning to pick up in a serious way.

Then it began to rain, a little, a needling rain. It stopped as suddenly, as if in prelude to some great gusher. The sky darkened a shade and began to swirl, then roil, to the west, toward Memphis and then calmed even as it turned darker still.

"Have you heard of something, Governor, called Imposter Syndrome?"

"Called what?"

"Imposter Syndrome—where you think you're basically a fraud, a pretender, and you're always about to be found out. Outed as a fraud, as not really what you present yourself to be, even if you're only a special assistant to the assistant director of absolutely nothing."

"Sounds like some made-up thing."

"Well, that's what I thought, in a manner of speaking. I thought—Imposter Syndrome, why, that's just the human condition, isn't it? That's all of us. It's like a line I read in book. This one character says to another, 'We're all of us just basket cases.' I think that's what the author ought to have titled the book. Hell, I think every self-help book ever ought to be called that. Because we are, or anyway I thought so, all of us just basket cases, waiting to be found out and outed as imposters."

"Well, I never really—"

"Exactly. Governor. You don't have it. I'm sure now you never did. That's how I came to realize Imposter Syndrome is a real thing—because not everybody has it. It's not the human condition. It's only most of us who have it. But you—"

"I don't quite follow." He was, indeed, slightly confused. Was she finally starting to come on to him?

"You're no imposter, are you, Governor? You're the real thing. You're what you purport to be. It must be remarkable to be you. And here I sit, afflicted as ever, with Imposter Syndrome. I just finished *Ulysses*, one of the most knotty books ever written, and I was there with Joyce, I was in bed with Molly for her monologue! *Yes! Yes!*—"

She *is* coming on to me, the governor thought. Why hell yes, the leggy wench. Never before done it on a chaise in a downpour on the high seas!

"Naughty," he said, "you say?"

"Oh, in all ways and spellings, Governor."

"Indeed." His eyes looked into hers as his body angled for somewhere to sit.

"But can I get twenty pages into *Finnegans Wake*? Can I make hide nor hair? Can I, governor?"

"Imposter Syndrome?"

"I'm an imposter at the thing I've always been best at. Feel like I am, anyway—and that's the condition itself. It's a total self-diagnosis thing."

Yes, the governor thought. Totally coming on to me. Throw our clothes overboard. Shameless, we'll be. All legs and lust.

"We should take cover," he said, lowering himself onto the end of the chaise, though still she had not moved her legs. "Have a drink, talk. Wait out the storm."

"Then why are you sitting down?"

He made a show of lifting the glass, something of the charmer and charlatan in the act. He took from it an elegant sip, licked his lips, said *Ah-hah.* His right handed his left the glass. The right reached for her shin. It was so pale that it shone, despite there being such little light.

"I'm not drinking," she said.

"Too much the other night?"

"Too much? What?"

"Oh. I saw you. The other night, I mean. You, over the side, getting—well, indisposed, let's say. I thought sea sicknesses, but—"

"I'm pregnant, Governor," she said. "Twins, they say."

His hand paused there, just above her shin; the inch between them might have been a mile, the shadow a demilitarized zone. The governor looked as if he might like to leave it there, that hand, hovering, floating, while the rest of him made a hasty exit. He'd been chastened twice in one day—certainly some kind of personal record. But still it didn't shake him, not really. He was Trey Flattery. Nothing truly bad had ever happened to him. He was the governor of Tennessee and might someday be president. Somewhere on board he had two mistresses, one a supermodel and the other a state pageant-winner cum country star, and there was always his wife, if it came to that. There was something there, still. Or at least there was as much as there ever was—a perfect-looking couple, they were: presidential. "What politics has joined together, let no god or goddamn fool put asunder," were Bate's suggested wedding vows.

"Of course, yes," said the governor now to the state historian's wife. "Just so." He about said *top notch!*

He slowly rose and turned and began to step away. That hand had gone to sleep and he felt like he was tugging some dead-weight, shameful part of him.

"But Governor?"

"Yes, Mrs. Blankenship?"

Yes, yes. Wait.

"If I wasn't?"

"Yes, Mrs. Blankenship. Yes?"

Wait for it, wait for it.

"Still no, Governor."

8

He turned on the crank radio, trying for a song, or something about the weather, or news of the condemned man, Cheatham.

Static, some shape-note hymnody, the Bible verse of the day, something about woe and treachery, and then the voice of the DJ on the pirate station out of Memphis: "Good people, good people, and all the rest of y'all. Listen up. We got news from across what used to was Tennessee."

There was a rustling of papers, then the clatter of a bottle being toppled, a muffled *fuck me,* and then, "Technical difficulties, y'all, bear with." Dead air. A moment of silence for the spilled booze, then a song called "Oh Baby, No, Never, Please, Uh-uh," a blues for snare drum, pawn shop guitar, and open weeping.

Then the sound again of papers rustling. A sound-effects tap-a-tap of typewriter keys, signaling the news, and then this, just in from the eastern provinces …

Tennessee Goddam

I got six men
They like to fight over my bones
When they're done I bury five
Then I take the one on home

—Lil Cripes & Her Mean Time Five
"You Got to Want Me Blues"

I wanna take a journey
To the devil down below
I done killed my man
I wanna reap just what I've sowed

—Bessie Smith
"Send Me to the 'Lectric Chair"

1

The bomb woke him. It about took a bomb, most days, to wake him. For Cheatham slept the sleep of the dead. "Good practice," Shagbark Turner, fellow denizen of that doomed place, liked to say. This was death row, at Old Black Prison, a great, gray palace of gloom at the foot of Old Black Mountain, in the Great Smoky Mountains, in the far eastern cranny of the former Tennessee.

Turner, he'd be dead now—ashes to ashes, dust to dust, Shag to bark. They'd all be dead, the dead fuckers. And who to mourn, light a candle, give a shit? Creek the Indian who really wasn't, and Old Man Merry—funny name for the nastiest bastard of the lot. First time Cheat heard it, he said, "Who'd you fucking kill, Merry. Santy Claus?" Old Man Merry made a growly sort of noise that put in Cheat's head the image of fur and fang. Cheat smiled; well, it was not ladies' tea and crumpets he'd come to. Wasn't nothing dainty about these digs or delicate about these denizens. Said, "Don't go biting my ankles, now. Just saying hidy, was all." Old Man Merry—likewise dead now, but not from old age. And all the rest. Manfred Bland, who had manners, laid out his victims like Sunday dinner and over them said prayers they could not hear and God did not acknowledge. The devil, even, turned a deaf ear. A truly sick fucker, was Manfred Bland, but not so death row noticed, so much. And Deuce Coleman, who was stoned, was all, and did not mean to do that thing he did with the machete to his bosom friend. Was just playing. Goofing. Fucking around while seriously fucked up. Real dope fiend, Deuce. Angel dust like dry rub on a Memphis rack of ribs. But not a bad man, not really. Deuce, who regretted it, truly, who broke down every time he heard the word *decapitate* at his trial. Said, famously, while on the stand, that if it were possible he would *recapitate* his bosom friend. "Recapitate?" said the prosecuting attorney. "You know," said Deuce, "put it back on. His head." The judge had to give the jury a talking-to about losing their shit in open court. But hell, judge was laughing, too. So, dead now, poor dumb Deuce, who might have had an insanity case, there being something of a fine line between dumb and crazy in the eyes of the world, except that Deuce snorted that fine line and everything else in sight—one time some actual Memphis dry rub. As the defense attorney said in his close, "It wasn't so much that Deuce took drugs but that drugs took Deuce."

"Be that as it may," said judge, jury, and the state of Tennessee.

Dead now. All dead. Rest in pieces, like your bosom friend who went and lost his head. Oh, and the Reverend. Dead as well. The Reverend Robert "Thee" Kingdom, Pentecostal preacher who did not just handle snakes but taught the slithery bastards to rob banks. Imagine you that. But a snake in a situation of such high tension and tight quarters will choose flesh over a fresh stack of hundreds, every time. A rattler has no need for a grand mansion or sleek roadster or whatever else ill-gotten gains would get him. He won't wear him some pretties, splurge on art. No need to see the David. A snake's a snake. We been knowing that since the beginning of time. And so Reverend Robert "Thee" Kingdom, charged with four counts of capital murder and seven of corrupting a snake. Defense argued, with passion and Bible passages, that you cannot corrupt a snake, for a snake is born bent. "Objection, Your Honor. The snakes they ain't on trial here." "Sustained, and so very true." Jury deliberated for six minutes, and the judge, at sentencing, said the Rev was to die by lethal injection of a cocktail of rattler venom and Disperse Red 9.[18]

Dead, all dead.

---

[18]The dye used to foil bank robbers. Bright, colorful, and awfully messy, though found to be essentially harmless in laboratory studies on sheep, rabbits and female Sprague-Dawley rats, as documented in "Toxicity of Military Smokes and Irritants: Volume 3." Disperse Red 9 is used in the state's execution cocktail, then, as Campari in a Boulevardier—splash of color, bit of tartness.

But not Lee Cheatham, for reasons he could not for the life of him explain, as he awoke, groggily, from his nightly death called sleep, to see all this destruction.

The bomb had blown through the northwest corner of Old Black Prison. It was all scree and rubble now. It was Sunday, first light. Gray skies and a flush of rain, ill wind out of the west and gusting. And death row, brought down around itself.

A bomb. On death row, of all damned places. But then what place more damned and thus deserving of a bomb? Gallows humor had it that Big Karma would claim responsibility, or that perhaps the state, in consultation with a higher power, or efficiency experts, had found something more expedient than electricity or otherwise juice for killing its most heinous and doomed, of which Cheatham was considered foremost. He was the most feared, because of his size and perpetual scowl, but also the most doomed: His execution date had been fixed for two weeks hence, and Governor Flattery, the heartless charmer, had not granted a stay.

Yet here he was, Cheatham, on the outside of Old Black, the prison, about a hundred yards up Old Black, the mountain, looking down on all that fresh ruin in the rain.

He thought for a moment that he'd died and gone to … where? The cheap seats? The colored section?

"Poor Cheat."

Said one prison guard to another, as they stood in the smolder, surveying what had happened.

"Bet he ain't so tall now."

Said the other.

"I think I saw a finger. Less'n it was a piece of iron bar."

"Guess he didn't get to go how he wanted."

"Ha—sitting down."

"Please, Mistuh Guv'nor, sir, your eminence. Ha. Like Guv Flattery ain't got more important things on his plate."

"His lap, more like. The mighty whore dog."

"You ever screw a country star, Donnie?"

"Not that she said, Mel."

"Well, I don't guess an album cover counts."

He was thinking of the *Best of Dolly Parton, Vol. 2.*

"Nup. I think she must be present to win."

"Well, anyhow, good on Guv Flattery, the mighty whore dog."

"It's the life, I tell you."

"And here stands us. Or we. Whatever."

"And there lies Cheat. Somewhere there. And there. He cheated death, but only for a while."

"Let it be said. Let the record show."

The one went to perform the sign of the cross but he was not of the faith and bungled the thing. It looked like he was giving a mule directions to Kingsport.

"Think he's in hell already?"

"On his way, s'pose. And nobody to save his—"

"I think I saw part of an ass."

"Some cheek, that one."

"Reckon we ought to do something."

"Gather up the remains for identification?"

"Yeah, let's us do that. You want coffee first? I got a little something we can put in."

"Good man."

2

God at his typewriter. Long fingers, lovely form. Good posture. Looking down upon the machine. Favors a 1931

Continental Klein Conti, smoky gold of color, like His eyes, with cream-colored keys, like His robe, this day.

God at the keys. God, playing that thing.

God, writing the story of a writer writing a story about the end of it all. The writer in God's story is an old, dying man with a dead wife who haunts him. God pauses. No, not haunts. That's not it, exactly. It's more complicated than that. The writer kind of likes having her around, actually. Her sharp tongue, tart asides. Her height and bearing, even moreso evident as she hovers, inches above the floor. Presence—that's what she has that she hadn't before. Seems like that'd be the thing you'd lose, in death, not gain, God's writer thinks. Wonders what it's like to kiss a ghost, or more. Could you gain purchase, achieve friction with an apparition? (The writer's old, not dead.) So no, not haunting, exactly. God scowls at the words on the page and reaches for the bottle, takes His own name in vain. He's gotten it wrong once again, balled it all up like always.

God goes through Wite-Out like the old writer goes through Three Queens.

3

They drifted on. Past an unmanned canoe filled with books, from which they plucked a Library of America edition of Carson McCullers' stories and other writings; a fistful of pulp detective novels including one titled, *That Girl was Trouble*, which began, " 'Armed and dangerous,' she said, brightly, as if these were the qualities she sought in a man"; a first edition of Peter Taylor's *A Summons to Memphis*; a seventh edition, seventh printing *Boy Scout Handbook*, bookmarked by a small blue "applicant's record" card for the Reptile Study merit badge, between pages 424 ("Stimulants and Narcotics") and 425 ("From Boy to Man"); a University Press of Mississippi edition of Eudora Welty photographs; and a Tupelo, Mississippi, phone book from 1941. He clutched this latter as if it were of divine provenance. He paged to the letter P, sought the name Presley, Vernon.

"If only we had a telephone, Mrs. Flood."

"And the lines weren't down, Mr. Flood."

"Well, yes."

"And it were 1941."

"True."

"And little Elvis wasn't away at school. About a first-grader, he'd be."

"He started East Tupelo Consolidated that year."

"We could talk to Gladys."

"We could, if they had a phone."

"If only."

"I don't guess this old party barge can take us back in time. I'm beginning to wonder if it'll make Memphis."

"Would Vernon be in or out of jail, at this point in the life of young Elvis?"

"He'd have been out. Done his time. Eight months for forgery. Wasn't like he killed a man."

She raised an eyebrow. "Still, shiftless by nature."

"He worked. Helped build that shotgun shack they lived in."

"Little ol' thing," she said, and sang at him, "*You got a gal, six feet tall, sleeps in the kitchen with her feet in the hall.*" She was that height, and a hair more; upon her big feet, big shoes: women's elevens.

"I think it was hard for Vernon, you know, how close Elvis and Gladys were. They were so close I'm not sure there was room for him."

"All that baby talk between them. No telling what else."

"It would be fascinating, wouldn't it? To talk to Gladys. Us calling long distance, to the past."

"She'd be sitting at the kitchen table, drinking a can of Schlitz, I bet, waiting on Elvis to come home from East Tupelo

Consolidated. Just waiting to ask how did first grade go, Little E? Did you get any, baby? And Elvis blushing, saying, *Now, Mama*."

She was paging through the Boy Scout Handbook. She read passages from pages 424 and 425. She summarized. "Don't smoke. Don't drink—anything but milk. Not even tea or coffee. Jesus, these scolds. Oh, and don't jerk off—that's apparently not what the Boy Scouts have in mind by reptile study."

She looked at him across the length of the party barge. He was looking down at his shoes, his men's nines. He looked up and laughed, may even have blushed, difficult to say in the crepuscular murk of the day.

"Mostly," he said.

"Mostly, what?"

"You were about to ask me if I was a good Boy Scout."

They drifted on, silently. An hour became two. He was studying the photographs by Eudora Welty, mostly of 1930s life in Mississippi. They were like reading a Eudora story, sly and playful and sadly wise. Her pictures told stories, spun tales, cracked windows to lost worlds. There was a picture of an old Black woman, seated, in white rumpled house dress and wearing what looks like a man's hat, a Homburg, and the shadow from the brim covers her eyes save for the lower lid of the right. She's smiling, just shy of a grin. In her raised right hand she grips an ice pick, but not to pick ice. On the opposite page, there's an old, blind, white woman at her weaving.

There were pictures of dusty small-town Mississippi streets and country shacks, plum pickers, and a hog killing. There was a woman chopping cotton and another holding a baby. There were farmers in town, in their suspenders and hats, a Baptist deacon with a mustache that could have spanned the Yazoo River, a couple of Confederate veterans on a park bench.

State-fair floats and women with wings in a pageant of birds. Shanty boats and a man buying a ticket from a booth under a sign that read "Colored Entrance to All Performances." There was another of a group of tomato packers in Copiah County. They're on a break, huddled around a man playing guitar. His right hand, the strumming hand, is a blur. Just to his right, a man in rolled-up shirt sleeves and no hat, looks on with a grin. The musician and the other workers are elevated, on some sort of platform or porch. There's a boy in overalls and ballcap, on the ground, gazing up at the guitar player. He has one arm on the platform and the other is bent slightly backward with his hand on a hip. He's in awe, looking up and gazing as if at some Tuesday-afternoon comet streaming across the Copiah County sky.

John showed the picture to Cora.

"What's in that boy's head, you think?"

"What's he thinking, you mean?"

"Yeah."

She thought about it, but not long.

"He's just come to realize," she said, "there are two kinds of people in the world."

They drifted on. A couple of minutes became ten. He watched the sky for Tuesday-afternoon comets but all was calm up there. It was as if God and His angels were waiting to hear what she would say.

"Two kinds, huh?" John said, finally.

It was another ten minutes before she answered. Maybe she just assumed he and God and His angels already knew the answer, since it was plain even to that boy in Copiah County, Mississippi, in nineteen and thirty-something.

"There are tomato packers," she said, "and there are guitar pickers."

Later, apropos of all that, they fell into a long conversation about Elvis.

"You're asking," she said, when he had gone on for some time about the question of cultural appropriation, "would I have fucked him?"

It was not what he was asking. And yet …

4

He was a big man, that bad man, Lee Cheatham. Square head atop a wide span of shoulders. A body that tapered just slightly, wedge-like, down the long length of him. He went six-foot-seven, a solid two hundred and sixty-eight pounds, even on prison food. But prison food, shit—you'd have thought he ate pig iron for breakfast and picked filings from his teeth with hundred-year-old hickories. Parts of him looked carved and others forged. Feet the size of keelboats, cloudburst fists. He could have given a giant a go. Could have survived anything—but a bomb.

Yet here he was, spared. Saved, in some premeditated way. But by whom? For what purpose? Was it the hand of God? Not too goddamned likely. But what? He didn't sleepwalk, and damn sure not through prison walls.

Best guess, he'd been drugged and then dragged from his cell, dark of night, and dumped that hundred yards up the mountain. Surely that was it. What other explanation? Then the bomb planted, a timer set. But the bomb just a diversion, a feint, though Shagbark and Manfred and the rest would not have agreed.

Who could be so diabolical? Who could have plotted it and made it so? Who with both chops and connections? God? God, no. The government? Well …

All this thinking made his head hurt, which he took as a good sign. He felt as if he were coming out from under this chemical effect, whatever it was. Like anesthesia, or a lost weekend. He felt like he'd been rewired and his limbs switched around, an arm where his leg ought to be. But it was fading, the fuzziness. His ears were ringing but that was the bomb. He'd have rather'd Coltrane's "Ascension," or some Albert Ayler, some wild, free jazz, but hell, it was good to hear at all.

He looked about. Well, fuck me, he thought. Fuck me roundly with a small crowd around. A few feet away was an Army-green backpack, and in the backpack a change of clothes, boots, a knife, a pistol, a length of rope, a hundred dollars in tens and twenties, a crank radio, some jerky, a jug of water. The pants were dungarees. His size, as were the boots. The shirt was one of those numbers like an old country and western star would wear, egg yellow with pearl buttons, and white stitching to look like, the fuck are they called, lariats. More designs in other colors, sagebrush or some shit, a wagon wheel, on which posed a scarcely dressed cowgirl with a lasso. Looked like the first thing a hick would buy after he'd won the lottery, or had a hit record on the Hot Country charts. Size XXXL Tall, looked like a fucking circus tent, sure enough, and him the goddamnedest sideshow act ever witnessed west of the Great Smoky Mountains or east of the Mississippi River.

See the man who escaped Tennessee's death row without even trying!

Cheatham—the man who cheated death!

5

The Floods had drifted somewhat to the south. More statues of more soldiers, of horses' heads and sabers, the odd obelisk. It was as if the war were being fought again, at flood stage. To whom the advantage, this time?

"Shiloh," she said.

"Holy ground," he said. For John loved places that held their history, that heaved under the weight of it. "You can go to church on Shiloh. You can talk to God."

"There's a good catfish joint around here somewhere, or there was," she said. "Maybe ask God directions. He's good at pointing a finger."

"I was here once, one summer, long time ago. That summer I—" He had begun sentences this way since they met. *That summer I—.* She always let it pass. He didn't know if she didn't care or had an almost preternatural understanding that some stories took time to tell and could not be, should not be, rushed. His money was on the latter, her being a woman with an untold story of her own.

"Catfish Hotel—that's what it was called," she said.

"We just roamed all over," he said. "In and out of the woods. We saw things. Or felt them. They were there, as sure as we were. Most places, the ghosts have an element of surprise, you know. At Shiloh, you expected to see them. And we did."

"We're all bottom feeders now, I reckon."

"Ghosts," he said, eyes peeled for one now. "Stepping out from behind a tree in the woods or over a rise in a clearing."

"I've gotten myself hungry. Hand me a can of those beans, husband. And a pack of crackers if we have any left."

"You think ghosts can swim?"

"Damned but if we aren't eating like goddamn field hands. It's come to this."

"You think they can?"

"Ghosts? Swim? Nah, husband, I think they just sort of hover. Get the hem of their garments muddy, but otherwise no harm done."

Along about nightfall now. Or it was high noon and just another dark day.

"I can't see much of anything."

"Good time for a story." She struck a match and lit a protection candle. "Tell me one."

"One what? Ghost story?"

"Nah, husband. I know all those. Tell me the story of you. Tell me how a sheltered white boy came to be sitting here with a ruint Black woman. Tell me how you came to be at my big feet, and why you look at me like you do—looking at me now, that way. Like I'm the boss and high chief, the woman king, and you'd do whatever I said, dive over the side, swim to the bottom and get me a couple of filets, fried, from the Catfish Hotel, if I said so. You'd do that for me, wouldn't you? You'd rob the place for me, if I said so. And you, who'd never done one crazy thing in his life before he married the likes of me." She paused for the length of a cigarette puff, though she wasn't smoking. "Or did you?"

So he told her.

6

A breeze blew through the cemetery at dusk, mussing the leaves of ancient oaks. Shadows up and danced. It felt like rain.

This was how it began, his story, his story of ...

That summer I—.

It had been silent for some time, and so the boy thought they'd leave soon, before dusk gave way to dark. The girl, though, was just settling in. "I wanna be a blues mama, big-legged and brown-skinned," she said. "But I'm even skinnier than I'm pale. I'm about to blow away. Hold me tight and hang on, Johnny Flood."

She wanted to be many things—a blues mama, a gun moll, the first girl chief of the Chickasaws; anything but the poor, plain-faced, skinny-legged girl she was.

The boy turned, but not quick enough to suit the girl—she thought lightning bolts dawdled.

He held her, but she said, “That ain’t what I call tight.”

She spoke low in a voice that had some lilt when she slowed it down, though she rarely ever did. Words came out the girl’s mouth like birds sprung wild from busted cages. But a sky full of birds wasn’t enough for the girl. Mere flying would not do. She wanted them to be like the crop dusters that buzzed the Mississippi Delta in that summer of boys and girls. She wanted them to swoop and plummet and do the loop-de-loop. She wanted them to strike fear, awe, wonder, and want in the boy.

“I don’t see what skinny’s got to do with it,” he said. “I—”

“You innocent thing, you,” she chided, and he thought about why they were here, in the cemetery at dusk.

She lay on the cemetery grass. She stretched her skinny self endless.

“A blues mama’s got to have some fat on her, boy,” she said. “She’s gotta throw that big leg over. Meat shaking on the bone, like the old song says. *My, oh.* Meat shaking on the bone.”

She seemed about to break into that old song, then stopped and sighed again, and then said, “You don’t listen to the blues, do you, Johnny Flood?”

No one had ever called him Johnny. He was John or Jonathan or even John Baen, to include the middle name that had been passed half a dozen times or more from male Floods, back to fair Scotland.

The boy lay beside this most strange girl, brushing against the bare paleness of her skin, not because he moved against it, but because he was as still as those cemetery stones and so was there to be brushed against—Spell’s First Law of Motion. For Spell was the girl’s surname. First name, Jenny. And everyone called her Jenny who didn’t just call her the Spell girl.

The boy thought again about why they were here, in the cemetery at dusk.

“Well, um—”

"Memphis Minnie," Jenny Spell began. She had scolded him and chided him and now set about to teach him, about life and the blues, about women and men, and what one poet of the dark chord called the stuff you got to watch.

Some days it was gun molls, Bonnie Parker and Lottie Coll and Smitty White, and other days it was Indian chiefs, Crazy Horse and Billy Bowlegs and the great Tishomingo. Today it was blues singers. She seemed, in her mind, to have struck, finally, on something she could be, notwithstanding her pale skin and skinny legs.

"Yeah boy, Minnie. Her real name was Lizzie Douglas, from down in Louisiana. She sang about her ice man and her coal man. She sang about getting her ashes hauled. *My, oh.* And she sang about her butcher man and her strange man and another man who was a sandhog in the sea. I don't know what a sandhog is, but anyway he died. I guess he drowned doing a sandhog's dirty business. But what's one man, more or less? Minnie didn't need 'em, just kind of liked having 'em around. But only kind of. She'd cut a man if he crossed her. I mean, drain him pale. Slice me if I'm lying, Johnny Flood."

This seemed to him to be the last word on the subject, but then she said, "Minnie went through men enough to fill this cemetery, boy. Corpses stacked double, bodies piled high."

She stopped and turned to face him, as if to watch the chill settle upon him. For this was the first little bit of power she'd had in her life.

"You look a little drained, Johnny."

She looked some woozy, herself.

The breeze, barely more than a whisper before, now seemed to be getting its voice. The shadows darted where before they danced. Was that a drop of rain?

Now he thought they really might go—but Jenny was off again.

"Oh, Minnie. I mean to tell you. She played guitar better than any man. And Minnie, she was glamorous." Now the girl seemed to be moving not just side to side but up and down; she seemed to float and hover and touch down again beside him. "Minnie wore dresses with slits up to here"—she slashed at her pale neck as if with a knife—"and she showed her fine brown skin and she wore big hoop ear rings, too. Birds came to rest on 'em. Crows and grackles, one time a parrot that sang, *Sing it to 'em, sister. Give 'em proper hell.*"

They were doing it now. Her words, that is. They were swooping and plummeting and doing the loop-de-loop. They were striking fear, awe, wonder, and want. The boy took them in, every one. He closed his eyes and saw them. And said not a word. If he could have said anything, if he could have started a sentence, much less have finished one, it would have been, "Jenny, Jenny, Jenny. Oh Lord, Jenny Spell."

"Well Minnie, she sang songs about black cats and roosters and good biscuits. She sang about Joe Louis the Brown Bomber and the New Orleans Stop Time. She sang 'em funeral slow and she sang 'em party hard. Sometimes she gave the blues the back of her hand and sometimes a sweet, loving touch."

She turned to face him. She stared until he blinked. She kept staring until he blushed. He blinked and blushed, but he did not turn away. He just looked at her, in something ten times deeper than a trance.

Jenny Spell had a plain face, but you'd have stacked dictionaries in one stack, Bibles in another, and you'd have burned the one stack and sworn on the other that plain was the one true ideal of human beauty. That's how it was with Jenny's pale skin, too. You'd have thought pale was something rich folk would pay good money to get their golden skin to be. This is how she seemed to young John Flood, son of privilege, scion of wealth and power, innocent for the ages.

The boy was fifteen years old, a son of something like Kentucky royalty—his father trained horses on a farm between Lexington and Paris, and his mother was a professor of history at the university. He had been sent for six weeks that summer to Mississippi, to live with an aunt and uncle and a stew of wild cousins, in the little town of Roost, in the Delta. The boy was slight, bookish, and altogether his mother's son. They could spend whole afternoons in a room together, just reading, thinking, never saying a word; it never occurred to the boy that she was distant, or had issues undiagnosed. As for the boy's father, well, the boy got on better with his father's horses. He could spend whole afternoons with them, too, but tended to favor the disappointments, the racing failures, or anyway the puzzles not yet solved by human minds. The three-year-old chestnut colt Imperious, his father's Derby hopeful, frankly scared the boy, so much was the horse like his trainer in bearing and comportment; they even ate the same way, like ancient kings of some uncouth age. Some horses were even too human for little John Flood.

His parents planned to spend those six weeks "sorting themselves out," whatever that meant. A vague idea only, had the boy. John did not ask, could not, in his innocence, guess more. But he knew his father went riding with the woman who owned Imperious, and his mother seemed more than fond of one of her graduate students.

The Delta relations had issues of their own—they scarcely acknowledged the arrival of the young mister from horse country. The cousins were near feral, for all the family's money—the boys off chasing girls, and the girls men. The aunt was opening a restaurant she claimed would be the finest between Memphis and New Orleans, and there spent all her hours, fussing over linen, the brunch menu, and the chef she'd hired away from The Golden Apple in Jackson. The uncle had "business concerns" that took him out of town often—meaning "off chasing some tail in Biloxi," the aunt said.

So John Flood was left to himself those six weeks, to wander the town and wonder as to the fate of his parents' marriage, the behavior of adults just generally, and the meaning, exactly, of tail. More often, he sat swinging in the porch swing of the big empty house, just off the town square, on the east side, the wealthy side.

One day, from the west side, the poor side, came walking the girl. He was sitting in the porch swing, reading a book about a boy trying to find his place in the world. He had just come to the place in the book where a girl appears. The boy believed in fate, in magic. He believed in everything but himself.

Jenny walked by on the sidewalk below, stopped suddenly on the heels of her cowboy boots, cocked her head. Her hair was so blond it was nearly white, a sort of poor girl's platinum that spilled all down her back. It swished and then settled as she stopped.

She looked at him for the longest time.

"Hey, boy," she shouted up at him. "You need a ticket to ride that thing?"

Jenny sighed now, a lull between her last words and her next ones. And then said: "There were others, too, and you should know them. There was Muddy Waters and Howlin' Wolf and a couple of Sonny Boy Williamsons—the second's the one you want to study on. He sang about fattening frogs for snakes, and about how his baby had hydraulic hips, and an air-conditioned stomach."

"Hydraulic hips," John said.

It was Jenny who turned away. She looked off toward town, then turned back, as quickly, to face him—and caught him, like she hoped she would, knew she would, looking where those hydraulic hips would have been.

"I'll be wanting a pair of them, too," she announced.

And then she was off again. His continuing education in the blues. An alternate history of America to that which his mother taught back at the university. She told him there were more blind men than you could find dogs for. She said blind men were some of the best guitar players, but not because God felt sorry for them. (She said they were strictly on their own, God-wise. She said we all were.) She said it was because before they were blind men, they were blind boys, and couldn't work the fields, so they were given guitars, or made them, out of barn slats and baling wire, whatever. She said those blind boys played those makeshift guitars until their bones showed through their skin. She said it was one of two ways to get real good at guitar.

She told him about the Memphis Jug Band, and the Mississippi Sheiks. She shaved a good syllable and a half off of hers and those Sheiks' home state, the way she said it. "They sang about having blood in their eyes," she said, not seeming to know, quite, what that meant; knowing only that it sounded evil, righteously so. She told him about the one who called himself the Devil's Son-in-Law and the High Sheriff of Hell, both, and also went by Peetie Wheatstraw, but his real name was—"I forget," she said. "Missed that day in school, I guess."

John thought, *School?* But she was off yet again, telling him of Barbecue Bob and Bo Weavil and Furry, Peg Leg, and Jaybird, and Scrapper.

"And there was plain ol' Robert Johnson. No nickname for him," she said, in a voice more grave than before, as if the rest had been recess and now the boy was to study deep in the canon of all blue knowing. "He went to the cross roads and fell down on his knees. You know why, don't you?"

"I guess it had been a long walk and he was tired," John said. But even an innocent new to those parts knew the second way to get real good at guitar.

"Nuh-uh, Johnny Flood. Robert Johnson went down to the cross roads to meet up with the devil. He was there to give his soul to Scratch to get to play guitar better than Son House and them."

"So this Son House," the boy said, as if reading the name from some sacred text, "he was the best of them all? He was King of the Blues?"

"I guess you won't get run out the Delta for saying so. My Uncle Pete, he says Son House sounded like a giant of a man when he played, like his guitar was strung with Mississippi River bridge cables. But there were others. There was that rascally Charley Patton. Uncle Pete said he was some Indian and some white along with being lots black and blue. He'd beat his guitar like it was a bad girl. He'd play drums and guitar both on it. He'd play that thing behind his back and between his legs, all that field of stuff. He'd leap in the air and hang there for days. Fire department one time had to come get him like a cat in a tree. But they saw he was mostly black and blue and just let him be. Poor Charley. And he had a voice sounded like he ate gravel on mistake, like his bad girl painted those rocks yellow and called 'em scrambled eggs! Poor ol' Charley's mouth cut and bleeding—and his bad girl saying that's just hot sauce, Charley, is all the hell that red stuff is." She *almost* took a breath. "But Minnie's my most favorite. She was a strong woman who brought the stuff, Johnny. I want to be a woman who brings the stuff like Minnie did. I'll cut a man who tries to stop me. Swear to the devil and say amen."

The boy took a deep breath, as if for the both of them.

7

He could barely make out the mountain for the smoke, and the smoke for the rain, and his feet for the fucking muck and mud. But then, Cheatham had not expected to see freedom's splendors again in this life and was not of a mind to be fussy.

He dressed in his new duds and buried the old. Cheatham, in his sartorial splendor! Cheatham, anew! Free as jazz. He began running up the mountain. Loping, in those long strides of his. Loping faster up that big rock called Old Black than a lesser man would have tumbled down it.

He made it to the top and then stood leaning on a bitternut hickory that might have been some kin of him. He stood casually, as if waiting for a ride, or a drink. He looked down the mountain at the prison, or what he could see of it through the smoke. The smoke was clearing, a little. The rain had let up, too. He hadn't noticed. Hell, any time now the sun might come wandering home from whatever bender it had been on. Shake off that black lung, baby; it's me, Cheat.

He checked himself for injuries, the bomb's toll. No injuries, just the wet smudges of bomb soot on his face. I look like some fucking minstrel stunt man, he thought.

He crouched there atop the mountain, more to think than to rest. They wouldn't find his body in the rubble. They'd find all the rest but not him. Old Man's Merry's trigger finger, the Reverend Robert "Thee" Kingdom's snake eyes. Maybe Deuce would be decapitated; karma's a fucker.

He had an hour, maybe two. Then they'd come. They'd come with men and dogs and guns. Hell, even the dogs would have guns.

He stood. He gave his body a great shake and then steadied himself. He took a first step down the other side of the mountain. He knew the country. Had people there. Sure, they'd welcome him. *Hey, Cheat? Long time. What you been up to? Gallows pole?* Down the mountain to Deer Creek Gap, toward Inadu Knob, on toward Camel Gap. Cross over into North Carolina. He had people there, too. Big brood and every one a drunk. They'd shoot but not straight. So down the mountain, Cheat. Down the mountain and goodbye Tennessee, sorry I couldn't sit a spell. Hello, North Carolina. Tar Heel state.

But they'd expect all that, wouldn't they? The authorities. They'd know. They knew everything else. They knew his waist size and inseam. They knew his fucking shoe size. He looked for the first time at the boots. They looked to be snake skin, though Cheatham had not seen one that color. Was it turquoise? (No, azure.) Looked like something more befitting a peacock. More strut than slither.

Anyway, they fit. And all the rest of it. Whoever was behind all this had done their homework. But why? *Why spring me just to fuck with me?*

He took a moment to think, gather himself. Turned on the crank radio, to see if he'd made the news. He had.

This just in. Breaking news. Cheatham escaped from Old Black. Set an explosive device and killed everyone on death row. Cheatham, public enemy No. 1 with a bullet—hell, bomb. Armed and dangerous. Believed to have plans to hunt down and assassinate Governor Trey Flattery, who denied his stay.

Cheatham turned off the radio.

Believed to what? Assassinate the governor?

Well, he thought. They might have fucking consulted me.

8

The girl called Jenny Spell wore loose bib overalls and one strap was hooked and one strap wasn't. She wore a red T-shirt under. Written in white script on the T-shirt were the words "Sweet to Mama," the name of a bar in Ruggles, Texas, where her Uncle Pete played music for money. Pete Spell was Jenny's hero, the source of all her knowledge of bluesmen, and of gun molls, and of Indian chiefs, too. He sent her gifts from the road—skeleton keys and spent shells, Indian arrowheads, and one time an empty half-pint bottle that had been passed, he said, from Little Walter to Muddy Waters and back again.

He played guitar and sang in a band called Cherry Ball. He was good with that guitar. John heard him play, just before the band set out on its latest tour. The boy hadn't known mere fingers could dance a stomp and tip-toe, too, but Pete Spell's did. He had a deep, scuffed-up voice that John would have hated to hear in the cemetery dusk, much less the boneyard dark, but he liked it just fine in the broad light of day. Pete Spell would sing the dirty blues and then smooth it over with a gospel number. He'd tempt lightning like that and think nothing of it. Then he'd tell tales of faraway towns and the bars he'd conquered, places like the Sweet to Mama and the Stomp that Thing and the Dog Me Around. He'd tell tales of Memphis and Dallas and of places with names like Arkadelphia and Belzoni, and of New Orleans, too, and some other places without names at all. Then he'd flash what even innocent Little Johnny Flood took to be a whiskey grin.

John wondered about the taste of whiskey: Did it take the tartness out of cuss words, make them easier to say? He wondered what else a taste of whiskey might ease. He thought of bank robbery and stealing away to Memphis in a stolen car, and he thought of sins of the flesh.

He turned again to face Jenny. He let his eyes take in all that hair of hers, no less white though it was dusk, in the cemetery. When she stood it went down about to where those hydraulic hips would have been.

It was near night. Jenny shook her head at the moon, as if they were in cahoots, as if only the moon, which was given to growing big and round—nay, voluptuous—understood the girl's notions.

"I want curves," she said. "I want curves that make the big river straighten up and notice."

She was up on one elbow now, leaning over him. That white hair like poor girl's platinum fell loose and long over her little bit of shoulders; her shoulders weren't much more than coat hangers.

All he said about that was, "Oh." Then he stuck a finger through one of her belt loops and listened for what she might say next.

But for possibly the first moment since they'd met, the girl said not a word. There followed something more silent than silence, as if silence had ceded the floor to Jenny Spell and gone off somewhere to wait her out. You could have heard a ghost, that night in the cemetery, were there any about.

9

They met on the top deck of the *Clementine*, the chief of staff and the newspaper reporter. The one had summoned the other. It was private but not quite quiet. The nightly party was breaking out, earlier than normal—it was earlier every day now—below on the Tennessee deck, the pleasure deck. The floor of the top deck fairly thrummed with it.

"Ah, the hicks and slickers," said Bate.

"The hicks and slickers are your people," said the newspaper reporter.

"Yes, thank God for them. I just wish sometimes He hadn't made so many."

"I didn't imagine you believed in God."

Dusk now. They drew silent and drank.

"I don't," said Bate, finally, "but the hicks and slickers do. The hicks, more so. But in the end, the both of them. The former for salvation and the latter for propriety or show or maybe just liability insurance."

"I marvel at them, you know," the reporter said. "The way they thank God for getting them through their trials—but never blame God for hoisting those trials upon them. To say nothing of their tribulations."

"God fucks with hicks and slickers for sport," Bate said.

"They would say He's testing them," the reporter said. "But yes, to these old eyes it does seem to be a rather serious case of fucking with."

"It's God's favorite sport."

"I always figured Him for a baseball fan. Something pastoral, you know. Timeless."

"Baseball, huh?" said Bate. "I'd think something more bareknuckle."

"You'd think, but nah." The reporter laughed. They might have been talking about some local eccentric with money.

"You've thought this out."

"My old man," the reporter said, "he said God was a big sports fan. He said God loved the races—horses or dogs, didn't matter. He didn't bet. Just loved to watch a fast thing go. God—the original railbird. But it was baseball He liked best, my old man said about God. He said God didn't have a favorite team. Didn't hate any team, either, even the Yankees. It was the game He loved, the perfect order of it. He didn't say about the pastoral nature, or the timelessness, either. I added those."

"God must have looked down and smiled at the two of you. Unless of course He was off at some ballgame somewhere, in the bleachers with a dog and a beer. *Gawd*."

The reporter smiled at the thought. He said, "My old man said God preferred little scamps to big sluggers, Rabbit Maranville to Jimmie Foxx. That's why, my old man said, ballfields in heaven don't have outfield walls. You just hit the ball and run. You run until you make it home." He shook his head, in something like wonder. He took a drink. "My old man, he was a crafty fellow. He wanted me to get religion, but he wrapped it in cowhide."

"Dipped it in cornpone, more like," Bate said.

"Well, it is a beautiful thought. Those fields that go on forever, no walls, and the little man out there, having his day. It's a beautiful thought, you have to admit."

Bate smiled. "I admit to nothing, ever. That's *my* religion."

"Well anyway, I didn't get any. Religion, I mean. But I did grow up to be a sports writer," said the reporter, whose name was Freddie Davidson. "I don't know whether my old man's plan backfired or worked just like he figured it would. He was a baseball fan, on top of being a crafty fellow."

"So you're a sports writer, then. Not a real reporter." Bate looked at his empty glass, as if one more thing had gone and disappointed him. "So, say if Cheatham, that death-row inmate who escaped from Old Black, were to, for instance, find his way on board this ship and assassinate the governor, like they say he's set out to do, you wouldn't be fit and qualified to cover it, huh?"

"Not unless he plans to use a baseball bat to kill him," said the sports writer, with no apparent shame.

"Well, anyway, you'll have to do for my purposes."

"You have purposes, Mr. Bate? Oh, well. Course you do. They say you run the state. Even a reporter from the toy department knows that much, hears things."

"Why, I'm just a humble civil servant. I serve at the will of the governor, and he serves at the will of the people. It's civics, is all. You went to school, surely. Even a sports writer must have to get to fifth grade to be fit and qualified to write balls and strikes."

"You make it sound noble—government." He said that word to sound like *no bill,* like he was craftier than Bate imagined, or else just had a strain of hillbilly somewhere in his lineage. Either way, Bate knew the man's weakness. He poured them fresh drinks.

"There's another on board. Reporter, I mean," Freddie Davidson said. "I haven't seen sign of her lately, but ... Two of everything, right?" He laughed. "And she's a real reporter. Covered the state house. Uncovering corruption, her speciality."

"Seems we're down to one," said Bate, looking over the side of the great steamer and giving his glass a splash. "So it'll have to be you."

10

Governor Flattery was beside himself. (No, really.) He was standing alone, or so he thought, on the stern of the top deck. He was watching the sternwheel turn. He was thinking of his own course through life. Was there only so far that charm, wealth, sexual prowess, and a chin like ship's prow take you? Was he on a slight losing streak, only, or was this something more, a long, slow descent to deeper shit? Either way, though: Losing streaks were for losers and deep shit was for Bate to shovel—he told himself this.

He turned his thoughts to the people, his people, the teeming Tennesseans over which he ruled (er, served). They would look to him now, the poor bastards. They would want to know there was a plan, though he never was much for those. A man who can float through life leaves the planning to others—Bate again. But a bit of heroism might be just the thing, for the people, after all. Some derring-do to divert attention from the soggy state of things. A grand gesture, end of the world and all. But what?

He had never felt quite so alone. It was down to his leadership now. Bate, his best friend, might well be turning on him. Washington was no help. The federal response, a shrug. What was it that junior fucker from FEMA had said, just before the lines of communication went down, or were cut?

"We have our own problems up here, Governor. You ever tried to reason with a swamp creature? Some days I think I'd rather the fires, or take my chance with a sinkhole or hurricane. The situation everywhere, Governor, it's fluid."

"Fluid? Fluid! It's a goddamned flood, man!"

He gripped the rail now. He dropped his head, thought of throwing himself over and into the sternwheel. But really, now? Trey Flattery, suicide? He laughed, laughed so loud he surprised himself. It was a full-throated, deep in the chest—no, lower—rumble of ... what, exactly?

A return of the hail fellow, well hung?

A slide into madness, like afflicts kings from time to time?

Did I just refer to myself as a king?

The laugh had left a smile on his face, but it fell away as he looked up and opened his eyes to the great flood. A shudder, then, as that smile fluttered to the deck at his feet, and now followed a proclamation, of sorts: "Once we were the forty-eighth greatest state in the greatest nation ever known to God or man," he said, with more or less equals parts anger and petulance, "and now look at us, we're a fucking … goddamn … catfish farm."

The sound of laughter came now from outside his body.

And then a voice that sounded like a pretty fair country approximation of his own, saying: "Catfish, huh? So your people will eat, at any rate."

The governor turned starboard and saw … himself.

Well, anyway, close enough. He himself was just slightly taller, and wider in the shoulders, broader in the chest. But the face—good God. Those blue-gray eyes that pierced even as they danced. Cheekbones like the work of some master carver. Proud prow of a chin, perfect down to the small cleft, which squiggled in a southwesterly direction, like Tennessee's border with North Carolina near Johnson City. This was a high-level knockoff. Top notch!

They were even dressed alike—a tan sport coat over a pinkish polo, white trousers, deck shoes. (Like it was Fiji for which he/they were bound, not fucking Memphis.)

The governor stepped back and then leaned in toward his double.

Is this what the state historian's wife meant by Imposter Syndrome?

11

Back went Cheatham. Back down the mountain toward Old Black, from whence he came. Creeping where once he loped. Stealth as could be now, notwithstanding that egg-yellow cowboy shirt in size XXXL Tall. Looked like a fucking walking billboard for a farm-fresh breakfast. Did it somehow disguise him in plain sight? Quite possibly. Was that all part of the diabolical plan? To be dressed like the fucking Egg Council's float in Nashville's Faron Young Day parade?

A quarter of the way down the mountain now, near the place where he'd awoken. Saw his own footprints, big boats in the mud. He looked down, could see now the water creeping toward the prison. The great flood—he'd heard tell of it. Old Man Merry had said it was God coming to get them. Merry seemed to revel in this thought, for to get to see God and look the Old Cuss in the eye, finally. Manfred Bland had said make your peace, boys. Seek salvation and forgiveness. Trying to get a rise out of Reverend Robert "Thee" Kingdom. Said, "If only you had an ark, Reverend." And the Reverend said, "I don't need but a boogie board. Ain't like I'd be taking any of you fuckers with me." "Why, you snake, you," Manfred Bland said and hissed, in mock offense.

Cheatham came to the bottom of the mountain, still a hundred or more yards from the prison. It was day but the sun had not appeared, perhaps cowed by the sight of Cheatham's shirt. Fog and bomb smoke mingled, like some ghost waltz. The rain fell, as ever. Just east of the prison, he saw a dulled glint of gun-metal gray something. A boat? Cheatham moved up into the woods and made his way toward it, thinking, if it's a boat there'll be men in it with guns, and they'll shoot me on sight. Began moving toward it, no matter. Laughing at a thought he had.

Cheatham in his sartorial splendor, thinking, *A damned shame it'll be, to have holes in such a pretty shirt.*

12

Class was in session, on the forecastle of the *Clementine*. Bascom Holcomb "Bud" Miller was finding teaching not altogether different from that one time his band Tom T. Y'all played a benefit show at Old Black Prison—the difference between a captive audience and a captivated one could be vast, indeed.

But he found this to be freeing. He could teach what he wanted. So he read from favorite books, like *Satan is Real*, by Charlie Louvin, of the legendary Louvin Brothers, and Nick Tosches' *Country*, which included such chapters as "Orpheus, Gypsies, and Redneck Rock 'n' Roll" and "Stained Panties and Coarse Metaphors." He read lots of essays that got at the essence of country music, and the corruption of same by the evil forces in vile Nashville. On this day he read a personal appreciation of one of his own favorites, titled "Drinking Beer with Patsy Cline Up in Heaven:"

> *She drank beer and cussed a blue streak and told dirty jokes to make the men blush. She called herself "the Cline" and most everybody else "Hoss." This must have been an altogether new sort of behavior up in heaven, back when she arrived, all of a sudden, that long-ago day. But I suppose heaven must have made quick peace and accommodation. Because how could you possibly keep Patsy Cline out of heaven?*
>
> *The last show was in Kansas City. Then it was back home to Nashville, in a little, single-engine Piper Comanche. It seemed like a good plan. But there was "inclement" weather—that's the word used in these situations, like how you're driving a car and then suddenly you've died, or "perished," in an "automobile" accident. Death changes the whole conversation, the way you*

think about people and their places, in this world and the next. And so the little plane plummeted from the sky and crashed in the woods outside Camden, Tennessee, on March 5, 1963, and its most famous occupant, the country star born Virginia Patterson Hensley, became an angel with a honeyed voice and a string of hits you didn't have to be a hick to love—beautiful songs, it's true, but as much pop as anything. Torch songs, really. You know them. They're timeless, classic numbers, some of the best records anybody ever cut, in any genre—the likes of "Crazy" and "I Fall to Pieces" and "Sweet Dreams (Of You)."

That's not the Patsy I'm thinking of here. I raise my cold can of Schlitz (Patsy's brand) to heaven and salute the earthiest citizen of that place, Patsy the country singer. I play not those pop hits with the strings and sheen and the Jordanaires singing background, but the pure-country numbers like "Turn the Cards Slowly" and "Don't Ever Leave Me Again," the honky-tonk stuff. I picture her that way, too—dressed like the cowgirl she was early in her career, before the mink coats and cocktail dresses. Mostly, though, I just shut my eyes and my mouth and I listen.

Damn, how that woman could sing—the big, pure voice, the boom of the thing, the swoop and ache of it. She could growl, and whoop, and she had this other thing she did—it may be the one thing she can't get away with in heaven—that sounds like she's swallowed a yodel.

That's the Patsy I love best, before she crossed over (in the chart sense, not the corporeal one). On "Honky Tonk Merry Go Round," you can almost hear bottles breaking, along with the fiddle, steel guitar, and stand-up bass. "Don't Ever Leave Me Again," a song she co-wrote, is as tough as the blues. I'll bet she had a hell of a lot more fun singing it than "Walkin' After Midnight," which she dismissed as "nothing but a little ol' pop song."

I like to think my version of Patsy Cline—the cowgirl in boots, before she was whisked uptown—is the one the late folk singer Bill Morrissey had in mind when he wrote his great song "Letter from Heaven." It's one man's wry supposition of what it must really be like, up there. The character in the song is dating Patsy, and how I know it's the cowgirl version of Patsy is that in the next line he talks of last night in the bar, buying Robert Johnson a cold one. Oh, and he ends the song with a yodel. Amen, brother.

I know what's in the Good Book, but I like to think heaven is a place where the beer is cold and the music smokes. And I like to think Patsy Cline's up there, getting lots of requests, no doubt, for "Crazy," but singing mostly hillbilly and honky-tonk. Down here, we've made her an angel. We have this image, and the soundtrack to go with it. We've pried the beer can from her cold, dead hands. But I don't think that's quite how it's played out, up there.

All these years later, I suppose she's got run of the place and sings what she damn well pleases. She's "the Cline," after all. As for God, well, I guess by now He's come to terms with being called "Hoss."

The snotnoses were intrigued by it all. The boys all seemed to think this Bud Miller had the hots for Patsy, and the girls all started calling the boys and each other "Hoss." The girls pretty much had the run of class, that day.

13

They had gathered to wait, two gravediggers with their shovels and the town soak and a boy of ten whose father was the mayor. This was down in North Mississippi, in the little town of Burden. They milled at the end of the dirt lane, waiting for the old writer to die. For two days they stood staring up the dirt road to the middling hill, and the white mansion there. Two days milling and waiting for the old writer to die, and those two days spent musing on his life and his fame and his eccentricities, and they touched now and again on his drinking—all but his life's work, because of the four only one, the town soak, had read a word he'd written.

"He's a stubborn dog, I'll give the old son of a bitch that," the first gravedigger said. "Still, though. Can't hold out much longer."

"What in hell's he dying of?" said the second.

"The rot, I heard."

"Ah, the rot. Sure enough that'll get you."

The second gravedigger said it in a sing-song voice that set the first to musing. Their moods were light, these two, for they were at work but not at labor. Still, they were beginning to resent the old writer's reluctance, or refusal, even—hell, who knew what he was capable of, the old writer—to succumb. The very order of things seemed somehow in play, and what with the weathermen and preachers alike going on about the coming flood, saying not even the hill country would be safe.

A light rain fell from a sky the color of their shovels.

"The slow creep of death's upon him now," said the first, musingly, with a nod up the dirt lane to the middling hill, on which sat the white mansion, like some affront to the rest of the town, be it ever so humble. "The great writer, indeed."

You could have sifted the first gravedigger's words for deadly sins and found no fewer than four; he was as good a Christian as the next man.

"I'd ruther be hit by a train, myself, if it's all the same to God," said the second.

It might have been a fair fight, or anyway a good question as to whether a locomotive with a fair head of steam could knock the second gravedigger off his spot. He was no taller than his shovel but his shape owed more to a hole that a shovel might be used to dig, if the hole in question was not a grave but a small pond for fishing.

"Make quick work of me, when it's time," continued the second. "Not the rot, pray God." He paused to think, and then added for good measure, "Or the crud, either one."

"Crud won't kill you, man," said the first. He was by a far stretch the taller of the two, fairly towering over his shovel, though he had the general build of it. He was tall and thin with a large, flat-faced head. "But I'd watch the croup, mind you."

"Oh sure, the croup," said the second. He shuddered just slightly at the thought.

Now the boy spoke up. It was inevitable that he would.

"Daddy said meanness."

The boy's daddy, the mayor, was a man of many thoughts and theories, and much connivance, and the source of most all of the boy's knowledge and leanings.

"Can't die of meanness, boy," said the first gravedigger. "Why, it's meanness keeps a man alive. More so a woman."

"Meanness didn't keep his alive," said the second, with a nod up the dirt lane toward the white mansion, which would have been the tallest building in the town even without the help of the middling hill.

"Reckon she wasn't mean as him," the first said on the subject of the old writer's wife. "Though you wouldn't have said so, if you'd met her. I did, once. Tall woman, you know, looked down at me like I was something she nearly stepped in. A splotch on the ground. She smelled of gin and old money. Nice legs, though. Fair gams."

"Guess you got a good look at 'em, being just a splotch on the ground."

"I seen better."

"And had worse."

"I guess all of us here but the boy would say the same."

The second gravedigger spat his assent, just missing his left boot, which anyway was the same shade of brown as his tobacco juice.

The two gravediggers drew silent and the boy grew impatient. Two days waiting and the old writer had yet to up and die. The boy was beginning to feel misled. He might be missing the neighborhood football game or maybe some actual fighting.

"The rot ain't a real thing," said the boy.

If he had not heard his father speak of it, it did not exist. This made for a long list that included, but was not limited to, science, tact, transcendentalism, true love, piety, poetry, free jazz, Black intellectualism, and Sole Almandine.

"Jackson died of it," said the first gravedigger, gravely.

"Why, that dog of mine was struck by lightning on a Wednesday," said the second, sharply and to the contrary. "You know that."

"Ain't talking about your damned dog, man. Talking about Andrew Jackson. Old Hickory. King Mob. Died of the rot, eighteen hundred and something," said the first gravedigger, with the gravity of one whose forbearers, gravediggers all, had turned the dirt when the original old cuss died. They may well have.

"Oh, him," said the second, as if they were old cronies, or anyway had mutual friends or frequented the same feed store, maybe had briefly courted the same girl in younger days.

"Man had a hell of a head of hair," said the first, almost dreamily. "Great expanse of forehead, mind you. Could have walked your dog across it. Grazed sheep, played a game of ball. But a hell of a head of hair, Andrew Jackson."

"I miss that dog."

"I was speaking of the human one with that name."

"I know, but still and all. That dog."

"He was good, for a dog."

"He was good, just generally."

"I meant no disrespect toward the deceased hound."

"He was more than a dog. He was almost— "

"Had a serious countenance, I'll grant you."

"I don't know what that means, but I'll accept it, in his name and memory, and thank you for it."

"Way he looked at you, I mean. Those eyes, you know. Almost like a wise man or founding father. He never did talk, did he?"

"Not words, no."

"Words was what I meant."

"Well, he'd whine, you know. Bark, of course. And had that other thing he did, remember? Kind of like a cross between a horse whinny and a—what's that one horn?"

"Trombone?"

"Nope, bigger."

"Tuba."

"Smaller."

"Hell, man."

"Bassoon!"

"Bassoon's a woodwind, fool." The first gravedigger had not gone far in school but he was what you would call a shithouse scholar; he knew a very little about a great many things. He could name you all of Stonewall Jackson's major battles and Clark Gable's wives, and use electrode in a compound sentence while sitting on the can.

"Well, anyway, that one sound he made, you know."

"Orchestral, that dog!" sang the first.

The second gravedigger spat tobacco juice from the edge of the dirt lane onto the county road. It had arc and contrail and a sort of hurtling grace, for being a viscous, brown glob. (A metaphor for the coming flood? They would not have said so.) It landed about six feet out into the county road. It landed with a sharp splat. The boy was impressed by the feat but tried not to show it. His father had told him that gravedigger was about as low in life as a white man could fall, or a Black one could rise.

The first gravedigger did not seem to notice. He was thinking, still, about Old Hickory's hair, and about the old, dying writer's hair, and the hair of other great men, real or so-called, some with powdered wigs, George Washington and such, the founding fathers, and the wise men of the Bible with their locks long as God's—and that one pro rassler he saw one time, up in Memphis, with a wide streak of white in his hair. From where he was struck by lightning, went the legend.

The first gravedigger, sinking into one of his occasional reflective moments, thought about how high a man could rise in the world, with a good head of hair. Why, there was hardly any limit. A man could be president. He could be heavyweight wrestling champion of the world. He could do nothing so much as write books nobody read and be called great.

"Maybe he's done gone bald in his dying," he said, nodding up toward the white mansion, hopefully though without real conviction, for the old writer had been blessed with such a full head of hair—a shock, you would say—that it surely would take twenty-odd years of dying to lose it all.

The second gravedigger, though not of a contemplative bent, was staring at that tobacco-spit stain on the ground as if to puzzle out its shape and meaning. Was it the form of his old, dead dog? A bit, yes. The state of Mississippi, belly up? That, too. Well, damn. Did it mean that his old, dead dog was trying to reach him, to come back home? Was the afterlife just so much shaggy wandering? Why, how in blue hell should he know?

The second gravedigger finally broke from these deep mysteries. He said, without looking away from the tobacco-spit stain, “The old writer, bald? I don’t reckon, nope. You’d about have to scalp him, for him to go bald. Where’s an Indian when you need one? Ol’ Tishomingo, he’s long dead and gone.”

The mention of the long-dead-and-gone chief might have shaken the first gravedigger from his sad contemplations, for his mother had once told him that he was descended, on his father’s side, from the great leader of the Chickasaws. Last honorable man in the line, his mother said, and the last handsome one, too. She laughed through her cigarette smoke and told the boy to go play in traffic, right after he made her another toddy.

But the first gravedigger just thought of hair, all the more. He thought of long, straight Indian hair, black and glistening in the sun, pretty as some school girl’s. His own hair was thin and limp. As to hue, it was redolent of nothing so much as dirt, tobacco spit, and boot.

The first gravedigger looked at the sky. It was gray but hadn’t yet opened up. The light rain continued. Maybe it would turn dark, and come a storm, and lightning would strike what he had of hair and give him a wide streak of white, like the wrestler up in Memphis—Sputnik Monroe,[19] that was his name. But the first gravedigger doubted it, for he’d never had a stitch of luck in this world.

The town soak spoke now for the first time.

“Greatness,” he said.

---

[19]A dirty, cheatin’ heel in the ring, with a name inspired by a Soviet satellite, yes, but Sputnik Monroe was a great American and civil rights pioneer of the late 1950s and ’60s. Read it in your history books, snotnoses. Sputnik desegregated Memphis pro rasslin’, insisting his Black fans be allowed to come down from the balcony and sit wherever they wanted in Ellis Auditorium. Another time, he was arrested on a disorderly charge for “drinking in a negro café with negros,” according to *The Commercial Appeal*, the Memphis daily. He was represented by a “negro attorney”—first time the judge could recall seeing that, for a white defendant—and fined $26.

"Huh?" said the gravediggers as one. They were always doing that. They were like an old married couple, except for they mostly got along.

"It's what he's dying of," the soak said, with a nod toward the white mansion. "Can you boys imagine a heavier load to lift, much less to tote?"

For the soak was the one among them who could speak with any authority on the facts and circumstances of the old, dying writer's life and works, which were otherwise hidden in plain sight on school and library and bookstore shelves, where they were rarely mussed or even dusted.

"Greatness, you say," said the second gravedigger.

"Folderol!" said the first.

The soak just sighed and smiled. And they call me the soak, he thought.

"Now, that'll kill you, sure enough," said the second gravedigger. "Old Folderol! That shit's pure, high-beam rotgut. Got a bad bottle of it up in Memphis this one time. I woke up next to a—"

The soak made a *baaa* sound, but not so the gravediggers could hear.

"Ain't talking about whiskey, fool," said the first. "Talking about the state or condition of stuff and nonsense. That's folderol."

"Ah. Stuff and nonsense'll kill you quicker'n lightning will," said the second. "Best to avoid."

"I wouldn't touch it with your shovel," the first said.

They both spat tobacco juice out onto the county road, like old fishermen casting lines upon the water. They drew silent again, and then the second gravedigger said: "I saw a cow killed by lightning. Lit the old gal up from the insides, bones and such, like on the cartoons."

"It was a cartoon you were watching."

The second gravedigger gave this some consideration. "Well," he said.

More spitting, some nodding, here a scratch—some deep excavation on the part of the second. And in this way did the two gravediggers pass the time while waiting for the old writer to die. They were patient. It was their lot. It was not for them to say the time, but only to see that a proper grave was dug when it came. For every man should have a proper grave. It was God's work, but more so the town's.

The soak did not press his case, for now, as to the pending cause of the old writer's death. He took a seat on the old, stone fence that surrounded the old writer's estate, took out the makings of a cigarette, and began to roll himself one. He sang low a song as he went about the task, his voice like a low moan from the mash tun.

He sang:

I saw the devil one day on Sunnyland Avenue
Swear I saw the devil on Sunnyland Avenue
I said, "You must be lost, poor devil"
He said, "Poor boy, you must be, too"

The gravediggers looked at the soak as if the words were coming from a cow in a meadow, and not the cow's mooing end. For the gravediggers were not music lovers, and as for the boy, well, he was promised a death, and by God ...

"I don't care if it's greatness or Old Folderol or some injun kills him," said the boy to his sneakers, "long as something gets the damned old son of a bitch."

The boy kicked at the dirt with those sneakers and watched as the pebbles flew and noted where they landed. He did not look up. It was his first time to cuss in public and he thought it had gone rather well.

14

The storm was some ways off, holding its breath.

"If it's a tornado—" the boy, John Flood, said.

"Well it ain't," said the girl, Jenny Spell.

"But what if—"

"Then we're in the safest place there is."

It was the cemetery, still. It was summer's end. It had been a summer filled with adventure, fraught with it. They had "borrowed" Jenny's daddy's old truck and gone to look for ghosts at Shiloh, and they made a pilgrimage to Robert Johnson's grave outside of Greenwood, and then continued on up Money Road about five miles and stood on the side of the road looking through the vine-steeped ruins of Bryant's Grocery where that 14-year-old Black boy from Chicago wolf-whistled at that white woman. Jenny asked John if he knew what happened next to that boy, named Emmett Till. John said he didn't, no, not exactly, sort of, so Jenny told him about it all, about the kidnaping and mutilation, the river and the bridge, the cotton-gin fan they'd strapped to the boy so he'd sink proper, and the open casket for all the world to see. Jenny said to John, "What the hell history do they teach you up in Kentucky?" and John, thinking of famous Kentuckians and legends of the state, said, "Secretariat." Better that, he thought, than "Colonel Harland Sanders," who anyway was born in Indiana.

"Emmett Till dying changed the world, for about five minutes, my Uncle Pete said. He said every few years something real big and terrible happens that opens people's eyes to how bad the country can be, how mean it is, how it was built on bloodshed and hate and lust for power. He said there's an uproar and people get mad and sing hymns and demand change, and the politicians, they form committees and make speeches and then make just enough change that they can call it change. Then they give the people some bread and circus, he said, and things get back to how they were before, only with a little bit of change to the good. I asked him what bread and circus was, and he said, 'Cheap whiskey and college football.' I told Uncle Pete he ought to run for magistrate or president. He just laughed, said if he ever wants to get strung up and shot, he'll just go back to philandering. I said what's philandering and he said, 'Stamp collecting.' "

The girl now took a breath. The boy tried but could not.

So many adventures they had, that summer. Life smacked the boy across his face, buckled his knees. Books died. Words failed. Fear grew wings, flew to the sun and back in a supersonic crop duster. One day, they'd even stolen aboard a train and ridden it to Hattiesburg and hitchhiked back. John kept having to talk Jenny out of robbing a bank.

Now they were back in the cemetery and Jenny said it was time and John did not ask for what. She lifted a cigarette to her lips, struck a match and lit it. She tilted her head, closed her eyes. The boy watched to see if her lids would quiver, to see if it was just a show, an act, a demonstration for his benefit. But they did not quiver nor otherwise move. They closed to stillness, and he thought of the sacraments.

She puffed on the cigarette and made smoke. She blew clouds and the clouds became wisps and the wisps left a layer of dust, of ash, on the cemetery stones. That's how it seemed to the boy as the girl smoked the cigarette.

"Like so," she said. But he said no, *uh-uh*.

So she leaned over and kissed him and he tasted that smoke on her tongue and he liked it, that smoke on her tongue. He took a drag. Now he knew it was time, and for what.

Her hair was up. He liked it up. He liked it down. He liked it mussed. He liked to muss it. Her blue jean overalls still had that one button unbuttoned, that one strap hanging down. She took his hand and led it to where the other strap was hooked. He unsnapped it and moved his hand away. Jenny leaned just slightly forward and the strap fell to the cemetery floor. She pulled off that red T-shirt. She did it one-handed, like a movie stunt girl might have.

"Well, Johnny Flood," she said, "it ain't much but it's yours."

15

They had talked God and baseball and the difference between a hick and a slicker. They had talked country music, bemoaning the sorry state of it, wondering whether the hicks could rise up and steal it back from the slickers. It was Chief of State Bate's theory that a hick could be counted on to steal but that rising up was simply beyond him. Freddie Davidson the sports writer called Bate a callous bastard and Bate said wasn't that just like a sports writer, to use two words when the one would do.

They grew quiet. They looked out beyond the rail of the top deck to the gray nothingness beyond. They looked up. The sky was like a black and white picture of gray.

"Well, I've enjoyed your hooch and hospitality," said Freddie Davidson, finally, almost as if there had been a script, written by the one and read by the other, "but suppose you tell me what you want, Mr. Bate."

He was holding his liquor well enough but he knew it wouldn't last much longer. It would hit him all at once, with a fine, wet wallop. So it was for all the Davidson men back through history. It would begin with a slight slurring of words and a distinct gutter mouth; an attempt to dance, perhaps, and the failure to so much as walk straight, would follow. Davidson men had, through the ages, come to believe this inability to out-drink their fellow man was what kept them from reaching greater heights in the world, though there were other factors, as well. Sports writer, in fact, was as high as a Davidson man of modern times had risen, except for one who made dog catcher.

"Did you ever think about why the public hates the press?" Bate said, turning to Freddie Davidson.

"We still talking about the hicks and slickers?"

"I mean the public as a whole, everybody, John Q. and his wife Martha. Their kith and kin. The hicks and slickers, the rubes and bumblers, the risers and strivers, the artists and others of the so-called intelligentsia."

"Oh, all them."

"They pretty well all hate the press, you know—more even than they hate politicians," Bate said. He reached over to pat the other but stopped an inch shy, as if sports writing was somehow contagious. "But it's worse than that. To be hated, that's sort of a badge, isn't it? But the thing is, the thing that galls, is they trust you less. Trust! I don't mean you specifically, Mr. Davidson. I'm sure you almost always get the score right, and never quote out of context except when there's no other way to make a point. I mean your kind. Your lot. *Journalists.*" He said it in the same way he had, earlier, said *Gawd.* He seemed to have about as much regard for one as the other.

Freddie Davidson had started to slump a little in his deck chair. Was it the turn of conversation? Oh, a little of that. Was it the drink, starting the windup to the fine, wet wallop? Most definitely so.

He reached for the arm rests to straighten himself but missed one and banged his elbow. "Motherfuck," he announced. It had begun.

"Less trusted than a politician, by damn!" Bate said, moving in. "How can it be, Mr. Davidson?"

"It's a got-damned head-scratcher, for fucking sure," said Freddie Davidson, taking the full brunt of the drink now, as always. Just a minute ago he had executed an alliterative independent clause, now he was fully potted. Fuck's sake.

Bate, meanwhile, seemed to have drunk himself to a heightened state of evil. No, no, this was just his normal self. He was, in fact, wholly unaffected by the alcohol. It was another of the skills he had developed over the years. He could out-drink any man, because when he drank with another man his mind was on another track entirely. He didn't drink to be social and he didn't drink to get drunk. He drank because it made the other man drop his guard. It was then Bate went to work, to get whatever he was after at the time. It was a sort of mind control at work, or sublimation, maybe a little bit of a wooden leg. Whatever it was, alcohol held no sway over Bate, except when it could do the least harm: when he drank alone.

"But it's simple, isn't it, Mr. Davidson? Uh, Mr. Davidson? You still with me?" Bate said now. "Politicians lie to people, right? Politicians—"

"Cocksuckers!"

"Most, yes. They soak their lies in half-truths and sunshine and—"

"Aspirational fucking hooey!"

"Why, sure. Well said. That's the worst sort of hooey. And then they wrap all that in—"

"The got-damned American flag!"

"I thought you said this was a head-scratcher. Why, you're halfway to understanding already, Mr. Davidson."

"The hell are you talking about?" Freddie Davidson was passing briefly through the state of belligerence on his way to stupor; he was barely upright in his deck chair. Shall we dance, Mr. Davidson?

"Whereas—" Bate made a grand sweeping motion with his right hand, still holding his drink, not spilling a drop. "Whereas the press—well, you're all about the pure, unvarnished truth."

"Hear, fucking hear!" Freddie Davidson sounded like the student section at a Southeastern Conference football game, and looked it, too, flushed and disheveled, like he might need at any moment now to puke down the front of his date's sundress.

Bate sighed. He took a sip. He continued.

"I always wondered," he said, "why you all want to go and give varnish a bad name—to say nothing of what you do to the truth, the poor pretzel of a thing."

"The fuck're you saying, man? Wait—no, I see. You're saying—"

"Yes, see? You're a drunken sports writer and you can see it. People—the hicks and slickers, the rubes and bumblers—they don't want the truth, unless it's served up like they like. We know how they want it, don't we, Mr. Davidson? They want it on a plate heaped high. They want it with mashed potatoes and white pepper gravy, and rolled biscuits good for sopping. They want it with green beans with ham hocks, and chicken that seems not to have been fried for eating but bronzed for some museum display on the Southern culinary experience."

Bate took a moment to marvel at himself, his eloquence, his cunning, the casual manner in which he pulled it all off. "And then," he said, "they want grace said over it. Grace—*Gawd*. The lie on top the lie on top the lie."

A bead of spittle began to form on the lower lip of the esteemed member of the Fourth Estate toy department. He was moved to speak but more so to drink. He lifted his glass but stopped. He suddenly seemed morose. This, too, was typical of Freddie and all the Davidson men before him. But it had a steadying effect, something like clarity. At any rate, he was able to speak.

"People don't want the fucking truth, the cocksuckers," he said. "They sure as shit don't want it unvarnished."

"It's a noble profession, journalism, to be sure … " Bate said. "But what if you were to, as they say in sports, switch teams?"

He turned again and faced Freddie Davidson, who seemed to be going from morose into some new state, a sort of greatest hits package, which contained aspects of all those previous.

"You wanna hire me?" He seemed about to point a thumb at his swelled chest, in a sort of Mike Fink gesture.

"You're a newspaperman without a newspaper, Mr. Davidson."

"I fucking am that, Mr. Bate."

Freddie Davidson did now pass into a final state, which he saw as liberation and Bate as acceptance.

"So what you want me to write, bucko?"

"I'll tell you, when the time comes."

Freddie Davidson, the sotted sports writer, turned now to Bate, the governor's evil chief of staff. He leaned close, with tilted head and jutted chin and all the suspicion with which a boy of twelve would examine a freshly baked apple pie left to cool on the wide sill of an open window on a summer morn in the Midwest.

"How much you pay me, boyo?" said Freddie, a Davidson to the end.

16

"It's uncanny."

Said the governor of Tennessee to his double.

"He said you'd say that."

"Who? Who said it?"

"He said handsome men with more ambition than brains are a penny a hundred. He said they all look pretty much alike anyway."

"Who? Bate?"

"He said people see what they want to see in a man."

"It's Bate, I know it."

"He said—how was it he put it? Said, the great ship Flattery's an empty vessel. Said to add a couple, few silver streaks to my hair, and how to comb it just so. Said to comb it like there was an island breeze blowing in it. What to wear, how to walk, how to talk, all that. Said I'd be close enough to pass for you from across ballroom or bed."

The governor was interrogating his double. He was trying a light touch, so he started by offering the man a drink.

("I'll have what you're having, Guv!") They had decamped to the former's stateroom. They sat at a small table in the anteroom.

Four drinks in, the governor had gained only a nice buzz. He was starting to be impressed. What was it they said about imitation? The highest form of …

The governor smiled real big. He raised his glass, to himself and his other self.

"Cheers to me, myself and I," he said.

"There's just two of us, by my count. But sure, why not. Same back at you, Guv."

"You even sound like me."

"Not my natural voice, of course. It's how he told me to talk. Gave me recordings to study."

"Say something in your natural voice."

"Afraid I can't. He said not to break character, ever. I go around spouting your politics, even when I'm off the clock."

"What are *your* politics, if I may ask?"

"Hard left, but a man's got to pay the bills," he said. "I'm for gun control and regulating the banks, but I'll stay out of your bedroom—it's too crowded already. I'm against Big Pharma, Big Tech, and Big Country. I'm against capital punishment even on the off chance the prisoner's guilty."

"Be still my bleeding heart," Flattery said, mockingly. "What's he paying you?"

"I couldn't say, Guv. A man who has no ethics and standards is no man at all, I heard said one time."

"Whatever he's paying, I'll double it. No—triple. You're working for me now."

There was hardly a pause.

"At your service, Guv." The double said this in his own natural voice. You could have cut high grass with his twang.

It went on like this. The double told all about how Bate hired him, early in the governor's term. He said he was sort of on-call. He said, "Some weeks I'd have engagements and some not. Engagements, is what I called them. Your man Bate, he didn't call them anything. Just said for me to be where, and when. He's brusque, your man. I'm not saying asshole. I can be a handful myself."

"What were your, um, instructions?"

"That's the thing. Not much of anything. Empty vessel and all, I guess. No offense, Guv."

"Some taken, but go on."

"Sometimes I was just supposed to walk through a room. Be seen, he'd say, then go. Other times he'd leave it to me. Said I could have a few drinks and see what happens. One time—I remember this, damnedest thing—I gave an interview to a reporter. Sort of an impromptu thing, you know. This was after a long, wet lunch in the Gulch. Funny thing, that. Reporter, he asked me something about the Department of Corrections. I said, well, I get to telling so many lies we need a whole department to clear them up. Just fucking with him, you know."

Six drinks in now ...

"So, tell me. Did you ever—"

"Fuck your wife, Guv?"

"I was going to say make a speech, but ..."

17

"You going to get run over," the shorter of the gravediggers said to the boy.

The boy sat lounging in the middle of the county road, half on his back and resting on one elbow. He was a rough-hewn son of privilege in idle defiance. He was that dangerous—ten years old and wouldn't have budged for an oncoming car if God was behind the wheel. He said, "You'd like that." He was stout for ten but sounded half again as old. Already he could drive a tractor and shoot a rifle and carry three twelve-year-old tacklers across a goal line. The one time he'd gulped his father's whiskey hadn't gone so well, but he was devising a scheme by which he would try sipping the stuff.

"That ain't nothing but make work," the taller of the gravediggers said. "We already got us a job here."

"If he'd just up and die," the shorter one said.

"If he just would, yup," said the taller.

"Who the hell sent you two, anyway?" It was the soak. "His daddy the mayor? Ol' Scratch Himself? I heard of waiting up with the dying, but Christ. Most folk bring flowers for the ill or food for the family. Have you not heard of a casserole? The shovels are a little, I don't know, boys—pushy. Rude. It's just not done." The soak smiled wryly.

The taller of them took a step forward with shovel in hand; the shorter aimed to, but he'd planted his too deep and so stayed put and settled for a scowl. He'd have sooner disrobed there on the county road than to walk three feet without his shovel.

"No," the soak said. "I know. You two're straight out of one of the old man's stories. I don't recollect which. No, I do—that one where the young man who ain't yet lived is talking to the old one who ain't living long. Let me see. That's right. Well, the reaper, Ol' Grimmy, he's said to have his eye on the old man, and has sent a couple of his minions out for a look. That's you two—the minions. Hell, you're not even real. Ha! Well, no more so than those shovels, and a shovel's just a thing, a tool."

The taller of the shovel men twisted his mouth in a downward slope. His lips, though, were too thin to project true menace; they looked like two worms in a dead heat across his face. He took another step forward, too close now to take a good, wide swing at the soak. *Goddamn it,* he thought.

"But anyway," the soak said. "I was telling you about that story. How did it go? I recollect now. The old one asks the young one, 'Where does eternity go?' and the young one, he says, 'Well—' " He paused and then came to a full stop.

"Well what?" The three of them said it as a chorus.

"Well, the young man didn't know what to make of it. But he filed it away, for to try and figure it out later, when he was older, wiser."

The chorus was displeased. The taller of the shovel men twisted his mouth up further, those two worms seeming to try for some artful cross between a scowl and the symbol for eternity. The shorter one glared, his own try for true menace, though his eyes, black and shining, called to mind nothing so much as a puppy's wet nose. The boy shook his head and said, "Hellfire," the way his daddy did when some damn fool had disappointed him. Damned fools were forever disappointing his daddy. And then the boy said, "Anything ever happen in those stories of his?"

"Why sure," the soak said. "This one time a bear ate a boy about your height and size."

The boy glowered where another would have shuddered. He put up his dukes, lest his cocksureness was lost on the shovel men—or perhaps in case a bear were to toddle upright from the woods, looking to mix it up.

"But," the soak continued, "by and large, no, not a lot happens, in the way you mean it. He never was one for low theater. There's generally a shotgun handy in his stories, but it's like he's had one box of shells to last him. He's more for the slow death."

The soak put one foot on a vine-covered gate at the entrance of the old writer's property. Slow-peck vines, the soak called them, because the flowers were the shape and shade of red, painted-up lips. They made him think of his late wife, Alma, her ways and affections.

The soak patted his pockets for the makings of a cigarette. He began to roll one. He liked the sound of nothing doing, didn't figure it would last. He missed sweet Alma, the way they'd lay waste to a day, together. He'd read to her, poetry or one of the old writer's stories, some bit from the Memphis newspaper. He'd croon it. He could even make a headline from the Memphis newspaper sound like something you'd set fiddles to. Hell, ball scores, pro rasslin' outcomes, dog-racing results from the track in West Memphis. He was a bard and a pard and a card, Alma used to say. Only Alma and the old writer knew him as something other than the town soak; one had taken the secret to her grave and soon the other would, too. Then he'd be who they said he was, if for no other reason than a town needs a soak, for to wipe its feet on. He sighed again but did not smile.

The boy said, "I don't reckon I'd read his books if they put one of those shotguns to my head."

"Well," the soak said, coming out of his mood, but just a bit. "I don't guess it'll come to that. But I'd mind those bears, if I were you."

"Well, you ain't."

18

Cheatham circled wide, giving the men in the boat wide berth, and then approached from behind. Through canebrake, into marsh. He was shin-deep in water and the water rising visibly, as if the great state were some clawfoot tub and a bath were being drawn for a man the size of God, or Paul Bunyan. He brushed against something with feathers. Did not say, *That you, Hope?* Just said, *Shhh the fuck.*

He had trees for cover now. He thought of old dead Shagbark, but these trees were no hickories, had smoother bark. *Fagus grandifolia?* How the fuck was he supposed to know? He stopped and leaned forward, between two trees. It was getting on to full morning now, but there was scant evidence of it. He could see the men, or at least the outlines of them. They were two, in officers' uniforms of some sort. He pushed back from the trees. He took a step right and was knee-deep, another and he was up to his thighs. He stopped. The men had their backs to him, looked like they might be Fish and Game, but had been given rifles. Pressed into service, must be. They held them like they were some newfangled poles for fishing. He was submerged, nearly. The water lapped at his chin. He moved closer to the boat and stopped. He listened. They talked like two old anglers on a Saturday morn.

"You really believe it?"

"Believe what?"

"That this Cheatham character built him a bomb, while he's on death row, then managed to escape before the damn thing blew? The hell'd he make it out of? Plastic cutlery and beard whiskers?"

"Crafty fucker."

"I'd like to meet the man who could do that."

"Well, I guess that's why they give you a gun, Dan."

Cheatham was on them before they could move, but move they did, as he rocked the boat from behind. The one named Dan went down instantly and the other turned on one foot to face whatever the hell it was that was assaulting the craft, sea beast or death-row escapee. Cheatham grabbed his rifle and then jabbed him with it, the man falling backward, toppling over his fellow warden, Dan, and into the drink. Dan dove in after, leaving his rifle.

Cheatham was the proud owner of a boat, and two rifles to go with his pistol. He clambered aboard and motored on out of there. He headed west—hoped it was west. The motor sputtered and coughed and then caught. The boat was gray and sleek, like a floating shiv.

19

A tornado is sudden, a rant of nature, a ghost until it appears.

John's grandfather told him this, one calm night over the clinking of ice against glass. Old Man Flood loved to talk of foul weather on fair nights. "You don't name tornadoes," he said. "There's no time and there's no running. A tornado will suck you up and spit you clear to the Midwest or somewhere, one of those 'I' states." Old Man Flood, who traced his Kentucky roots to Daniel Boone days, said you couldn't tell one from another, those 'I' states.

"Mr. Flood!" the boy's grandmother said. "Nothing will do but what it blows up a storm just for your personal amusement."

John's grandfather loved to tempt fate; also his wife's hearing and God's sense of humor. The boy listened to his every word and filed away each one.

"A storm's coming," John said now to Jenny.

"Yeah, well let it," she said.

20

And the Tennessee deck, the pleasure deck, did thrum with dancing and fighting, carousal and every kind of country music there was; some of it was even real.

There was a meeting of the governor's two mistresses, who got on surprisingly well. They were fans of each other, it turned out: The supermodel had always wanted to sing and the country singer had always wanted to be tall.

"I bet you about need guy wires to stay upright," said the country singer, who stood five-foot-one at full perk, craning her neck at the six-footer.

"Let me tell you," said the supermodel, laughing. She gave the country singer a gentle elbow jab meant for the latter's rib; it cleared the country singer's head entirely.

Not far away, Commissioner of Correction Lynch could be heard explaining his theory of more dying but less killing to a Nashville record label A&R man, who kept interrupting, at which point the commissioner would exclaim,

"But I'm not a pussy! Hear me out, man! I'm not soft on anything!"

Meanwhile, a super group had formed among some of the musicians, and they had taken the stage to tremendous applause, which, when it gave way, did so to silence, for the super group was made up of four lead singers and no instrumentalists. It was awkward, but only for a moment. One and then another began singing a cappella. Something about the lack of instrumentation, just having the sound of human voice, put them in a reflective mood. For they chose a classic song—alas not the same song.

"Is that 'Lovesick Blues' or 'Honky Tonk Heroes'?" Adjutant General Spears asked Senior Counsel Bills.

"I might could tell you," said Senior Counsel Bills, "if one of them would shut up."

At this moment, the other two in the super group started in singing. One song seemed to be "Behind Closed Doors" and the other might have been "Crazy Arms." Each of the four began to sing all the louder. They seemed to each think it a good idea, some new idiom of country music they were creating, some new market to mine, new contest category for which they might take all the nominee slots in one fell swoop. Their four voices swelled as, well, four.

21

And so another day dawned in North Mississippi, in the small town of Burden. The rain had cleared, for now, and the floodwaters had stopped, shy of the county line. The sky, alas, was gray as ever. The sky was the shade of spit on slate; it glistened, a little, like spit. Wait—was that a drop?

The old, dying writer stood at the edge of the porch, leaning out, looking up.

Coming a storm, he thought. Wind and rain and hail the size of bad pennies.

He settled back into the old, iron rocker. He smiled. For he was alive, yet. He had written this latest story, this last one, though he didn't like the beginning and it still lacked for a proper ending—it just sort of stopped, like life does, sometimes. And too much of the middle drifted where it should have flowed. There was too much middle in the middle, was the thing. Oh, well. That was writing. He would cut what needed to be cut. Writing is cutting, he liked to say to young writers, though they never took him seriously. Writing is revision. He said that, too. Revision was the real work of the thing. If a writer were to land on a distant planet, never before seen, much less foot set upon surface, by human man, and if the writer were to touch down on this distant rock with the softness of a feather, a shadow, just so and perfect, the first thing the writer would say is: Let me go back and try again; I'll get it right yet. The writer never got it quite right, but not for lack of revision. The work was hard but his head was harder. But mostly, revising meant he was still writing. It was his breathing. It was what kept him alive. It was better than Three Queens and most sex and the promise of eternal salvation. God, it was fun.[20]

He sat and smiled and gave a wave as he watched them go, the gravediggers to their digs, the soak for a drink, perhaps from the bottle he kept by the grave of his late wife. She wasn't a ghost, like the writer's late wife, she was just dead, but that was all right with the soak. It meant he could get a word in.

The boy left, too, in a huff he seemed to have borrowed from his daddy the mayor. He would report to his daddy that

---

[20]Another fair country writer from these same parts, William Faulkner, once advised students from Princeton to write for pleasure, so as to feel passion in the act. He said writing should be fun. Faulkner must have had fun himself, unspooling a 1,288-word sentence in *Absalom, Absalom!* Faulkner's writing advice also included stopping when you're hot, which may have explained why that 1,288-word sentence was incomplete.

plans to capitalize, in a civic way, on the death of the famous writer would have to be delayed or perhaps shelved. For the old buzzard would not die, and he was useless to them upright, doddering, and still writing.

The old writer sat, pages on his lap, pencil in hand. He read what he'd written on the first page. He frowned, in a pleased sort of way. Oh, what clutter. A right mess, this was. He'd have to keep going until he knew it was good, or good enough. Worthy, to use another word.

He remembered another book he'd written, years ago. Labored over, died for, years of his life given to—but, hell, that was every book. He was trying to interest some small publisher in the North Country. He was out of favor, those days. The New York houses had all said no. They'd called it experimental. He'd said it was nothing of the sort. He hated when people called it that. If you were still calling it experimental when the thing was done, the experiment had failed. So he had gotten it all in order, this latest book, this tome. He printed it out. Seven years of his life, from first draft to last revision. He brought it to the post office and the stern woman there weighed it. Just shy of four pounds, it was—would have been seven, but for all that cutting, all those revisions.

She asked if it was perishable.

The old writer looked up, incredulous, aghast, distraught.

"I hope to Christ not," he said.

Death is Not the End

I wonder what the devil keeps grumbling about?
He's down in hell and he can't get out

—Taskiana Four
"Creep Along, Moses"

Why don't they call them Acts of the Devil? You know, hurricanes and floods and the like, that earthquake they say they're going to have up in Memphis. Every time there's a flood or something and somebody calls it an Act of God, I bet God's got to pay the devil royalties, like Aretha did to Otis when she sang "Respect."

—Ivy Coldwater, folk artist,
Taint County, Mississippi

1

Cheatham and his craft cut through the water. The hum and the gurgle and, good God, the sight of him. You could have spied him three states away, but he met not a soul for the first hour of travel. Had all of his fellow Tennesseans drowned? Would their deaths, too, be laid at his cowboy boots?

He ate jerky and listened to the crank radio, for news of his exploits. Had he set off more bombs, torn a big-ass hole in the ozone, knocked off any liquor stores?

But it was music only. Blues songs and country, soul serenades and bar-napkin symphonies.

Then the weather report.

"Gloom seems to have paid off the sun again," said the weatherman, gloomily, and turned it back over to the DJ, who played a set of rain songs—"Rain Dogs" and "I Can't Stand the Rain," and then "Just Walkin' in the Rain," by the Prisonaires, cut by state inmates on Sun Records out of Memphis, 1953.

The motor sputtered and coughed again. It gurgled and stalled. It sounded like it had been out in the rain too long and caught its death. Cheatham called the engine a motherfucker, or perhaps he was speaking of his condition and the state of things, generally. He sighed. He fell reflective. He thought, for the first time since his "escape," of the woman—but which one? The one he once loved or the one who once obsessed him? The one they said he killed or the one who set him up (he said) for the murder?

Would she be in Memphis? Hell, she'd be woman king of the place. If the flood waters got too high, climbed the bluff and threatened her favorite Beale Street dive, she'd levitate the whole of motherfucking Beale while she sang "Killer Diller Blues" and "Shave 'Em Dry."

He put her from his mind. Tried to. She made him crazy, loose in the head—a dangerous state for a man on such a precarious streak of never having killed (he said) another human soul.

He sighed. He looked at the jerky, the jerky looking like some swamp fossil from protohistoric times. How they marketed that shit as snack goods, Cheatham had no earthly notion.

He turned practical. He wondered how much gas he had left. How far had he gone? How far to go? Was he even headed west? Would she be there, waiting, the woman king?

Well, if he ran out of gas, he could always lash the two rifles together for a mast, and use that XXXL Tall cowboy shirt for a sail. The shirt was soaked and needed drying, anyway.

What a sight he'd be, what a sight. Cheatham on the high seas. Tennessee's most hunted. He'd don that cowboy shirt, once it'd dried, and perform, impromptu for you. Anybody asked, he was going to Memphis to cut a record at Sun, a modern-day Prisonaire.

2

He moved close enough to hold her, and then held her.

3

Back aboard the steamer *Clementine*, the teacher was beginning to make some honest progress with the snotnoses. He was doing his damnedest, playing his banjo behind his back and between his legs, and making up lyrics as he played. One day he stood on his desk in his cowboy boots and sang, a new one, a love song:

Drink a dram to the town of want
in the state of grace

I'll run a finger up your leg
Honey, all the way to your face

The snotnoses clapped and hooted. The snotnoses had all sorts of questions. Where's the town of Want? Is it in Dickson County? Somewhere up in Kentucky? What's a dram? A boy named Colton asked if he could do that finger thing to a girl named Casey. The girl named Casey asked if she could smack Colton's face all the way to the town of Want.

Bascom Holcomb Miller, better known as Bud Miller, said just the once, Miss Casey, and then had the snotnoses all gather in groups of six to write their own country songs, from the scene they'd just witnessed or maybe one they remembered from their own homes. Several of the budding tunesmiths said they'd spied their parents in various states and stages of undress in unusual places, up top the butcher block in the kitchen being the teacher's favorite. There was much violence, too—likewise, much of it taking place in the kitchen, where knives and sausage grease and cast-iron skillets were readily available.

The teacher said for the snotnoses to work hard at their craft, like good little snotnoses, for at term's end they'd perform their compositions on the top deck of the *Clementine* for the governor himself.

4

He kissed her bare shoulders and then let down her hair. He ran the fingers of both hands through it, some strands lank and some wild and a-tangle and all of it white like poor-girl's platinum, like ghost hair, like a dream, all dreamy.

5

The two Nashville songwriters, Leo Chance and Cig Murphy, were in their usual place, doing the usual things. They were drinking bourbon and talking about writing a song.

"You know what it feels like, Leo," Cig said, "to wake up in the morning and realize 'Lost Highway' has already been written."

"To say nothing of 'Crazy' and 'Crazy Arms.' "

"And 'Hey, Porter!' "

"You know, I've been thinking about Porter Wagoner," Leo said. "His name, which was real, by the way, and perfect. That great pompadour with those countless miles of golden coastline. Those Nudie suits that he wore, so blue the sky bowed down before him, became the ground under his rhinestone boots."

For Leo was several toddies in and turning rhapsodic.

"Porter, on the stage of the Grand Ole Opry. Porter, singing duets with Dolly. Johnny Cash singing 'Hey, Porter'— a train song, it's true, but still."

"Hey, Leo?"

"Yeah, Cig?"

"You think Dodge Ford's real name is Dodge Ford?"

"I think it may well be."

"What about Colt Remington?"

"Yep," Leo said. "But you know what?"

"What's that, Leo?"

"I heard he's from Connecticut."

"Well, I'll be."

6

He was aside her now, his hand on her pale skin.

"They say open fields are good and a ditch, too, if you got a ditch handy," Jenny Spell said to John Flood. "But a cemetery is the best place of all to be during a tornado."

He rose onto one elbow.

"Because everybody here is dead?" John said.

"So far as the tornado knows," she said. "*Shhh.*"

She grabbed him by the buckle of his belt. He seemed to fly and land all in one swoop. He was over her, suddenly, his hands, open-palmed, on the cemetery floor.

"You know what?" he said.

"What?"

"What if—"

"*Shhh*, Johnny Flood."

He didn't want to *shhh*. God, anything but *shhh*. He wanted to gab on about Robert Johnson and the cross roads myth, about Memphis Minnie and her many men. He wanted to talk about the weather the way some people talk about religion. He wanted to tell Jenny how he liked her the instant he saw her, that day from the porch swing, though *like* wasn't near enough the word for it. *Like* was a tame little word with no fuse. *Like* didn't light the sky. He wanted to say these things and others, too. He wanted to leave that storm out of breath, from all his talking, and then, after he'd weathered a real storm and a figurative one, then he'd—

But Jenny Spell said it again. "*Shhh.*"

John kept his hands, open-palmed, on the cemetery ground. That tornado, if it became one, could yank trees and gravestones from the cemetery ground, could fill the sky with rant and granite and limbs of ancient oaks, but John didn't suppose those hands would move, could move. He looked down at her, at that white hair at once lank and a-tangle.

"Love your sweet baby, Johnny Flood," Jenny Spell said. "Love her like there really is a tornado coming. Love her like God ain't looking. Like I really am, sure and finally, that big-leg blues mama I'm dying to be."

Now she said it again, one last time, "*Shhh.*"

So the one thing he couldn't do, he did. He had one hand loose. It rose and hovered, it touched down and set about tracing rivers and constellations on pale-white Jenny skin. John's senses settled in his fingertips, and so Jenny was all he saw and smelled, heard, tasted, and touched.

The storm bruised the sky and the winds began to swirl, but one force of nature was all John could manage at a time. The storm became the sky, but Jenny and John seemed a thousand miles away, and the boy with a thousand years in that one hand loose. He kissed his way down Jenny's face. He lingered. He tasted and touched. He seemed now to have that second hand loose, with its own second set of senses, its own thousand years to spend at its leisure, those thousand miles removed from that storm.

But no mere storm. It took on the color of iron and death and the form of a body. Now the body gave way to a new form and flew silver-tongued across the sky. Later, there would be pictures in The Roost Reporter and the newspaper out of Memphis. The tornado would be all people talked about, for days on end.

But John still was those thousand miles away, with those thousand years in that one hand loose. He didn't see that sky the color of iron and death, for seeing Jenny's blue eyes through that white hair. The storm began to howl, singing background for the blues in his head.

"Jen—" He was about to say he wasn't scared any more. He was about to say he was ready. But she said, "*Shhh,*" like *shhh* was the greater wisdom, a song older than the blues.

Now came a thousand freight trains bearing down on that sad, small town as the very ground shuddered and shook.

Now silence you could hear, and they heard it.

Now wind you could see, and they saw it.

7

Cheatham didn't know whether he'd run out of gas or the motor had died, or both. So he drifted with the currents. He drifted a day or more. He ate jerky and sipped judiciously from the water jug. He didn't mind dying but by damned if it'd be from dehydration. No slow death for a man who spent years of death row. Make it something quick like. A piano falling from the sky, like in a cartoon. Hell, a full jazz combo or outright orchestra. It had rained everything else.

He was tired, sore, beaten down, tending toward delirious. He was alive, about it. He saw no signs of life but some birds of the air, and another of their brethren, a turkey buzzard, that gruesome-looking fellow, perched atop the unloosed lid of a grain bin that bobbed in the drink like a child's bath toy.

He tried the crank radio, that pirate station out of Memphis. He seemed to be old news already. There was a brief mention of him still on the lam, armed and dangerous, but the lead story was the trial of an alleged river walker, in West Tennessee. The newscast did not say how far the perpetrator had walked or what in hell harm he had caused. The news ended, and then a commercial for Sunrise Bread, "best bread under the sun," and another for the Big Clydie's Two-Ring Circus, "shows afternoon and evening and all night in your dreams, buck and a bob a head and kids under three for free."

Cheatham drifted on. Various household items came floating by, pots and ladles, a rolling pin, spice rack, a small bistro table, couple of stools, a chef's hat poofed up like some portly little ghost. "Well, there goes the kitchen," Cheatham said. "I guess the parlor it'll be along directly."

He looked up, for falling pianos. He smiled—the thought of Fats Waller, old fave, at the keys.

Hell of a way to go, he thought, to die by falling piano with a man named Fats at the keys. Shit. Fats alone would kill you. The great man went something like three hundred pounds. He thought of what they taught him in fourth grade, that objects of different mass fall at the same rate. He never did quite believe it, even when the teacher took them to the window and dropped from it an apple and an orange.

Well, sure, apples and oranges.

Cheatham thought of a piano player named Fats and a guitar player named Slim.

What then, Isaac Fucking Newton? Tell me what then?

Cheatham stretched out in the boat. He was nearly the length of it. Cheatham, staring at the sky, breaking out laughing. Closed his eyes and saw it. Cartoon vision of his death.

Fats, you're killing me, man.

Still, it beat the hell out of sodium thiopental.

8

John held Jenny. Jenny held John. They clawed at the ground, at the graves. The storm swallowed their screams and spat back all manner of deathly curse. It howled, and that was the worst of it, that howl. It was a bellow from the bellows. It was every bit a tornado now. It yanked trees from the cemetery ground; the roots were bones of fingers, trembling against the blackness, beckoning. It flung iron benches, gravestones, a granite cross.

It seemed now to disappear, stealing over a rise on the country side of the cemetery, and John said, "Jenny," and she said, "Is it?" But it was the tornado that answered, that silver tongue with all manner of deathly curse upon it. The tornado moved in leaps and bounds. It took out a line of trees, turned to ashes a statue of a soldier in uniform.

They talk of holy moments in times like this. There is quiet in the din, there is calm in a thousand freight trains bearing down in one direction while a thousand more, heretofore unseen, rush from the other. The tornado holds its silver tongue. This is when God speaks. This is when God lifts His hand, guides His children to safety. That's what people say in the newspapers, after.

John did not know about holy, but he could vouch for the moment. They had it, John and Jenny. It lasted the length of a last kiss. It went for ages; a blink and it was gone.

The tornado was upon them now. It took again the form of a body. That silver tongue became a puffed-out chest. It tore through the cemetery floor with the force of those thousand freight trains bearing down. The sky was filled with those yanked trees, those iron benches, that granite cross, and the ashes of a soldier twice-killed.

It was nothing at all for that tornado to do what it did next, though nothing less than a tornado could have done it. Nothing less than a tornado could have torn them apart, separated them, and flung them to far opposite reaches of the cemetery like it did. It was a mindless thing, after all. It had no heart in that puffed-out chest. That silver tongue knew nothing but curses.

It was sudden, like Old Man Flood said. It was a rant of nature, a ghost made real.

John was airborne. He clawed at the sky, his senses in his fingertips still and trying for Jenny, for one last taste or touch of her. He thought, *I'm about to die, that's it, just die,* but even a tornado—even a mindless, heartless beast such as that—ought to grant a dying boy's request, for that one last touch or taste of such a girl as poor, pale, skinny-legged Jenny Spell. That was all he wanted, in this or any other world.

In that moment, John would have taken the hand of God and called it settling.

9

Cheatham slept for what seemed a day, or was it a week, then awoke sometime around dusk, or was it dawn, to see a ship, or was it a specter? It was about hundred yards away. He drifted near. It was a twenty-foot flatboat, with a sort of makeshift cabin in the middle. The back of the flatboat extended a good ten feet beyond the cabin, for a porch effect. There was a wooden rocking chair and beside it a small wooden table on which sat a book. A chicken, a white Leghorn, paced about the porch, in a distracted kind of way, as if it might be about to have a difficult conversation with a close friend. It reminded Cheatham a little of his lawyer, a young, earnest, white boy given the task of convincing the world a six-foot, seven-inch scowl with skin as black as cast iron did not do the thing they said he did.

"Hey, there," Cheatham shouted, but failed to get a rise even out of the chicken, distracted as it was. No acknowledgement came from inside the little cabin, and there seemed no light inside, no smoke piping out.

Cheatham waited a full minute. Thought he heard a noise of the sort a Leghorn might make, but it did not come from the Leghorn, which still was pacing about, oblivious to all else. Had the Leghorn thrown its voice? Was that even possible?

Had chickens evolved their stagecraft over the course of his long incarceration? Chickens? Stagecraft? Really? Cheatham knew a man one time, a traveling salesman, who kept an Andalusian that danced to flamenco music, and Deuce Coleman, his old death-row mate, said he came from a town in Georgia that was so small there was a banty rooster on the board of aldermen, and the dog catcher was a pit mix. Cheatham put all this from his mind—*focus, man.*

He took a deep breath. He listened. Stillness and the faint scratches of that Leghorn. He waited another full minute. Nothing. Then he slipped his pistol in his right boot, the knife between his teeth, and slowly boarded the flatboat, his eyes on the door of the little cabin. He had one knee on the flatboat's porch when the door creaked opened.

Well, fuck me.

Said Cheatham to himself.

10

The boy awoke to the gray-blue calm of the hour after, to the warm taste of blood thick on busted lip. That one hand loose hung limp from a broken arm. He crawled over the cemetery floor. He crawled over a rise, past flung graves, split trees, bent and mangled benches, fist-sized clumps of granite, shards of earth. He crawled some more and now managed to stand, and to walk.

His senses were in his feet now; he walked mindlessly with great purpose. His feet took him to the clearing. They broke into a run where one night he and Jenny walked, where they held hands and he gave her a squeeze and she gave it back, where they lay looking at the stars and Jenny said she wanted to reach up and grab a handful of them, to walk the streets of Roost with a pocketful of stars she'd spend like money. He remembered that night, that sky bejeweled, as he came upon her backpack, one cowboy boot and the heel of the lost other, a dime-sized silver button, all neat in a pile as if God's hand has been at work already, and yet too late: a makeshift memorial.

11

The DJ played a gospel song called "Death is Not the End." He let the last notes fade and then said, "Something to think about, eh, people? There's another place. Or so our bard with guitar tells us. He sings of storm clouds, cross roads, cities on fire. But he sings of salvation, too, and the tree of life. The bard with guitar is telling us, good people, that *life* is not the end but just the start of it all, that how you live here determines how—and where—you live after. How are you living, good people? Where you headed when you die? How you getting there? What will it be, good people? Glory train or hand basket?"

The DJ let the weight of all this settle, then he played a record by another bard with guitar, with a sort of flipside take on the same theme, "God is a Real Estate Developer."

12

The sky was scarcely any color at all; gray would not have claimed it as kin. The sky was all plummet and regret. The sky rued the day.

Cora Flood sat watching it. She said not a word. It had been an hour since John finished his story. His girl had died and he hadn't. Pale-skinned, skinny-legged Jenny Spell, with her hair of poor-girl platinum and dreams of being a blues woman, big-legged and brown-skinned, was off to West Hell or wherever. And the boy, John, thisfuckingclose to getting his young, white ashes hauled, was left to watch her go.

"Which makes me what, exactly?" Cora managed to say, finally.

Ten miles of slow crawl followed upon the floodwaters of the former Tennessee before John answered, and then it was only to say, "Yes. I know how it seems."

Another five miles of drift, two drinks, a cracker Cora stared at as if the face of Jesus, or McKinley Morganfield, were sketched out there in grains of salt.

"The second coming of—" She stopped, but not to eat or drink or even stare. The drift of the party barge, even, seemed to stop.

She moved close enough to hold him, and then held him.

13

Cheatham raised his hands high and wide, in a friendly sort of way; he might have been about to embrace a nine-foot bear from which he'd been long estranged. It seemed his one play. He had the knife in his teeth and the pistol in his boot, neither weapon particular handy versus whatever he sensed was on the other side of the door of the little cabin.

The door was open a crack and a shotgun barrel came nosing out.

"Hey, now," Cheatham said, as well as he could with teeth clenched on blade.

No response from the barrel or the man behind it.

"Howdy," Cheatham said, trying to sound as bright as that egg-yellow cowboy shirt. Maybe he'd be taken for a country singer just trying to flee the flood. Maybe he'd sing a verse of "Kiss an Angel Good Mornin' " or "Is Anybody Goin' to San Antone" for his supper.

Now the door opened just slightly more. Barrel gave way to action. The toe of one boot appeared.

"Armed to the teeth, are ye?" said the man behind the door.

"You mind terribly if I take the knife out?" Cheat managed to say.

"All depends on where you plan to put it."

14

Bate retired to his top-deck stateroom. He was alone, but for his two bulldogs, Cracker and Nathan. He patted their heads, said Daddy had done well. His time, after all the waiting, all the bidding and biding, was about to come. And to think, God, of all people, had set it in motion, with this last great Southern flood. Maybe it was time to believe in the old coot. *Gawd.*

He went to the stateroom's bar and poured himself a good, stiff one—whiskey in a brandy snifter. Alone but for the bulldogs, the alcohol hit him almost immediately, as always it did. Because now he was drinking to drink, to be drunk. It was his due, and he received the corn as something like a sacrament. It was sweet relief, to lay down his guard as others did their burdens.

Four glasses and an hour in, with Bate well-soused, trousers off, and starting to sing a show tune, a woman, well-soused herself, stumbled mistakenly into the stateroom.

"Did I send for a hooker?" said Bate, thinking it entirely possible.

The woman was low-slung and ample, with wild, raven hair; she looked somewhat exotic, for hailing from Sneedville, in Hancock County. She put a hand a-hip and said, mock-huffily, "I'm a country singer."

"Six of one … " said Bate, a bit blearily.

"Don't I know it," she said.

They laughed. He poured her one. They drank. They talked. Loose lips and all. Bate began, in time, to brag of his plan to topple the governor and his government, to take control of Tennessee and a vast territory beyond, over which he would rule, from Memphis, City on the Bluff. He said he'd rule it with a gloved fist, like Boss Crump did for all those decades. And then, when the time was right or the mood struck, whichever, he'd take off the glove. He'd be the full-on dictator the place needed all along.

The country singer, being an East Tennessee girl, asked why not rule from the mountains there. She said she'd rather a mountain than a bluff, especially in a time of a flood. Bate smiled. He liked her—her spark, and drinking prowess, her build all low-slung and ample, how she didn't seem to be altogether repulsed by the trousers-down sight of him. He said it was smart of her to wonder. He explained. He said East Tennessee was easily ruled, because East Tennesseans behaved in a predictable ways and voted as they were told, whereas Memphis, poor old shine, was the state's unruly relation. It couldn't be counted on to behave at all, or to act predictably. He said Memphis was prone to accidents, and these accidents had repercussions.

"Everything great that came out of Memphis was a damned accident. Elvis—accident! Every visionary was a madman, crazy person. Sam Phillips—the man needed electric-shock therapy to get through a Wednesday! Clarence Saunders, he created the modern supermarket—and still went broke! Called his grocery store the Piggly Wiggly. Christ, what passes for delusions of grandeur in that town. And Saunders, he started building his grand mansion then, his monument to himself. The Pink Palace, people called it."

"Pink Palace, huh? Sounds like a titty bar."

"Ha—you'd think! And I've just covered the white folk!"

"So tell me again why we're going to Memphis?"

Bate was beginning to seriously consider the country

singer for a roll on the floor, two falls, no elimination, or maybe a cabinet post. He poured them another and then said, "Because a town like Memphis, left to itself, gets to be trouble. It makes messes for the rest of us to clean up. But—but Memphis wants a savior. It knows, somehow, it needs one. So it's always on the lookout for one. That's the entire history of the city, look it up—wanting somebody to come save it from itself. Boss Crump knew it. So did the mayor they called King Willie. And so did that gap-toothed huckster, I forget his name, who showed up when they were building that pyramid down on the river bank. They handed the thing over to him, practically—a sixty-five million dollar pyramid! Ah, Memphis, she's a sucker for a huckster. You can be gap-toothed, and lack the appropriate social graces, doesn't matter. You can be shaped like a brandy snifter—I saw you looking, don't lie. Hell, a handsome man with airs would just raise suspicion in Memphis. It's why Flattery carried every city and town in Tennessee but one. Yup, Memphis. Poor old shine."

"I don't trust a handsome man, by and large," said the country singer. "Maybe I'm a sucker for a huckster, myself. They do tend to keep things lively for as long as they're around. It's only a homely man who has any real staying power. I stuck with one six, eight months, one time—a personal record. You may be onto something, your own self."

"You ever see a picture of Boss Crump? Bushy-headed hoot owl with jowls down to here!" He scratched his balls. She moved in.

"Oh, the press'll love you." On his lap now, whispering in his ear. The Sneedville Songbird, they called her.

"Hell, darlin', I'm bringing the press with me. I bought a newspaperman just today."

"Bought a newspaper?"

"Nah, just a newspaperman."

"Bought. Like with a hooker or something?"

"Just like with a hooker," said Bate, "only cheaper."

"Well, hell, honey. So cheers. To Memphis, then."

"City on the Bluff, darlin', where we'll be high and dry."

The country singer laughed.

"First time I ever heard Memphis called a dry town," she said. "But what about the pirates? I heard tell there were pirates."

Bate smiled. "There are no pirates. I made that up," he said. "It's called intelligence."

"You have it all planned out, huh? Your grand takeover, I mean."

"No, that's too easy and not half the fun. I set a few things in motion—some for a reason, some not—and let them take their course."

"Kind of like God, huh?"

The country singer laughed again. She wondered if this man held any real power in the state. She couldn't imagine so, by the look of him. He was a slob, and he talked big, told everything he knew. A blowhard, basically. But she liked him, for some reason. She was basically a blowhard, herself. Buzzards of a feather—her mama used to say to her daddy. So what the hell? "Hey, honey. You think you got a place for me in your cabinet, once you rise to power, like?"

"What do you want to be?"

"I don't know. I've got a mouth on me."

"Where do you stand on capital punishment?"

"You want me to spank you?"

"That's corporal," Bate said. "We'll get to that."

15

Governor Flattery was between mistresses. (No, really.) There on his starboard side was the supermodel, whose real name was Bonnie but was now called Cham, and on his port side the country singer named Misty Dunhill, her real name, who was the former Miss South Carolina.

"How we know you're not your double?" Misty wanted to know.

Bonnie who was now called Cham raised the sheets, took a long look, and said, "It's him all, right. It's the governor."

"So, Guv," said Misty, as had so many other woman, dating back to the first lady of Tennessee when Trey was just fresh out of Vanderbilt, "you gonna take a switch to us?"

He loved when they said that.

16

Bate and the country singer from East Tennessee had finished one bottle and another and still were not sated. The country singer wobbled topless over to the liquor cabinet. She clattered around in there while Bate struggled to stand but could not. He plopped back in his chair and smiled real big.

"Speaking of dead soldiers," she said, turning to face him. She held a double magnum whiskey bottle by the scruff of its neck. There was something rather large and floaty inside it.

"Huh?" Bate was staring at her breasts, with something like seventh-grade awe. "What?" He'd heard them called many things but never dead soldiers. He about saluted.

She waved the bottle. "So the rumor's true," she said. "I'd heard y'all had Forrest's brain, pickling in a bottle of whiskey."

She had all manner of questions for him about it. Did it weigh the same as a normal human brain? Had it been studied to explain the general's brilliance as a battlefield technician? If you placed Forrest's brain in a simple, dumb animal, like say a jackass, could it be expected to think deep thoughts and devise cunning plans and lead men, or anyway other jackasses, into battle? You might have thought she'd ask how they got the damned thing in there, a human brain, about the size of both of her fists, or one of her breasts, through the mouth of even a double magnum bottle of Old No. 7. But she did not, for she had a better thought, all of a sudden. So she asked it.

"Could we—should we? Just a—"

Bate leaned forward, about the best he could do in his condition, and said to the country singer from East Tennessee: "Do you notice, lass, the bottle's about half empty already?"

They had themselves a nightcap.

17

God at His typewriter. Questioning Himself, as all the better gods and writers do. He created man and woman, this world and the rest, the flowers of the fields and fish of the stream, but damned if He could claim mastery over the written word. Word choice, sentence construction, plotting, theme, voice, sense of place, text and subtext, when to write in the vernacular voice and how far to take it. It never got easier. For all His lovely form and His lovely fingers, He was an amateur at it. His perfect posture helped Him turn no phrase. He had donned and then ditched His lovely robes and now wrote in an old, cotton Irish grandfather's shirt with a hole in the left elbow—had it belonged to Yeats? Synge?—and a pair of dungarees whose provenance was harder labor than writing, even.

It made no never mind. Writing *was* hard. And He could never quite bring Himself to employ *deus ex machina*—His birthright, to be sure. It seemed a cheat, somehow. No, this had to be done the hard way, which made it all the more satisfying, when the words fell together.

Creating the real world was nothing next to imagining one.

Writing. God, was it fun.

He loved stories—the characters and all that befell them; conflict up on its hind legs, crowing, and resolution off in the distance, hiding behind a tree. But just a few words, strung along just so, could get Him through the day. A sentence could save a month. For eternity was a very long time, even for God.

18

The author at his desk. He's hunched over a computer keyboard. He's a two-finger banger, never could learn to touch type. Pity the poor author. No—pity that poor keyboard. He bangs it so hard the letters on the most frequently struck keys have worn off—a hazard for a hunt-and-pecker like himself. His hands do not hover but hunch, like the rest of him. A lifetime at the keys and he'll walk away someday, if he's lucky enough to, looking like nothing so much as a Times New Roman italic *f*.

He sits and thinks, as he often does, of the writers to whom he is in thrall. They are mostly dead, but he has visited their old homes or their graves—Faulkner and Welty. Dickens and Shakespeare. In Dublin, he visited Joyce's house and then drank in pubs[21] where Joyce or his characters drank. One day he toured an old family brewery in northeastern Pennsylvania

---

[21]One of his favorites, McDaids, is believed to be the opening setting for the Joyce story "Grace," in which the central character is so drunk Joyce needed a new word for it: *peloothered.* McDaids is storied in other ways: It's said to have been the city morgue (McDeads, then?), later converted to a chapel by the Moravian Brethren, eventually taking its rightful guise as a pub favored by the literary likes of Brendan Behan, who was also known to get peloothered.

and across the street was John O'Hara's house. He means to go someday to Andalusia, in Milledgeville, Georgia, to see what's left of Flannery O'Connor and her peacocks. He doesn't run across the authors' ghosts, in these jaunts, but he feels a certain presence, stray words in the air, lingering thoughts, blessed curses. How can you not, he thinks, leaning into the room at Rowan Oak where Faulkner sat at the typewriter by the window, where he tapped out those words of his, *slanted* and *inexorable* and *pinewiney*. Where he wrote the outline of one book on the wall—something the old, dying writer in this narrative does.

Disclaimer: The old, dying writer in this narrative is not Faulkner. He is Faulknerian.

The author wrote a letter once to Larry Brown, a writer from down Faulkner's way. Larry Brown wrote back. This was in 2002.

You can do that—you can write to writers, asking for tips and wisdom, some understanding. They'll read your letters and write back. They'll look over your scars and show you theirs, like jailbirds comparing tattoos. And then tell you to keep at it, just keep dragging ass to the computer or typewriter, to the blank screen or page, you'll be published yet. Or not. It's the only advice, really, besides this: quit.

The author had been reading one of Larry Brown's books. It may have been *Fay*. The author told Larry Brown what a fine book it was and asked him what advice he might have for an unpublished writer. The author knew what Larry Brown would say, because there are only two things *to say* to an unpublished writer—keep writing or quit—and published writers never seem to prescribe the latter. Quitting is too easy. Quitting doesn't scar.

"I'm rushed for time so I'll be brief," Larry Brown began, and then ran for just shy of two single-spaced pages.

(See: what writers do.) "I do get a lot of letters like yours and can't possibly answer all of them, but I read your paper"—(*The Commercial Appeal*, in Memphis, where the author toiled at the time)—"every Sunday, so there you go."

He wrote about what he called "an apprenticeship period" and how his lasted eight years. He wrote about things he'd written and then shit-canned, five novels and some eighty short stories. "I burned one of the novels because I thought it would be strengthening for me. And it probably was. I know it was because I couldn't tell you one line out of that novel now. It wasn't any good."

Six paragraphs in, Larry Brown made note of how he was going to be brief, "and here I've run on." He had to catch a plane the next day to New York for a pre-premiere party for the movie made from his writing, "Big Bad Love." He wrote about Arliss Howard and Debra Winger, who made the movie, and he wrote, "They've been to my house and I'm fixing to go to theirs."

He seemed amazed at his good fortune, but rooted as ever in his place in the world and his struggle and the struggles yet ahead. The author guessed that by the time Larry Brown left New York to go back home, to Mississippi, his head wouldn't have been turned even a little bit by New York but the big city would have some mud crusting on its fancy shoes.

Larry Brown said he still got rejected. He said his favorite part of a novel was sometimes cut "because my editor shows me where it's not needed. And sometimes we argue. But it's a process."

Finally, he said had to run. "All you can do if you believe in your stuff is send it out until you exhaust every possibility. A friend of mine had his book rejected fifty times before it was taken. So think about that."

Larry Brown wished the author luck. He wished him well. "all best," he wrote, and signed his name. Then, having given the author all that time he didn't have to spare, he got an envelope and wrote the author's name and address on it in letters nearly an inch high. Couple of days later, it made it up to Memphis from down around Oxford, where he lived, where Faulkner lived.

The author read the letter several times that day and probably several more the next and then filed it away. He pulls it out from time to time. And he watches that movie, "Big Bad Love," at least once a year, when he's feeling particularly discouraged by the way the writing is going, or more likely by the shabby treatment he's receiving from the callous fuckers in the publishing industry. (Maybe he'd fare better with them if he didn't refer to them as callous fuckers?)

"Big Bad Love" is a movie about a writer who wrecks his life, over writing (and drink). He loses his family, he ends up in jail for a spell, yet he perseveres. He keeps writing. Keeps submitting. The critics—well, you know them. They're callous fuckers, too. One called the movie "a self-indulgent celebration of self-indulgence," and another said the movie "bewilders," with its "stunted, opaque characters."

The author loves the movie but the author's wife sides with those critics. She doesn't need two hours of cinema to know the angst of a writer. She can just turn over in bed.

The author's wife calls it "Big Bad Movie."

The author has the usual dreams, to put books on the shelf and see them praised and perhaps even read. He wants reviews that glow like Beale Street neon and he wants pitched battles over movie rights. He wants people to walk out of the theater saying, "The book was better."

But the author has another dream. He wants to be his wife's favorite writer.

Larry Brown died the day before Thanksgiving, 2004.

The author took the advice Larry Brown gave him, back in 2002. He kept writing. He continued his apprenticeship. He kept banging his hard head against the fucking wall.

By 2011, almost a decade after writing to Larry Brown for advice, the author had gotten a handful of stories published but had found no takers for his novels. In October of that year, on the occasion of his 50th birthday, he interviewed himself, on his blog, which he called "The Soundcheck & the Fury," in a dual nod to his loves of music and of Faulkner.

Interview with myself on the occasion of my 50th birthday:

S&F: *So, 50 and not a whole hell of a lot to show. A handful of story credits and two unpublished novels. I guess you're going to make the case that you're a—*

DWW: *I'm a late bloomer.*

S&F: *I was going to say misunderstood genius.*

DWW: *The misunderstood genius is never understood until he's dead. The later bloomer has his day, if he stays at the work.*

S&F: *You really believe that?*

DWW: *Nah, not really. I sometimes think I'll die with a stack of unpublished novels on my desk.*

S&F: *No time soon, let's hope.*

DWW: *Well, I'm not sure two novels is enough to call a stack, anyway. They're not even big, fat novels, like my wife likes. She thinks anything less than six hundred pages is a tweet. I tell her the bookstores should use grocery-store produce scales on her, charge her by the pound.*

S&F: *You've said before that your literary goal is to become your wife's favorite writer.*

DWW: *Fucking Dickens.*

S&F: *You need to write your Bleak House. That'll bring her around.*

DWW: *I'm afraid I'd be quite the poor man's Dickens. I'd write Bleak Mobile Home. I think I'll stick to being myself. I'll keep writing what I like, what moves me, and maybe the world will come around. Or not. My one novel is a coming-of-age, which my former agent (not the one who died, but the one who quit me) said is not what editors want these days. And my other novel is about a rock 'n' roll band, which a big-time New York agent told me at Sewanee last summer will NEVER sell. And my next novel opens in West Memphis, Arkansas, at the greyhound track—the ladies of the book club will love that one! Dog track Saturday night!*

S&F: *You're a hard-headed son of a bitch, I'll give you that.*

DWW: *I'll take it. Best birthday present ever.*

The author's novel about the rock 'n' roll band was published, a couple of years later.

It has sold a thousand and three copies, to date. It has gone out of print and the publisher was sold.

If the author tallied his proceeds from the novel, titled *Long Gone Daddies*, and divided it by the fifteen years he spent writing and revising before, following some seventy-five rejections, a small publisher in North Carolina finally said yes, he would discover he was paid something like three cents per hour. (Best not do the math.)

The author is not even slightly ruffled by all this, for he's put a book on the shelf. (And now make it two.)

The author thinks of Eudora Welty, her natural curiosity, her travel lust and taste for bourbon, the garden out back of her house on Pinehurst Street in Jackson, Mississippi.

Eudora Welty's eye, her sense of place, and Good Lord, her sentences. Neither God nor Faulkner could write sentences like that.

She wrote on a typewriter—a Royal HH, it's said, among others. She wrote *The Optimist's Daughter* on a Smith-Corona Coronamatic 8000, an electric, but she didn't like the hum of the thing.

She wrote in the upstairs bedroom, by a window that looked out over the nineteen hundred block of Pinehurst. The house is a mock-Tudor and remarkably similar to the house where the author lived with his family, in Kentucky, from the summer before high school.

One small difference: In the front yard of the Welty house is an historical marker touting her as "one of the most acclaimed writers of the twentieth century." In the front yard of the author's former home is, at this writing, a "for sale" sign.

The author has visited the Welty house, has seen her typewriter, but holds to a fanciful theory that Eudora could not have written such lovely sentences on a typewriter—on a mechanical contraption, a machine.

No, the author pictures her waking before the rest of Pinehurst Street, and going out in her garden, with a butterfly net to catch the words she'd need that day for her story. They'd flutter into the net, almost willingly, and then she'd take them inside. She'd study them, catalogue them, and arrange them just so on blank pages.

The author continues to strive to be his wife's favorite writer, even after finally getting around to reading *Bleak House* a few years ago and now fully knowing what he's up against.

The author believes the opening page of *Bleak House*, with its mud and mire, smoke and "nether sky of fog," is the best thing anyone ever wrote.

But still.

Fucking Dickens.

The author believes this book is the best thing he's ever done, the best he'll ever do—until the next one. He believes it's brilliant, ground-breaking, his grand statement. He's thinking of burning it, the piece of shit. He's like most authors, that way: an ego wrapped in an id inside a basket case.

One last note. A curiosity, really: just as the author was writing this novel, the author's son was writing a short story of the same general theme and plot—the world was ending, Nashville, the state capital, was destroyed, and Memphis, wayward city on the bluff, was the last hope and refuge. They never talked about any of this. The author's son didn't know what the author was writing. The author didn't know his son was writing anything at all. And so:

Memphis After the War

And I saw heaven open, and behold, a dark horse
And he who sat on it was called Man, of course
And in righteousness Man judged and waged war
Because Man's only vision of Man was Man nevermore
So he rid the world of Man, as if enough was enough
But in the end Man was thwarted by one mighty bluff

—Memphians 9:01

December 18, 2019. That's when the first of the bombs fell. Twenty years later, we're still not sure who pushed the button first. Everyone assumes it was us; hell, we assume it was us. Sounds like us. Twenty-nineteen, man. It was just one of those years.

Let's be honest, we all knew it was coming eventually. World. War. Three. The big one. I think we all just thought there would be more to it. Don't get me wrong, most of the world was wiped out. Seriously, a lot of shit happened. But it just started. And then it was over—in a flash.

A global wasteland.

Mostly.

We reached DEFCON 2 around Thanksgiving. The football games and parade still happened, don't worry. My fantasy team lost. But that was when the experts started to warn us. Evacuate major cities, stock your basements, consider church. Repent. That's what they told us. We never listened before. Why start now?

Again, we knew it was coming, but we refused to *do* anything about it. That's kind of how we got to this point, right?

It was a time of inaction and faux outrage. Social media brought things to light, but nothing actually fucking happened. And a lot of bad opinions were thrown around. Can you believe people thought hot dogs were sandwiches?

Social media is one of the things we don't miss anymore. And it was a major adjustment after HD-Day. That's what we called it. The day high-definition died.

At this point, you're probably wondering how I got here. How I'm able to tell you this. Well, here's the thing. As I said, the world was wiped out. A wasteland. Mostly. None of us have basements here. Church? Not for me. I was raised on a different deity. An old God. An almighty protectorate of the people. An earthen shield, a mighty bluff.

That's right. This is Memphis. Nuclear war? The bluff will save us, we joked. We mocked. We knew it wouldn't matter what we did. We knew it was over if the bombs ever fell. And fall, they did. But fall, Memphis did not.

The fucking bluff! Just as the prophesy foretold. The scientist who survived is still trying to rationalize it. But sometimes you just have to take it on faith.

I can't emphasize enough how quickly this all happened. I was on my way to work on a Wednesday morning when the emergency broadcasts started. By the time I had parked, there was no Nashville. I just sat there, door ajar. Glued to the radio in the parking lot. A coworker came by and nudged me, "It was the day the Music City died."

Too soon, in my opinion, but I couldn't help myself. I fired off: "All those poor bachelorettes.

"I guess Trisha Yearwood really was on the wrong side of Memphis.

"Bet that chicken is real hot now."

He looked stunned. "Jesus, man. You've ... put some thought into this, I see."

So here we are. Memphis 2039. It's not the Memphis we knew, per se, but it's still *Memphis*. Home of the Rock 'n' Roll Hall of Fame. Sorry, Cleveland. You never deserved it. Memphis is the last bastion of culture in what's left of the United States. But hell, we knew that before the blast. In an ironic turn of events, Memphis has been named the safest city in the country for twenty consecutive years. Sure, we're biased, but no one's left to argue with us.

The lack of global infrastructure, logistics, and other buzz words would have crippled most modern cities, but not Memphis. Even the hazmat suits have blue collars here. People always worked for what they had.

Phil Jackson, the famous basketball coach, once compared Memphis to "Dresden after the war." I didn't really know what he meant, at the time. I just knew I didn't like it. Phil Jackson was an asshole. But now I know what he meant. Well, I've never been to Dresden. But I've seen Memphis after the war.

—Adam Wesley Williams

The author's son doesn't hate Nashville or want it erased from the earth. No one does. "Memphis After the War" is a story—a story about the end of the world, the emotional reflex that is dark humor, and the very real, sometimes very raw, contentious relationship between Tennessee's two largest cities.

It's also a story, like in the book you hold, about the folly of man.

And of course the value of a good bluff.

Snags

Looking down upon the filthy river after dark, it seemed to be alive with monsters ...

—Charles Dickens
American Notes for General Circulation

West Hell is the hottest and toughest part of that warm territory. The most desperate malefactors are the only ones condemned to West Hell, which is some miles west of Regular Hell.

—Zora Neale Hurston
"West Hell"

1

Cheatham's escape from Old Black Prison and his subsequent journey west to Memphis were subjects of much rumor, conjecture, and even some outright reporting. This last was the least reliable, but quite entertaining, exceeded in that regard only by state "intelligence," which had it that Cheatham was traveling west on a makeshift battleship, on the bow of which he had installed a Davy Crockett Nuclear System—a recoilless rifle system capable of firing nuclear warheads—which he was said to have stolen from Fort Campbell Army base, on the Tennessee-Kentucky border.

The Davy Crockett, some seventy years old but said be in fair working condition, had a range of seventy-five miles, according to a recorded statement from the state's new press secretary, broadcast on the pirate station out of Memphis.

The new press secretary was an earthy sort, owing to her raising in Sneedville, in Hancock County. She referred to the nuclear weapon system as "Davy," and said it was the worst threat to polite company since her second husband. She referred to the citizens of the great state as "all y'all," and to Cheatham as the "strapping Black menace." A politician had nothing on a country singer for playing to the crowd, after all. She said he was heading west, set on assassinating the governor, on account of he'd been denied his stay. She said the state had commandeered everything that could float and called it a navy, for to stop the strapping Black menace. She loved saying that last bit. "Wanted dead or deader!" she fairly shouted. She said the state air force was buzzing the skies and dropping bombs. "Picture it with me, all y'all." Then she paused, for the citizens of the great state to imagine the sight, and for the country singer-turned-press secretary to take a swig and light a cig, for she was strictly a one-take gal. She closed the statement, which was partly scripted, partly improvised, and highly East Tennessee-twanged, with a guitar-accompanied performance of "I Didn't Hear Anybody Pray."[22] She was not the most politic or professional of spokespersons in state history but there was no doubting why she'd been dubbed the Sneedville Songbird. She killed that song.

Reports persisted, then, that Cheatham was out to assassinate the governor, and then have his revenge against the woman he claimed had set him up. There was a bounty on his head, ever rising, like the waters—a hundred, a thousand, a hundred thousand. Pretty soon he'd be worth more than Hank's death car, Graceland, or Forrest's pickled brain.

As always in these situations, there were numerous sightings of the escapee. Cheatham was "seen" in Paris, Frog Jump, Skullbone, Goat City, Graball, Hornbeak, and Sweet Lips—the open-seas version, apparently, of keeping to the back roads.

He was reported to be wearing full armor, Chickasaw Indian war dress, an invisibility cloak—everything but an egg-yellow cowboy shirt.

In fact, he'd been captured by an old seafarer named Trimble.

"Not much of a day for it," said Trimble.

---

[22]A sad country classic, involving whiskey, broken glass, and a fatal crash on the highway, originally recorded by the Dixon Brothers, Dorsey and Howard, in 1938. Dorsey wrote the song. It was no great shakes on the charts. But then country star Roy Acuff recorded it 1942 as "Wreck on the Highway," claiming it as his own and getting a national hit out of the thing. Litigation was threatened and Dorsey Dixon received some recompense, but who's ever heard of him? When Bruce Springsteen, hillbilly from New Jersey, came along some decades later and wrote the same song, only different, he used Acuff's title. It's a good song. Hell, they're all good. Sad, though. The best songs usually are. Roy Acuff said that. Or maybe it was what's-his-name, Dorsey Dixon.

They both looked up: a creaky sky, the color of old barn. A Mail Pouch sign would have looked better against it than clouds, of which there was just one—harbinger or stray, hard to know, really.

"Not much of a day for what?" Cheatham said.

"For whatever it was you'd planned."

"I look like I got a fucking plan?"

"I guess that bomb at Old Black Prison went off all on its own."

"In fact, that's exactly what it did."

"Everybody on death row died but you. You think they'll pin those murders on you, too, or maybe they count them to the good?"

"I didn't have shit to do with it." He said that thing again about the bomb going off all on its own, ridiculous as it sounded.

"What they call, um, spontaneous combustion, was it?"

"I ain't saying that."

"It would be a hell of a note, for to have it happen on death row."

"There was a bomb and it went off and I didn't have shit to do with it."

"You said that. Say it one more time and click your cowboy heels and it might start to seem true, but not to me."

"I don't expect you to believe it. I hardly do my own self." He was beginning to feel like a character in a story, like he was dreamed up and written down and dropped in the story, made to suffer all manner of threats and indignities, just so some writer could string along his dear reader and sell a million copies and keep himself in a high-shelf booze. One man's indignity was another's julep, he thought.

"You do have the look of a man things just happen to."

"Exactly," Cheatham said. He thought he might be getting somewhere, finally, with this Captain Ahab-looking fucker.

"It would explain the shirt."

Cheatham had placed his knife and pistol on the deck of the flatboat, as ordered, and kicked them toward his captor, who had come from out behind the door. He was a small man, or anyway seemed small in the presence of Cheatham. Most everything did, up to an American black bear. Trimble was slightly built and stood with a lean—no, more a tilt, as if he had spent too long standing in his seafaring life and could have used a new hip. That would explain the wince on his bearded face, which otherwise was weathered and lined, from a life spent outdoors. There was something more going on, around the eyes. It might have been wisdom, but Cheatham wondered maybe madness, like in that old movie.

"What next, then, Ahab?" Cheatham said.

"What did you call me?"

"Ahab."

"You know the book?" It was a very favorite of Trimble's, along with *Life on the Mississippi*, *Heart of Darkness*, *The Mississippi and the Making of a Nation*, *The Wild Palms*, *Suttree*, *The Log from the Sea of Cortez*, *Ship of Fools*, *Billy Budd*, *A Miracle of Catfish*, and *River Rise and River Shine: The Lost Love Poems of Mike Fink*. He wouldn't read a book unless it was at least seventy percent water.

"Saw the movie."

"Well. Root for the whale, did you?"

"The Black boy. What'd they call him? Pip."

"Oh. Poor Alabama boy," Trimble said, "beating his tambourine."

"Crazy Ahab, when he left the big ship—"

"The *Pequod*."

"—to go chasing Moby Dick, well, he made Pip captain."

Cheatham smiled. He said, "I turned the channel, just then. Took to watching the Braves game. I don't even like baseball but I liked the idea of the movie ending just like that, with crazy Ahab going off to his doom, and Pip commanding that big ship all by his own self."

Trimble didn't know what to say. He didn't know whether it was the craziest thing he'd ever heard or somehow the most heartbreakingly hopeful.

Trimble—first name unknown—was a riverman of longstanding, a former boy stowaway from a small Kentucky river town who grew up to captain tugs and ferries and otherwise work whatever else would float. Pushboats, freighters, broadhorns. He'd fished, hauled, worked rescue, cooked even. He'd done everything with boats but race; never saw the point: You're out on the water, what the hell's your hurry? To get back to land? No, thank ye.

He was born too late but did not dwell upon it. Nothing was promised and life was choppy seas, at best. He might have been an explorer, a Bering or Hudson, or perhaps some more humble seafarer, a wooden-legged pirate or drunken privateer, a one-eyed swabbie; it might have been him who scrubbed the decks of the *Pequod* as best he could with his one good eye, forever missing a spot. No, he made do with the times into which he was hatched and abandoned. Poor orphaned Trimble. Found in the bulrushes, mayhaps—that was a nice thought, but it probably wasn't anything so grandly biblical, he thought. Still, it was only on the water that he felt himself. He never could quite get his footing, on land.

So, Trimble: He knew every snag and bluff reef on the Ohio from Cincinnati to Cairo, and on the Mississippi south to New Orleans. Twain's *Life on the Mississippi* was his bible, and he smoked a pipe in the manner of the great author. Though not just now. He never lit up before breakfast, and it was breakfast time. He held a cast-iron skillet in his left hand, with that shotgun still in his right.

He took a step toward Cheatham, who managed a smile.

"You gonna blow my damn fool head off, or fry me up my last meal?"

"What would you have it be?"

"Shotgun or skillet, you mean?"

"Last meal."

"Oh, that. Catfish, suppose. I don't care if it is breakfast. I prefer it deep fried, but I'll take it out a skillet."

"There are those who would have *you* deep fried."

"I didn't do it."

"Do what?"

"What they said I did."

"And yet it was you they hunted down and tried and convicted and sentenced and then scheduled for execution—"

"Be all that it as it fucking may. I didn't do it. I just look guilty. Sound guilty. You be six-foot-seven, black as that skillet, name of Cheatham, and see what they do to you."

"Innocent as a newborn babe, huh?"

"I didn't say that. Just said I didn't do the thing they said I did. That's all they got me on, that thing I didn't do."

"That's a conundrum. Hell for you, but makes a good story."

"What I was thinking, yeah. You ever feel like you're just some character in a book?"

"Like I'm not real, just made up?"

"Like that, yeah."

"You believe in God?"

"The hell's that got to do with the price of beer?"

"If you believe in God and God made you and God's all knowing, then—"

"What about free will?" Cheatham said. His old death row chum Robert "Thee" Kingdom used to talk about free will, said every man had it and used it to his doom or salvation. He said man had free will to choose Jesus as his eternal lord and savior or drink a case of Blatz. And then Shagbark Turner, he laughed, said hell, man, drinking a case of Blatz ain't free will, it's just bad judgment. And Robert "Thee" Kingdom, he said that's exactly what I'm saying. Thus did the denizens of death row pass the time, talking of deeply spiritual matters, and refreshments.

"Free will, cheap beer, sure it's all the same," Trimble said. "God lets man choose but God knows, on account of He's all-knowing, what that man's going to choose, and woman, too. You see what I'm saying? Omniscience trumps free will."

"So me and you, all of us we're just some story God's telling."

"I guess, yeah. God at His typewriter, tapping away this tale."

"So it's not my fault. Not really."

"I thought you said you didn't do it."

"I didn't."

"But you did other things?"

"Didn't we all?"

Trimble looked about. "It's just me and the chickens here. We're not on trial."

"I only see the one."

"The other keeps out of sight. It was him who gave you up—alerted me to your presence aboard my humble flatboat."

"Thought I heard something. Thought maybe that chicken there was, uh, throwing its voice."

"You come across that happening before, in your travels, Cheatham?"

"I haven't seen much of anything."

"Well, end of the world and all."

"Is it, Ahab?"

Trimble sat in the wooden rocker and looked musingly out upon the waters. He dropped the cast-iron skillet to his side but the shotgun kept watch on the prisoner; its dull, dark, midnight eyes watched Cheatham with cold and cocksure nonchalance. Cheatham still had those rifles from the fish and game men, but not where he could get to them—a gun in his face was sure as shit worth more than two in the boat. But anyway, it was nice to be outside, if you had to be captive. It was like some death row field trip or something.

"It's not the end but you can see the end from here," Trimble said.

"I don't see anything."

"Why, just yesterday the steamer *Clementine* passed by, bound for Memphis. It was near night. There was music playing, people dancing, having a time. I don't know whether that's evidence for or against it being the end of the world. I didn't see Jesus about, but I think I caught a glimpse of the governor, standing on the bow, surrounded by a bevy of women. Or anyway, I saw a bevy of women and there was a man in there somewhere. I extrapolated it to be Governor Flattery in there amongst all that female flesh."

He stretched out that word, *extrapolated*, as if removing it from storage for public display. It had been a very long time since he'd had a conversation with another human being, and he was mindful that his vocabulary might have atrophied.

Trimble did not tell Cheatham what happened next—that the same shotgun now pointed at him was the day before aimed at the governor of Tennessee, or anyway at a man who seemed to be the governor, surrounded by that bevy of women. Trimble's finger on the trigger, his mind running the traps and algorithms, distance and angle from his boat to the bow of the *Clementine*, the wind speed and relative humidity, his own age and rustiness. Trimble thinking, *If I were only a younger man, and revenge were a dish best served reheated, and this shotgun, this old scattergun, were an official Tennessee state sniper rifle.*[23] *And I were a killer, like that escaped death-row convict named Cheatham.*

---

[23] *Tennessee's new official state rifle is so powerful it can 'destroy commercial aircraft'*—headline on washingtonpost.com, Feb. 26, 2016. The story refers to the Barrett .50 caliber rifle, manufactured in the small, Tennessee community of Christiana. Christiana: a name meaning "follower of Christ," that noted gunslinger.

Trimble didn't say any of that, nor the reason for his enmity with the governor, which was really with the governor's father, who had once been Trimble's closest friend, or so Trimble thought, but sold out all they had for a backseat roll with Trimble's best girl, and then, his tongue as silver and lithe as his dick was long and skinny, finagled his way into the bed of Trimble's best girl's mother, and never mind her own complicity, before moving on to other girls and women, and one time a state fair-winning sow. Or anyway Trimble liked to include the sow among his former friend's conquests, because it made him smile to think it, and he wasn't so bitter when he smiled. Trimble, anyhow and after all that, had had quite enough of dry land and the humans who dwelled there. He took to the water—the dream of his youth, foolishly abandoned—and there made his life, away from man and most of his traps and trappings. H. Walt Flattery II went on to accumulate great wealth and vast holdings, and slept with seventeen-hundred women, so he said, but only once did his seed find, as they say, purchase. His boy, H. Walt III, a chip off the old block, or rather switch off the old shrub, was his father's son in every way, only with better looks and even more ambition. Life was not fair and God was dog spelled backward, Trimble thought, but out on the water, a man's mind could settle and drift and find new vantage points, ways of seeing the world. He could spread his bitterness thin across the waves, watch it dissipate and disappear.

Trimble sighed. He let his mind settle, or mostly so.

"The governor let you down, I hear," he said. "Denied your stay. Can see why you're gunning for him."

"I got no beef with Flattery," Cheatham said. "Or anyway, I ain't out to kill him. I ain't out to kill anybody."

"That's not what I heard on the crank radio."

"Damn fool radio. Lies, all lies. Except maybe for that one song I heard, passing through Nashville. Or maybe it was Jackson. Every town looks alike, when it's taking a bath."

"What song was that?"

"I don't know. Something about how everybody's a rank stranger to me. I felt it, that one. Spoke to me, somehow."

"Oh, beautiful song. Was it the Stanley Brothers singing it?"

"Nah. They have a sister? Was a girl singer."

"Oh, Emmylou Harris did a lovely version.[24] Maybe it was her." Trimble dropped back his head and smiled at the sky; when some shipmate used to ask what it would take Trimble to forsake the seafaring life and came back to dry land, he used to say, "Emmylou." They thought he was kidding.

Trimble sighed. He looked at the shotgun in his right hand and the skillet in his left. He seemed to be weighing which it would be.

"C'mon," he said. "Let's us eat. Never shoot a man on an empty stomach, I always say."

"His or yours?"

They both laughed.

Breakfast was hash from a can. End of the world and all.

2

The faded star from Memphis leaned forward in the corner chair. It was a recliner but he wasn't dead, only faded. He was telling stories of the sidemen he'd fired and the ones he'd shot at and the one he shot. "I never killed a man," he said, and then paused, like always when he came to the chorus of a story.

Time was when that pause could stop everything but girls from being teenagers. But that was long ago, and so time went on ticking, the old steamboat swaying, and the faded star said, "That boy was no man."

---

[24]Trimble may have dreamed this. For Trimble dreamed often, and often of Emmylou.

This was on the Tennessee deck of the steamer *Clementine*, the pleasure deck, in the smaller, more intimate of the two lounges. The faded star from Memphis, a piano player, had taken up residence there, or anyway had his last remaining sideman move his recliner into a far corner of the lounge, where he could see everything coming and going. He mostly ignored those comings and goings, though, as long as they left alone the piano in the opposite corner, near the bar. He hissed when anyone went near it. No one was permitted to lean on it—*ain't a piece of furniture, you unconsecrated motherfucker*—and God or Satan himself forbid if someone made to touch the keys and play a note.

As the faded star talked, his left arm pitched forward, fingers cocked and poised, precise as a spider's legs. His fingers were skinny like a spider's legs, but a spider's had nothing on them for length, and it was the flip of a rare coin, even now, all these years passed, as to which moved with the finer grace.

The room was empty now but for the last sideman. He sat on a barstool across the way. He'd never been fired or shot or even shot at; *poor fucker never had a bit of luck*, was what the banished sidemen all said about him. He sat reading a month-old Nashville newspaper. There was no more to be done. But they would soon be back home, in Memphis. That was the word all about the *Clementine*, though Captain Bull Chandler had not confirmed it. The captain was rarely seen, appearing seldom at dinner, and then seeming not so much his old, imposing if amiable, self but something more toward inscrutable. His beard looked more unkempt than ever; if he'd have smiled, you would not have seen it for the forest. It covered the lower half of his face down to the bottom of his sternum, if indeed he had one beneath that beard.

The faded star had gone to Nashville for a tribute show, arriving just as the Cumberland River's rising was beginning to stir serious civic concerns. Streets were closed, warnings issued. It had rained for eleven straight days; it was beginning to be hard to tell the meteorologists from the preachers.

The tribute show was canceled—a relief, in a way, to the sideman, who had neglected to tell the faded star that he was not, alas, the subject of the tribute, but rather one of the fawning guest performers. He was expected to perform some other singer's song.

The rains continued. The Cumberland River fancied itself a great lake, then an ocean. The faded star and his last sidemen were granted passage on the *Clementine*. The faded star demanded the finest stateroom, with gold fixtures and stocked bar and a private veranda. He was shown to steerage.

He handled it like the faded star he was, like some Hollywood queen of yore. He mocked and preened, pissed and moaned, shouted and pouted. Divas could have gone to him to get their PhDs.

"Ah, you had you some times, boss man," the last sideman said now. "You'll have some more yet."

The faded star had a cigarette in his right hand. He held it low on the fingers, in the crook of the first and second, daintily almost, like a thirteen-year-old girl sneaking her first in the alley out behind her house and not knowing how, exactly, to hold the thing, much less smoke it; or, say, like a piano player whose fingertips were sacred things to him, not to be sullied by some purpose other than that which God intended. ("The devil may hold lien on my soul," he once said, famously, during a nationally televised performance with the president's wife in the front row. "But Ol' God Hisself give me these fingertips." Documentary footage suggested the first lady was smiling, behind the mask she'd been issued for just such occasions; she'd been a girl once, a teenager, even.)

He raised the cigarette to his lips. He reached for his wine glass. There was whiskey in it. He sipped the last and set it back on the table beside; the cigarette stayed behind on his lips, a fuse on his face. Now his right hand was empty and he raised it before him, as a priest would the chalice, but that his hand itself was the sacred thing. He examined it, fingers outstretched, as if preening for him. But they needn't have. He was in awe of them, as a rich man would a masterwork of art which he happened to own. He smiled like a man who had just been informed of a loophole in the devil's lien.

"You goddamned right I will," he said.

Only then did he lean back in the recliner.

The last sideman turned the pages of the month-old Nashville newspaper. He came upon a story and read it. He laughed—and immediately wished he hadn't.

"The hell you laughing at?"

"Nothing, boss man."

"There something about me in there?"

How could he have known, the last sideman thought, but then: of course; the faded star thought everything was about him.

"It's an old paper," the last sideman said. "From last month."

"What's it say about me?"

The faded star thought it might have been about the tribute show that never was. A tribute, he supposed, to his country years, after his star faded that first time. Faded, hell—his crown was lopped off and his head damn near with it. It had been an international scandal, though the faded star still, all these years later, wondered what in fuck was the fuss.

"Ah, boss man. You know the papers."

"What's it say, boy?" You could have sailed the steamer *Clementine* and a sister ship through the pauses between the words.

He called all his sidemen boy. That's all they'd ever been to the faded star, though the last sideman was three months older, half an inch taller, and the better man by every measure but the Billboard charts. He'd been married but once, for thirty-two years. They were something like high school sweethearts—him, at first sight; her, fast after being hard-cured of a crush on the then-still-budding star. She was gone now, dead, taken; it was six years past. She'd lingered in her dying, though her wit was dry and cutting to the end. He'd come off the road to be with her, had said to the faded star, "Go ahead and fire me if you want. You can even shoot me," and the faded star only half joshing said, "Well, maybe I will." She told him he'd be a widower soon, but she'd been a widow all those years, with him on the road, playing another man's songs for meager sums and scant acclaim. And you, she said, the better musician, even. It was true, as far as it went: He could play every instrument on the stage, didn't matter whether it had strings or keys or skin. He could coax sound from a stone, but lacked the nerve, the audacity, the gall, to stand out front of the sound and shout the devil's high hosanna.

But she smiled when she said it. Her eyes did, anyway. She understood it was who he was and what he did and how he made his way. She always thought he could have been—what? A star? No, God forbid that. But his own man, at least, a singer of his own songs. She nudged but didn't push. He wavered but didn't budge. He was a sideman and she was a sideman's wife. They'd lived the sideman's life.

"Goddamn you, boy. I said what's it say?"

"Nothing, boss," the sideman said. It was about as much as he ever wanted to say on any subject, any more. But he knew his place, his role. He could take a cue. He said, "Oh, just that they're having one of those auctions of stars' things. Country stars, you know. It's for charity. They got big hats and gold records, all of them signed, of course. And there's some stage outfits, spangly and all. There's this old outlaw singer's boots they say's hollowed out in the heel to hold—I don't know. The outlaw's stash, I reckon. You remember him, the outlaw singer. He was good people. Remember that weekend down in Texas, with you and him and his manager we called Rooster S. Christ. That was a weekend, near as I remember. Anyway—they got the outlaw's boots. I guess he didn't die with 'em on, or else he ain't died yet. And guitars, you know. They got lots of guitars. Some ain't even been smashed."

The faded star said, "Fuck a guitar player. Fucking chicken scratch motherfuckers."

The last sideman knew better than to get the faded star started on guitar players. He said, "And there's things from before the famous country stars went and got themselves famous. They got a book report, of all things, by that girl singer who's gone pop. This was from when she was a schoolgirl. The book report, you know, it was about"—he aimed to talk until the faded star forgot what the point of it all was—"that Gatsby fellow."

He didn't say "great." Just because there was a fuse on the faded star's face didn't mean some fool sideman had to light it.

"And anyway," the sideman said, "it wasn't much of a book report. She said there was some good parties in it, and she liked a good party, herself. It's only a page long but they say somebody might go eight hundred dollars for it. They say it's worth more now on account of she's a pop star."

"What's she sing?"

"Oh, you wouldn't like it. Pop stuff. Frippery. Mostly she sings about her ex-boyfriends. That's her thing, seems like. She goes through 'em. Seems kinda like seventh grade, to me. Sounds like seventh grade, too. Not the seventh grade I was in, mind you."

The last sideman figured if he kept talking the faded star would not ask the question he was sure otherwise to ask.

"Artistry's dead, ain't it, boss man? Talent's not got a thing to do with anything. You just got to look the part. Singer ain't got to have a great voice. They got laboratories to fix that shit up. But you can't teach long legs, can you, boss?"

The last sideman looked over at the faded star. He was gazing at his hand again, or still; if he had been a museum patron, and his hand had merely been Leonardo's tousle-haired lady, he would have gone for a piss or a sandwich ten minutes back. But the hand, this hand, his hand, held ceaseless wonder for him. The faded star was deep in meditation upon it, thinking with apostolic zeal, *You could have written gospels. You could have healed the lame. But you had a higher calling.*

The sideman was about to say something about something else entirely. The threat seemed to have passed. The faded star was studying the lines of his hand. But then he said, "They got something of mine, do they, boy?"

The sideman paused. But there wasn't much future in pausing. He said, "Old pair of blue jeans, is all, boss. Nothing you'd ever wear on a stage. Used to be, stars would dress like stars. Now they—"

"How much?"

"—when they wear anything at all."

"I said how much, goddamned you?"

"What's that, boss man?" He decided to explore the back of the bar. He perused the bottles all in rows. He spied the glasses, held a snifter aloft, as if checking for spot or imperfections.

"I said how much. How much they expect those blue jeans of mine to fetch? Tell me, goddamn it."

There was no lying to him; Ol' God Hisself would not have dared.

"Four hundred, they think," the sideman said. "Well, two to four. That's just somebody saying something they don't know."

"So half of what that pop whore's book report's gonna bring." The faded star seemed to be thinking how he might properly react to this affront; there was precedent for shooting at a sidemen but he was down now to the last. A wall, then, maybe. Or a TV. Random passengers. The faded star was about to tell the last sideman to fetch a gun and fast.

The sideman, sensing it, said, "Well." He struck the word as if it were a note, as if they were on stage again and a new show had begun. It was the one power the sideman had; he started the first song, the opening note was his, always.

The faded star, thusly played by his own sideman, laughed now. It wasn't like they were auctioning off his fingertips, he thought; he imagined only a handful of desert sheiks could even afford the opening bid on those pale lovelies.

"Four hundred for my jeans," he said, bemused now and with a snap of the fingers for whiskey, more whiskey, in his wine glass. "Why shitfire, boy, there got to be that much worth of pills left in the pockets."

3

The trial began at ten bells in the morning. Well, called it ten. Time had ceased to have any real meaning. For bells they had the bailiff bang a broomstick upside a tin shack that served as the makeshift holding cell for the prisoners.

The prisoners were dragged out, in their iron shackles and mud-caked duds, the sound they made a sort of minor-key death march, *Bedraggled in D*. "Pick those feet up, step it the fuck up," said the bailiff, more of a country waltz man, himself.

They were paraded through the crowd, which had, after all, paid for a show—fifty cents a person or a buck a boatload. That was general admission. It was a fiver for reserved seating. The crowd hissed and jeered, as if on cue. They might have been a studio audience and this a game show, though the prisoners would not have said so.

They were three. Two were accused of looting a church; one was a white man of late middle age and the other a young Black man. The former was apprehended while drinking white dog whiskey from a golden chalice. He was quite drunk and singing, while hunched atop a tree stump, in an otherwise flooded area. He was charged with larceny, religious antipathy, public drunk, disturbing the peace, loitering, and illegal performance of a bawdy song or skit after curfew. The latter was caught not far away, pulled down from his perch in an old sycamore tree, where he was quietly, rather piously, reading a pilfered Bible. He was charged with grand theft, impersonating a Christian gentleman, and general shiftlessness.

The third prisoner was the real prize, a man of uncertain racial heritage accused of being a river walker, a capital offense these days. His name was Suss Jones. He was some Indian and some white along with being lots black and blue. He was of roughly the same height as his fellow prisoners but stood a head higher, as they slumped in direct relation to their legal straits while he seemed as if he might have arrived for his own coronation. He had imperious eyes, a haughty grin. You could have told the time of day by the cock of his head.

The prisoners circled the grounds and were brought before the judge. They sat cross-legged before him. The judge was white-haired, in a red velvet bathrobe, with black satin pajamas under. He wore red slippers that might have been sold in an ensemble with the robe. He was sitting in a barber chair. Behind the prisoners, to the right and left, were picnic tables, on top of which were brief cases and stacks of documents, and in front of which stood men in dark dress pants and sweat-stained white dress shirts with sleeves rolled up. One was making a speech that clearly pained the other to hear.

The jury box, that is to say a small section of bleacher like you might find at a rural high school football field, was off to the side, and seated upon it: four men, three women, and, swaddled in a blanket and settled onto the lap of one of the women, a bluetick coonhound puppy.

Scattered about the spit of land were several dozen spectators, some on quilts and others in lawn chairs. Some occasionally clapped and others laughed mildly at something a near neighbor said but most just stared off at the cast-iron sky as an old man with a push cart ambled through the crowd selling canned fruit for a dime apiece, singing softly the old tune, "Have You Ever Seen Peaches Growing on a Sweet Potato Vine?" There was a fair line of patrons at an outhouse door, and off in the distance a juggling act was practicing with a two hatchets and a rolling pin.

The Floods dragged their party barge up onto the cusp of land and approached the proceedings. A smiling man with a four-chamber money changer stepped into their path and said, "General seating or reserved, folks?"

"So what in hell's this, community theater?" Cora Flood said.

"I'm sure I don't understand the question, ma'am."

The man had his thumbs in the front loops of his pants and his fingers splayed, all the better to display his prodigious belly.

"You wouldn't be charging admission to actual legal court proceedings, would you?"

"Unprecedented times, ma'am."

John looked to see if the money-changer carried a gun. He didn't seemed to be armed, but the buttons of his shirt seemed about to pop at any moment and might take out an eye. He fished in his pockets for change.

"How much did you say?" said John.

"What is this jurisdiction?" said Cora.

"Can't say exactly." The money-changer turned all about, still smiling. He had a drafty smile and it created a bit of whistling effect as he turned. He ended up more or less back in front of them. "Somewhere between Kitchen Sink and Lowball, pretty sure. County of Riffle—almost certainly."

"What's the money to go for? Buy the judge some proper robes?"

"Good one, ma'am. I like you." He turned just slightly and spat, then turned back, looked at John and said, "It's fifty cents a person or a buck a boatload. That's general admission."

"Is he a real judge?" Cora said.

"Ol' Bill Harsh? Well, fancies himself real wise."

"Has a robe, anyway, if not the right kind."

John paid the man a crumpled buck, and they made their way near the front of the crowd just as a witness was being called by the prosecution. He was sworn in on an old paperback copy of *Huckleberry Finn*.

"I may get religion yet," Cora said.

A man to her left laughed at this. He said, "Can I quote you on that?" He raised a pen and notebook with a short of shrug, said, "Tatum. I'm the press corps. Stringing for *The New York Times*, a blog called The Soundcheck & the Fury, and several seed journals of note."

The witness, a lanky, jug-eared youth who might have been pulled from a church choir, mid-hymn, was being asked did he solemnly swear. When he paused with a look something like panic in his eyes, the bailiff said, "It's OK. Not that kind of swear, boy. Not like damn or fuck-all," and the choir-looking lad grinned from there to Gloryland and said, "I do," to that and the rest of the oath. He took his place on the witness stand, which is to say a barstool—another first for the lanky lad of God.

Prosecuting attorney: Now son, did you hear—

Defense attorney: Objection!

Judge Harsh: On what grounds?

Defense attorney: Hear or overhear?

Prosecuting attorney: I fail to see the distinction.

Defense attorney: Overhear suggests a listening point from further remove and so could be considered less reliable. Plus which it's rude.

Judge Harsh: Overruled! The boy has a fine set of ears and the accused a large mouth. I suspect and suppose and so do rule that they must have connected just fine, aurally speaking. As for rudeness, the boy wouldn't know the first thing about it. Look at him. Prosecution, continue.

Prosecuting attorney: Did you, son, hear with your own ears the accused say he planned to walk on water?

Witness: As God is my witness.

Defense attorney: Objection!

Judge Harsh: On what grounds?

Defense attorney: Separation of church and state, your honor. That boy's the witness, not God.

Witness (coming up off the barstool a couple of inches): Objection! God sees everything.

Judge: Objection overruled.

Defense attorney: Which one, your honor?

Judge (wags a finger at the defense attorney): Your'n.

Defense attorney (muttering but loud enough to be heard): Christ.

Witness: Him, too!

It went on like this for some time. By the time an expert witness was called for the defense, two members of the jury were sleeping, though the coonhound puppy was starting to squirm and so was handed from one woman to another.

Defense attorney: Is it your expert testimony, then, that water is denser at high tide?

Expert witness: It is.

Defense attorney: So such conditions might aid in an attempt, however misguided, to walk upon water.

Expert witness: To some very slight degree, but yes.

Defense attorney: And do you further attest that floods such as this current one contain much flotsam, and considerable jetsam, too, in amounts that might make it possible to, while attempting to walk across the water, however misguided the attempt might be—well, let's say, for there to be a fair country chance that a step in any direction might find some of the aforementioned flotsam, and jetsam, as to gain, let us say, solid footing across which a man might *appear* to be walking on water?

Expert witness: Much flotsam in a flood, yes, and like you say, considerable jetsam as well. In equal amounts, I should say.

Defense attorney: So it might be possible then, what with all the flotsam and jetsam, and by dint of the aforementioned density of water at high tide to which you so expertly testified, to *appear* to walk across water.

Prosecuting attorney (who had dozed off but now awoke with a start): Objection, your honor!

Judge Harsh: On what grounds?

Prosecuting attorney: Obfuscation, sacrilege, and general hooey.

Judge: Sustained!

The crowd cheered, all but Cora and John Flood, Tatum from the press, and a man in a sling trying to light a cigarette who seemed to have set his shirt afire.

4

They sat not talking for the longest time. Trimble took up the Good Book, his daily devotional, he said. He read a bit from it. Mark 29:15-23. Twain was talking about Memphis, "beautiful city, nobly situated on a commanding bluff overlooking the river."

"Memphis," Cheatham said. "That place'll be the death of me, if your shotgun doesn't get me first."

"Yep, nothing but trouble for you there. The governor, he'll be there. And probably that woman you say pinned that murder on you."

"Probably. Like as not."

"What's she like?"

"She ain't like anything. Just every kind of trouble you can dream up and put a dress on, that's her. If she never opened her mouth but to sing, the world might be a better place."

"She can sing, huh?"

"She sure as hell can. Old soul, R&B, the blues. Could make 'Champagne & Reefer' sound like a gospel hymn, she wanted to."

"I'll take the sea over everything in this life and the next, but there ain't nothing like a woman's voice when she sings."

"Well," is all Cheatham said to that.

Ten minutes passed, twenty. Trimble sat the good book upon a table beside him and looked out at the horizon. He seemed about to hum a tune but did not. He said for Cheatham to try the crank radio.

Static and skillet hiss and then a song out of Africa. Friction sticks and foot stomps, sounded like a happy song but who could say? Trimble caught a word here and there. Sail the world and you pick up a thing or two. He said *moto* meant hot. *Sukuma* was to shake or rub.

"Sounds like the singer, he's fixing to get him some," Cheatham said.

Trimble smiled and said he reckoned it was thus. "Been a long time, for me, personally."

"You ought to try living on death row."

"No thanks."

They sat silently now, both dreaming of the female form, as the good ship *Emmylou* began to drift just slightly south.

The crank radio played songs from everywhere and all over, Congolese dance tunes and Galway jigs, Appalachian reels and Memphis soul. The DJ said they were all related, of one brood, and could be traced back to before God. He said music made the world small, so small it fit in a little old radio. He said to turn it up. Crank it.

He played "Moyo Wanitanga-Tanga" by the Coast Social Orchestra, out of Kenya, and he played "Fa-Fa-Fa-Fa-Fa (Sad Song)" by Otis Redding, out of Memphis by way of Macon, Georgia. "Same song!" he said. "Tribulation, with guitar and horns! Man's troubled and trying to sing his way out. Man sings a sad song, maybe a woman hears it, you know. Maybe she takes some pity, bats her lashes, shows some leg. Maybe she ups and dances. Why, all of a sudden, that man ain't so sad anymore, just his song is sad, and then even that ain't.

Peace on earth, people. Or anyway, they get together, the two of them, and they get on, have a good run, maybe it's the real thing, a love supreme, like the man said. Maybe it's just a long weekend. But let me ask you, people: Any y'all out there got a thing against a long weekend?"

Trimble said, "You think that son of a bitch DJ will shut up anytime soon and play another song?"

Cheatham just laughed. He stretched out for a nap. He saw that Trimble had set the shotgun on the deck, but he made no move for it.

Trimble began to talk, tell stories. It was afternoon, late, a bottle had appeared.

He told of growing up in a Kentucky river town, called Lowside. It was a small but lively port on the Ohio, he said. He said its banks flooded if a passing riverman so much as pissed over the side of his boat, but the citizens of Lowside were proud and stubborn and apt to rebuild rather than move on to somewhere higher and drier. Lowside endured, he said, until it didn't.

"You wouldn't find it on a map now," Trimble said.

"I wouldn't even know to look, if you hadn't just now mentioned it," Cheatham said. "Lowside, huh? Well, everybody's got to be born somewhere."

"Oh, I wasn't born there," Trimble said. "I was left and found there. Discovered there."

"Like with Moses in the Bible? Found you in the bulrushes, did they?"

Trimble said he really was an orphan, discovered in the doorway of a tavern run by a man named Ruck. This tavern keeper—Ruck was his surname; his Christian name was Christian—swaddled the lad as best he could, in bar rags and some burlap, and placed him atop an empty whiskey barrel in a corner near the front door. There he stayed, all safe and still, until such time as the tavern started to fill with lushes and soaks with their tongues all a-wagging and dripping with language most foul—and those were the women. There was a brawl, and bottles were flung and swung, a pistol was discharged, and one woman of stout bearing held a would-be paramour in a headlock until he said three Hail Marys. (Her name was Mary). Patrons were thrown through windows and one small fellow swung from the light fixture, went flying, and landed in the lap of his own wife, worst luck! Stray dogs and feral cats wandered in through the back door, which was off its hinges. The front door, once opened, never closed; along about nine o'clock, a man rode through on a sorrel mule, shaking a Bible at the whole lot of sots though he seemed as pickled as any man and all but a handful of women in the place. By this time the baby was agitated and could not be calmed.

"Why, that tale's as tall as me," Cheatham said. "How'd they come to name you Trimble?"

"On account of I couldn't lay still and they couldn't spell."

Cheatham laughed. They both did.

At this point in the story, Trimble skipped ahead several years. He was a grown boy now. He didn't say if he'd been raised or he was just feral, like those tavern cats. He said he gravitated to the water. He felt that ancient tug. He would sit on the banks and watch the river for hours. At night, he'd sleep—he didn't say where—and dream, and imagine himself on the banks of the Ohio, in the days of long-past, watching flatboats heaving with hogsheads of tobacco and barrels of whiskey and other such staples of life and the times. The town was a major tobacco market, and home to multiple bourbon distilleries. He imagined himself stowing away and floating down river. He imagined himself among the leaves of burley and amid the barrels of bourbon. He could smell both, and his own stench, for in his imagining it was the steamiest summer ever in what was then called, is still called, the Ohio Valley. It was all terrifically exciting to the boy. He imagined listening as ports were called out—Ashland! Portsmouth!—and then, as a scuffle broke out on deck, barrels were jostled, tipped and toppled. Bourbon flowed and the stowaway boy washed up—such luck!—and was hauled before the captain, a gray-bearded old man with a starboard cock to his ancient, weathered head. He took one look and put the boy to work, stout youth that he was.

He said no more for a stretch, and then he picked up the story again. He was a grown man now. He had lost his way. He had turned his back to the water, convinced he had been born too late. It was a lazy river now, just the occasional barge or fishing skiff, and the steamboats, what there were of them, were floating arks of nostalgia. He wandered the state, moving west, like some latter-day Daniel Boone. But he was too late for that, too. The frontier was a strip of fast food restaurants, payday lenders. The world smelled of fry grease and defeat. He took odd jobs—painted houses, bussed tables, drove a cab. Morehead, Falmouth (which the local delinquents called Foulmouth), Bowling Green, Lexington, Paducah, Powderly, Flintlock, Dubs—the towns and cities of the Bluegrass State through which he passed, taking now a southerly bent. Rarely did he tarry.

In time, he said, he ran out of Kentucky and it was Tennessee now.

"I became a something of a budding, little gentleman in Tennessee," Trimble said. "Worst mistake I ever did make."

He told how he fell into becoming a right-hand man for a music promoter named Early Mains. He was an old carny barker with a master's degree in economics from Providence and another in philosophy from Vanderbilt. There was a whiff of the South to him, and of older country. But wherever he was bred, or whatever he was bred to be, he could sell anything. It was his gift. Bear wrestling or a crucifixion, it didn't make a damn to Early Mains.

He wore dark, rumpled suits with a string tie and cowboy hat, looked like he'd come hustling straight from a lost weekend to Uncle Dave Macon's funeral. He was a drinker, all right, but had no time for the dead. You couldn't sell tickets to a funeral; at least, Early Mains had yet to find the way.

Trimble ran errands for this Early Mains, saw to the needs of Early's artists, meaning carried bail money, and on this one occasion, being a respectable-looking young man with an air of innocence and well-meaning about him, was an emissary of sorts. This is where his real trouble began, only it didn't start out as trouble.

Early Mains was promoting a music festival, to be held over three days on a farm outside of Nashville. To his fellow drinkers at the Teardrop Room he described it as a sort of deep-fried Woodstock; to his would-be financial backers he stressed the religious element: There was to be a gospel tent, and one of the headlining acts was claiming to have found God, though he was still singing his heathenistic hits, now framed as cautionary tales. Early had raised only half of what he needed, and had yet to secure a farm, when he heard tell of a rich man named Flattery, in Belle Meade, who might be persuaded to become partners on the thing. Early Mains sent Trimble, who was twenty-one and sober and starting to look near handsome, to the offices of one H. Walt Flattery II, with a written invitation to meet with Early Mains.

No more did he say. That's where the story stopped. He didn't say about how Walt Flattery befriended him, or seemed to. How Flattery invited Trimble and his best girl to his country house, on Reelfoot Lake, for the weekend. How Flattery took a shine, and later a switch, to Trimble's best girl, while Trimble was on the second-story balcony of the lake house, looking out at Reelfoot, that magnificent lake created by the New Madrid earthquake of 1811, when the Mississippi River ran backward. How Flattery said he enjoyed the company so much he invited the extended family next time.

Midnight. Stillness. Cigar smoke swirled and whiskey fumes filled the air and the now gave way to the near future. The recent past lingered for one last sip. The recent past then bowed and was gone, to haunt some other poor souls, or to sleep it off, one. A single guitar note was struck, somewhere far off, a song being written, some begotten ballad or reel.

Trimble sighed and nodded to the near-empty bottle of Three Queens on the table beside. The bottle now did levitate a little and pour a splash into the seafarer's glass, then likewise did the same for Cheatham's. The two men sipped and smoked and talked a little, not a lot, about love and levitation, the cruel turns of life, the high cost of free will, and the hangovers they'd have tomorrow, if the end of the world didn't come and save them.

Cheatham began to tell about the whole sordid tale of the woman he was supposed to have slain. Katherine was her name.

"Slain," said the first chicken, like he was part parrot now.

"Anyway," Cheatham said, then said no more for a few sips.

Another guitar note, a third and a fourth. A song beginning to suggest itself. Fingerpicked notes began to swirl, like that cigar smoke. A horn section came in, from some other time or place. A mournful sound, like the earth heaving its last. A female voice from up above, drums from down below. No, switch that. The singer singing:

Long thin strands of cotton blow
Like limbs of ghosts across the road

And Cheatham told it all, the whole sordid tale, or anyway told parts enough that could be pulled together, stitched and cobbled, into something like a narrative or police report, or cautionary tale.

The night turned darker. Their cigars like tiny flares, the only light for miles. If the world was ending it was not making much of a fucking show of it. The world ending not even with a whimper but with an unpaid light bill.

"You still there?"

"I am."

"You think the world's ended and it's just us?"

"Hmm. Looks like the meek were misled."

The first chicken said that.

The small hours. Talking in the dark.

"You remember that year, ten year or so ago?"

"The Year of I Can't Breathe, they called it?"

"The Year of We Never Fucking Learn, more like."

"Hell, that's every year in America. Where you want to start? The beginning's a good place. But just pick a year at random."

"Twenty-twenty."

"You think we're paying for it now? Like divine retribution?"

"Sure, why not?"

"I don't know how divine, but yeah. Maybe."

"It's for sure some motherfucking retribution."

"That's the only kind of retribution I know of."

"Can't change our ways to save our lives."

"Change is slow."

"Why's it got to be that way?"

"You ever walk in shackles?"

"I have, yeah. Fairly recently."

"Well then."

Later still. The chickens asleep, even.

"Change this, change that. Change gonna come," Cheatham said. "Change, *shit*. Shit don't change."

Trimble reached in his pocket, pulled out his hand and turned it palm up. Five dimes, three nickels, couple of quarters, smattering of pennies.

"That's change," he said. "It don't ever add up to much."

5

The old, dying writer and his ghost of a wife took a walk. Or rather, she took a walk and he fell in a few steps behind. She carried a sheaf of papers that constituted the latest chapter of his last story. She walked from the house heading east. She lingered outside the window of the room where he wrote, looking in, half-expecting to see him inside there, the ghost of himself. And there he was, sure enough, hunched over that old Hermes Baby, trying to sweet talk the thing. That's a writer for you, she thought—at his writing even when he's somewhere else, out for a stroll with his best girl or old lady. Or maybe it was really him inside and his ghost who was standing behind her, dying to know what a dead woman thought of his latest last attempt to play God. But what difference between them, man and ghost, when the one is a writer?

She picked up a pebble and tossed it against the window. *Ping*. But he did not look up from his writing, lost as he was in his words.

She went on, out of the yard and into the town cemetery. He fell back a few more steps, stopped at the gate and watched her. The cemetery was sprawled on a failed hill, just outside of the town proper. It was as if the local dead had all quit the town but hadn't made it so very far away. The stone walls that surrounded the place were crumbling and the gate was rusted and half-hanging from its hinges. Must be the groundskeeper was on a bender or maybe he'd died, as well.

He stepped inside and stood leaning against the stone wall while she walked up that failed hill and found a tree to sit under. He rolled a cigarette and she took up the sheaf of papers and began to read.

Like handing her his beating heart, he thought, for her to study and weigh and pass judgment on like it's a rhubarb pie up for a ribbon at the county fair.

He walked through the cemetery, lingering when he recognized a name or recalled a story associated with the deceased. Made up a few, even. The ways people die, he thought: heartbreak, gunshot, shove down the stairs. Shiv or shot of poison, lightning bolt or snake bite. Drowned. Trampled underfoot. Bad whiskey. Regret. Duels, though not so much anymore, sadly. He'd liked to have lived in the age of duels. It wasn't the guns, so much, but the gall it took. Oh, to have lived in the Age of Gall. He even missed all the really big wars.

He walked on, down into something like a hollow, the graves leaning in against the slope, like the dead slipping away, then up a rise and saw it, the tree split in two, all those years ago, the night of his youth, that night a tornado killed a force of nature, if you can believe that.

He stood for the longest time just looking at the tree, then went back to find his ghost of a wife, to see if his latest last story was worthy of that ribbon.

"It's sensationalist—pulp work," she said. "It's beneath you. Or I should have thought so."

Her father's daughter, still and all, he thought.

"Everything's beneath God," he said.

"So it's God, still."

"It's always been God. You remember what you said to me that one time? You read something of mine, when I was just starting out. I thought I'd done something bold, thought I'd plumbed the depths and come out the other side, the first one who ever had. But I was strip mining, only. You knew it. You said, Don't play at God. *Be* God."

"I said that?"

"Or it was another woman looked like you."

He didn't look to see if she smiled back. He sat down beside her beneath the tree. It was an old sycamore, looked like it was shot full of holes but still standing.

"You and me both, bub," he said.

"What?"

"Talking to the tree, was all."

He pulled a whiskey flask from his jacket pocket. He unscrewed the cap and took a pull.

"So you don't like it."

"Like doesn't even figure into it. It's not meant to be liked. It's meant to shock, offend."

"Well, I don't know about all that."

"Not just a Black man but one as black as the ink on the page, and strapping as John Henry, and mean as Stagger Lee—"

"Not mean. Just looks mean. A man can't help it, people take him to be mean just because he looks mean, any more than he has a name that sounds guilty."

"—And a woman, named Katherine, who's not just white but white as the page, white as cotton. And not just that but the daughter of a cotton merchant; so, rich, too. And if there was any doubt about that, she drives up in a Bentley. A Bentley, in North Memphis. Of all things in all places. But why?"

"Why a Bentley?"

"Why any of it? Why a fair, pure, white, rich girl—"

"Who maybe didn't want to be any of those things—"

"Is that it?"

"You'd have to ask her. I'm just speculating like anyone might."

"You're the writer. You're her God."

"When has your God ever stopped you from doing what you set your mind to? Hell, your daddy was a might powerful force and you still married me."

"Point taken," she said. "So she was running away from all that, was fair Katherine. But I notice she took the Bentley rather than just hoof it."

The old writer smiled. "I gave her beauty and breeding and a willful nature," he said. "She came by the practicality all on her own." He took another pull of whiskey from the flask. He was beginning to feel better about it all.

"Well," he said, feeling the burn of the whiskey, liking it, that burn.

"But even that wasn't enough, was it?" she said. "A big, mean-looking, ill-named strapper of a man black as letters on a page, and a rich woman white as the page and the cotton her daddy sold in markets across the world. And even with the rich, white woman arriving by Bentley, you were still just two-thirds of the way there, weren't you? So in walks the third, bold as Bessie Smith in her headdress, singing the dirty blues. And of course trouble came with her, or close behind. A love triangle, only minus the love. I guess you have your reasons for the killing being done with a railroad spike and not a pistol. I guess the railroad spike was a metaphor, or maybe just messier. God knows. Or I guess you'd say it was one of those cases where God's creations get up to whatever the hell they want, God forbid."

"I don't really think I'm—"

"Yes you do."

"Well, it takes a lot of nerve, you know. You have to sort of build yourself up first."

"To create a world and all the life in it?"

"Yes."

"Even though it's not real."

"Isn't it?" He handed her the flask, an old silver thing with the initials "WF" in a fanciful font across the front. "I don't think I'd have ever bothered, if I believed it wasn't real."

She took a sip and then thought better and took a swig.

She looked down at the flask, at those initials there.

"William Faulkner?" she said.

He said, "Whiskey flask."

They walked to the gates and there stopped and looked back up at the cemetery, asprawl on that failed hill like some foreclosed heaven. They went walking, on toward home. He walked beside her, or tried to. He walked with the fading gait of a dying old man and she more or less floated, being a ghost and all. "Keep up, old man," she said.

They walked silently back to the house and then he sat in the old, iron chair, and she walked—floated, more or less—to the door. She stopped there.

"OK," she said.

"OK, what?" But he knew.

"What becomes of him, John Henry Stagger Lee Cheatham, or whatever his name is? He get the chair?"

"He didn't kill her."

"I know that. Or I suspected it, knowing you. But does he get the chair? Or maybe the chair in its original form."

The old, dying writer laughed, despite which there was no whiskey left in the flask. He said, "It's true the governor won't stay him, but maybe God will."

"Which God?"

"The one true one," he said.

"Well, it is your book, after all."

6

Meantime: The steamer *Clementine* had drifted off course and come upon a patch of dry earth, about the size of a ballyard or contained battlefield. A tent city of refugees had been erected. The governor was compelled to speak to the crowd. Standing on the bow of the boat, he launched into a long oratory, bits of every speech he'd ever given, no substance whatsoever, let 'em eat cotton candy.

Finally, someone near the front of the crowd, an old man wearing, inexplicably, an old woman's bonnet, said, "Did you bring help?" He pronounced it "hep."

"Not help," said Governor Trey Flattery. "Only hope."

"But is help coming?"

The governor talked around the question, at great length.

"Just tell it to us straight," the bonneted old man said, finally. "We can take it. Tell it straight. Tell us the truth."

The crowd took up this last word and turned it to chant.

Truth! Truth! Truth!

Silence now.

All eyes upon the governor.

A piece of paper was handed him. He read it over a couple of times, and then looked up to the crowd with something like a grim smile.

"The truth," he said, with attempted profundity. "Well, the truth is a whole other matter. It's an elusive bugger. Some would say extinct, by natural means the nature of which is more a matter for Mr. Darwin—"

"Or Buck Owens, either one," someone piped up.

"Yes, well. But dead, either way," the governor continued, glancing again at the paper. "Maybe not from natural causes, though. Foul play, could be. For truth can be dangerous, when disseminated in group settings and situations such as the one in which we find ourselves in today."

"Just tell us the blasted truth," someone shouted from the back of the crowd.

A winning smile now from the governor. It might have come from the ghost of a victorious soldier or a ballplayer who battled and prevailed on this very ground, lo those years ago. He crumpled the paper and tossed it over his shoulder. "Why, I couldn't tell you the truth if I wanted to," he said, arms spread. "Not a simple public servant and man of God like myself."

The crowd, as a chorus: "What's God got to do with it?"

The governor turned petulant and snapped at the crowd.

"God made it rain as punishment for your wicked, wicked ways."

"Not mine," said the old man in the bonnet, brightly.

"I'll refer you to commandment two," the governor said.

"I didn't know she was your wife!"

A scuffle broke out. A shot was fired in the air. But it all died down as quickly. Order was restored, the wisecrackers shouted down.

The governor raised his hands to the crowd, as if he might have been about to attempt some stunt or miracle.

But he only said, sober as all that, the rest of what had been written on the paper: "My fellow Tennesseans. Hear me: Truth, like proof, is alcohol content times two."

Silence all around. Heads scratched.

From somewhere deep in the middle of the crowd a voice shouted out: "Fuck's that supposed to mean?"

A man nearby said to the man who shouted, but loud enough for all to hear, "I believe it translates to the Latin as *in vino veritas*. You know. He's saying if you get a man soused enough, he just might let a little truth slip!"

The crowd, as one, nodded knowingly. The mob mentality turned thoughtful, of all things.

Silence again, and then the old man in the old woman's bonnet took a step toward the steamer *Clementine* and said: "Stand you a drink, Guv?"

7

The old priest they called Father Time watched the rain from the picture window in the front room of the rectory. He could hear, faintly, over the rain, the return of his friend, the one they called Old Man River. The latter walked in from the kitchen with fresh coffee.

"What was it you said earlier?" said the old priest, whose name was really Father Tim. "That thing I said you ought not to say?"

Old Man River, whose name really was Rivers, was old but not as old as the priest. He joined his friend at the window and handed him a mug. "I said God doesn't live here anymore, Father. He used to, but He's gone. He moved."

"Moved," the old priest said.

"Higher ground, I'd suppose. I would recommend the same for us. They say the flood has reached Mulberry Street."

The old priest stared out the window and tried for a smile. "I don't know about the flood, my friend. But God is everywhere." It sounded rote as he said it; it was like a prayer that way.

"Oh, I've been lots of places God isn't, Father."

"Now, now."

"You ever been to Scab, Oklahoma?"

"There's not a town in Oklahoma called Scab. I feel sure of it."

"Not saying it was a town, Father. Just saying there's a place and that's what they called it. What they called it, the day I was there. Didn't take much imagination to call it that, what I saw of it. I was passing through. When I was driving the truck, you know. Had to make Topeka by dusk. Always having to make someplace like Topeka by dusk. That's a real place. Topeka. I think that's an Indian name, meaning—"

Old Man River took a seat near the window—the old wingback, the bishop's chair, when he came to visit old Father Time on one of his diocesan jaunts from Little Rock. He sipped the coffee and wondered. "I think it means, 'Here comes the white man again. Hide our pelts and daughters.' Something like that." He laughed a little, then looked to see if he was having any success taking his old friend's mind of all that worried him—his Sunday sermon, mostly, but this rain, too. Weeks of it, and now harder than ever. He'd never seen such a violent display; maybe, he thought, this is the beginning of the end of it all. Well, fine, he thought. I've had a good run. Or, anyway, a long one.

The old priest just stood watching the rain, grim-faced. He closed his eyes and listened to it now: like fists, it was, thousands of them beating on the Italian-tile roof of the old rectory, like something desperate to get in and have their say.

This was Friday morning, a small Arkansas river town. The old priest was writing his Sunday sermon—well, thinking about thinking about writing it. This was his routine, his ritual. He wrote it first in his head, usually standing by the window or pacing across the plank-wood floors of the rectory's front room. The creak or sigh of a plank might suggest a word, God working in those mysterious ways about which so much was made. Sometimes he'd sit—but in the straight-back wooden chair, the one he'd brought over from the school library, the most uncomfortable chair in the diocese, he liked to think: a chair for thinking in. Then, when it had all but come to him, nearly whole, he went into the upstairs room he called his office, and tapped it out with two fingers on a 1932 Underwood No. 5. There, in the room he called his office, bare white walls on which hung neither cross nor Christ, those words and thoughts coalesced, and new ones appeared. He sat at a desk by the one window in the room, but never looked out it, and no one—not even God, he thought—looked in. He liked to think it was the one place God wasn't.

It was routine, ritual, but seldom did the words come easily. So he would play with the routine, tinker with the ritual. Some weeks he'd think in solitude, pacing the plank-wood floors. Some weeks he'd go for long walks; always on these weeks he'd wind up at the banks of the Little Red, as if summoned there. Sometimes he needed noise, company, a sparring partner, and so he'd call his friend, and Old Man River would wander over and drink the priest's coffee and prod him with bits of blasphemy and whimsy and bitter wisdom gleaned from a long life, vast travels, and AM radio. He had spent twenty years as a long-haul truck driver and had an encyclopedic knowledge of country music, which he claimed, to small avail with the old priest, explained not just life, but life after. He claimed to be a heathen but the old priest suspected Presbyterian.

"We've been through this," the priest said, glad for the diversion from his Sunday sermon. "God is everywhere. God was, is, and always shall be. God created the world." It sounded more rote even than a prayer; he might have been telling the girl behind the counter at the White Light what he wanted on his sandwich: oil and vinegar, please. *Oleum Sanctorum or Sacrum Chrisma, Padre?*

Father Time sat in an antique cane-bottom chair with his back to the window, facing his old friend. He took a first sip of the coffee and then set it on a small table. "That's house rules, as they say."

"God didn't make honky tonk angels," Old Man River said.

The priest said, "I give you God and you give me Patsy Cline."

Old Man River stood. He seemed to be weighing some decision. He looked at the floor and nodded. The decision thus weighed and decided upon, he went to a cabinet against the west wall and took out a bottle of bourbon. He gave his coffee a splash. "Kitty Wells, that was, Father," he said. "Patsy sang it, but it was Kitty Wells first. She had the hit."

"Anyway, it was just a song."

"I could say the same of 'Amazing Grace.' "

"That would be something like blasphemy, though. So good that you didn't say it."

"A wretch like me," he said. "I never liked that line. I'm no wretch. I have my moments, but still."

"It's just about being humble before God."

"Do you think Patsy Cline is humble before God?"

"Do you think Patsy Cline is in heaven?"

"If it's any kind of heaven at all."

"Oh, it's some kind of heaven."

The priest almost smiled, but only almost. He felt tamped down by the rain.

Old Man River stood before the old priest, gave his coffee a splash.

"Father?"

"Yes?"

"Is it particularly hard to write the big ones?"

"Sermons, you mean?"

"Yes, Father."

"You mean like Easter? Christmas?"

"I mean the end of the world."

"Oh, that."

A smile, then, but not a drop of joy in it.

8

They tried the crank radio. News of the great nation. News of crime, punishment.

A Black man was shot seven times in the back for walking away from a police officer who asked what the Black man had in his hand; the shiny, silver object turned out to be a harmonica. A white man, singer of songs, was charged with cultural appropriation, theft under two hundred dollars; at trial the judge threw out the case and awarded him a lifetime Grammy, in reverse compensatory damages.

News of natural disasters. Comets and fissures and the earth opening up and swallowing whole states. News of loss and woe, and of Cheatham's attorney, who claimed to have found, and then lost, in the flood, evidence which would clear his client of all charges. He quoted from Tennessee annotated code, the New Testament, and Hank Williams's Luke the Drifter alter ego. He appealed to the hearts of good men. He appealed, even, to God. He had given up on the governor.

The DJ came back on and said, "Sad times these are, soggy people. But you remember better times, don't you?" He paused as he cued up another record, "When the Catfish is in Bloom."[25]

He followed the song with a skit, an imagined interview with the governor or his double.

DJ: Tell us, Governor. Are you bringing religion to the savages of Memphis?

FLATTERY: No, they have religion. We're bringing country music.

---

[25]A musical collage by self-dubbed American Primitive guitarist John Fahey, incorporating a police siren, sounds effects from a B-movie about insects or aliens, a military brass band, a sample of blues great Charley Patton, a gospel choir, bombs bursting, a church organ playing the "Wedding March" at somewhere between carnival and warp speed, and the ambient sounds of an agitated crowd, all over the gentle chiming of Fahey's guitar, tuned to open C. A national anthem, perhaps, for a new country rising from the muck and bones of another.

9

The old, dying writer sat alone at the diner counter, drinking his coffee. His ghost of a wife was not in the old house, that he could sense, and the place felt altogether too quiet without her. So he walked into town. It was a quiet afternoon but not calm. The afternoon was freighted, it was fraught. The forecast was calling for more rain, and heavier. A flood coming to the hill country—what would they think of next?

He sipped his coffee. He took in the silence of the diner. Between sips he looked for clues in the coffee, he studied the dark viscosity of its swirls. He saw fronds and streams and other small, furled wonders. He saw curlicues, and spelled that word in his mind and saw the shape of its letters: You could pour coffee into a "u" and drink from it. You could sail down an "s" upon a raft or skiff, disappear down around the curve of its bends. You could scale an "l," or use it as a walking stick. An "i" was a baseball and bat, was it not? You could hit flies and have a buddy shag them, pretend you were Pepper Martin and Frenchy Bordagaray.

Other words came to his mind, or rather passed into it, and the words formed phrases and place names—facts with which a fifth-grader might win a geography bee, or a grown man a bar bet. There was a city or town or village named Jackson in nineteen of the fifty states. Pass Christian was not something to yell at a stock car race, but rather a town on the Gulf Coast of Mississippi, some hundred and seventy miles southeast of the state capital, Jackson.

A waitress appeared and asked him was he enjoying his coffee.

The old, dying writer said he couldn't remember ever enjoying a cup of coffee so much.

The waitress said, "Well." And then, "Can I get you more or do you not want to push your luck?"

He smiled. He sipped the dregs and then stood and left a five-dollar bill on the counter. He told the waitress to keep the change, and then said, "Land of Goshen was in the Delta, but not the Mississippi one."

10

The sun played children's games with the clouds, but the clouds grew tired of such trifling and turned dark.

Two days out of Memphis, a sort of desperation set in aboard the *Clementine*. Nerves were frayed from the long journey west and patience was as short as the supply of whiskey—a cross look could get you a poke in the eye, a sarcastic remark might prompt a pot shot from one of the cheap pistols that suddenly proliferated on board. Children carried them, even. The snotnoses—armed!

The infirmary was overrun with cases of ennui, lassitude, and the blue funk. The ship's doctor, a kindly old GP named Gravesit, ran every test he could but found no real physical symptoms to treat. He declared it to be a psychiatric event, and called on all the mental health professionals aboard to volunteer their services. Only two came forward—a country session musician with perfect pitch, and a washer woman who had once served on the custodial staff at a Nashville suicide prevention hotline that had closed when its neighborhood gentrified. The doctor instead drafted the ship's bartenders into service.

The most-asked question among the ill: *What if we don't make Memphis?*

The second-most-asked: *What if we do?*

All over the ship, arguments broke out, fights ensued. Small boys challenged grown men to duels. Families huddled together in fear, entire country bands hurled themselves overboard. Other of the country artists had artistic crises and vowed to abandon their pop leanings and go hard country, if only God or the ghost of Merle Haggard would spare them.

Passengers started seeing things—snakes, feral gangs of pistol-packing snotnoses, also wild dogs, long-dead kin, and Hank Williams in the flesh, looking for a drink, or the smallest sign that country music as he knew it still lived and breathed. The governor was spied talking to himself—that is to say, another actual version of himself. Some passengers reporting seeing two of everything. Ark Syndrome, was one bartender's diagnosis, for which he prescribed a double.

The good food began to run out.

Want some crackers?

You are what you eat, they say.

Mistrust seemed to be the ship's new religion, giving way to whisper campaigns—innuendo as a second language. The banjo player-turned-teacher, Bascom Holcomb "Bud" Miller, was accused of teaching ideas in opposition to the Big Bang Theory of Country Music. One of the snotnoses had ratted him out, repeating his blasphemies about the banjo's Black roots, and Uncle Dave Macon recording up north in New York City some three years before the Carter Family cut their first records in Bristol for Mr. Ralph Peer in what was accepted by all true believers as the proper birth of modern country music. Charges were brought and Bascom Holcomb "Bud" Miller was thrown in the clink; really the drink, as it were—the former chapel that had been dubbed the Tavernacle by the songwriters Leo Chance and Cig Murphy. So, anyway, he was lonely but well lit, thanks to all the hooch the two had hoarded.

The ship's loud speakers, heretofore used for announcements from the captain, a morning prayer, and the nightly playing of "Rocky Top," now blared nothing but hillbilly songs from the 1930s, hopped-up tunes with smutty lyrics about banging Lulu[26] and the like.

The snotnoses, the ones who weren't running around shooting pistols, gathered on the top deck with their musical instruments, to play a concert for the governor, as their teacher promised would happen, if they worked hard at their craft, like good little snotnoses. There were seven, mostly the sons of country stars who had, under the tutelage of Mr. Miller, come to denounce their parents' music, had come to see it as cheap, plastic, damn near not even there. They still loved their parents, but *damn, people, show some artistic integrity*. For a band name, they called themselves what Patsy Cline called most everybody: Hoss.

They had raided the supply of famous country singers' things, which had been liberated from the Country Music Hall of Fame and Museum as the floodwaters rose. That boy named Colton was wearing one of Willie Nelson's red bandanas and the blue denim shirt Townes Van Zandt was wearing when he wrote "Delta Momma Blues," in the pocket of which he found a pack of smokes said to belong to Waylon Jennings, and a joint that was probably Waylon's too, unless it was Willie's. Colton played a 1957 Gibson J-45 guitar said to be the one Steve Earle bought when he first got to Nashville. Colton was outlaw as fuck, pretty much, though he was scared to sing in front of a crowd. That fell to the girl Casey, doing her best to fill out the dress Carlene Carter supposedly wore that night in 1979 at the Bottom Line in New York City when she announced, "If this

---

[26]Recommended listening, dear Reader: "She's Selling What She Used to Give Away," a 28-song collection of dirty hillbilly music on the Bear Family label, by the likes of Gene Autry, the Light Crust Doughboys, and Roy Acuff and his band performing under cover of the pseudonym the Bang Boys. Randy couplets abound, but the women give (or take) as good as they get—the star of the compilation is Betty Lou DeMorrow of Hartman's Heart Breakers on the likes of "Feels Good" and "Let Me Play With It." Five stars. Smut you can dance to.

don't put the cunt back in country, I don't know what will," not realizing her mama, June Carter Cash, was in the audience with husband, John. That boy Colton tried to get that girl Casey to recreate that moment, but she refused, being a good girl who did not cuss in public, or really at all. She made instead a statement on the sad state of modern country music, introducing the snotnoses' first number by saying, "If this doesn't put the *try* back in country, I don't know what will." Then she went into a Patsy Cline song from when Patsy was pure country, before Nashville ruined her. She sang "Honky Tonk Merry Go Round" and then she sang "Turn the Cards Slowly." The other musicians were mostly just serviceable in their support—Colton could not smoke and strum at the same time, turns out—but the girl Casey's voice carried the day. It carried it back to before Nashville ruined Patsy. Then the child band huddled for a nervous moment and went into its original song, a two-stepper that Hank Snow wouldn't have kicked out of bed for eating Goo Goo Clusters.

I had enough of your naggin'
You ain't my cross to bear
I'm goin' to Sin City
I got people there

By the end of the number, the young musicians had about gotten their shit together enough to be worthy of that girl Casey's voice. Somewhere about the bridge, the tempo gained tremendous speed. The song became a train. Casey raced to catch up. She was near breathless, but somehow sounded even better, just barely holding on. It was a beautiful thing—for the summer of 1950.[27]

---

[27]A stellar year for pure country music, 1950. There was no such thing yet as Elvis or rock 'n' roll, and so the genre could just be itself, none of that pop goes the fucking country shit that's plagued it pretty much ever since. Or are we misremembering? One of the biggest country hits of the year, Red Foley's "Chattanoogie Shoe Shine Boy," was so pop it crossed over. It went to No. 1 on the pop

There was polite applause from a middling crowd and no call for an encore.

Elsewhere about the *Clementine*, passengers gathered at the ship's rails, on the lookout for sea beasts, great whites, or perhaps some sign.

They saw the latter, poking up out of the choppy waters, blue-lettered, campaign-style, proclaiming:
FLATTERY WILL GET YOU NOWHERE.

That night there was an assassination attempt on the governor, but the cheap pistol of a self-described "shade-tree anarchist"—really a protest singer named Henry Lee, aka Durango Slim, aka Joey Coffee—failed to fire. That was one version of the story. Another had it that the assassination was a prank or perhaps political statement, as the pistol was a silent-movie prop and fired not a bullet but a white flag, on which was written in black, block letters: FREE CHEATHAM.

Henry Lee was arrested and charged with incitement, protest singing on an expired license, and dark sympathies. He was arraigned on the top deck, with Bills, the state's senior counsel, standing in as judge. A fair-sized crowd of weary travelers gathered to gawk, glad for the diversion from all their own troubles.

Henry was a young man with a mess of brownish hair and darker brown impish eyes. He was small and thin and wore a shabby tuxedo coat. His battered old acoustic guitar was slung over his back, and a harmonica mounted to a metal contraption like some coat hanger's crazy uncle hung from his neck.

"You play taps on that thing, mister?" Bills said.

"That's not my specialty," said Henry, bemusedly.

"So, you have a specialty?"

---

charts and was covered by Bing Crosby. But hell, it sounded like a Bing Crosby song when Red Foley cut it.

“He’s a protest singer, ain’t he?” someone shouted from the crowd. “I make it protest songs are his specialty unless he dances, too.”

Henry turned in the general direction of the shout. “I got nothing against dancing, if that’s what you mean by protesting.”

“You got something against our state?” shouted another in the crowd.

“Because if you do,” shouted yet another, “we could have you … ”

“You mean like a grudge?” the singer said in the direction of first, and then off toward the second, “You mean like, um, strung up?”

Bills called for order. When the crowd simmered down, he took a step toward Henry Lee. He walked all around him, in his country moseying way. Back around the front, he faced him again and said, “Are you what they say you are, young man?”

Henry Lee laughed. “I’ve been called a scamp, a tramp, a git, a simp, a dirty commie, and the voice of a generation. People have their nerve, calling me the voice of anything. I just sing songs, take ’em or leave ’em.”

“Song and dance man, are you?” came yet another shout.

When the crowd again drew silent, Bills said, “Are you, young man, a protest singer?” Henry Lee pulled his guitar from behind his back. He struck one note and then another, and then laughed as they seemed, those two notes, to chase one another about the top deck and over the side.

“Nah, judge,” he said. “It’s just my love songs, they come out all askew.”

Bills said on the strength of the evidence presented, the state might could make a tight, little case against the alleged protest singer. Henry Lee was ordered held until trial. He was thrown in the clink, with Bascom Holcomb "Bud" Miller. They got on famously, Henry Lee being one of the few musicians on board who had heard of the banjo player's namesakes, Bascom Lamar Lunsford, aka the Minstrel of the Appalachians, and Roscoe Holcomb, inspiration for the term "high, lonesome sound." These were vaunted names to Henry Lee, who said he was only named after the dead philanderer in a murder ballad.[28]

The next day, the two were joined by the songwriters, Leo Chance and Cig Murphy. They had to pick the lock to get in, but were happy to have the company of a couple of real musicians, however incarcerated they were.

They all drank and talked shop and in time fell into a jam session that lasted well into the night.

11

They tried the crank radio. Music and weather and then a breaking news report from the trial of the river walker. Suss Jones had been found not guilty of river walking ("Only

---

[28]"Henry Lee," aka "Love Henry," aka "Young Hunting," a folk song that dates to late-1700s Scotland, later collected as Child Ballad #68—and, most famously, the first song on Harry Smith's *Anthology of American Folk Music*, in a version by West Virginia coal miner Dick Justice. The basic story: When Henry Lee spurns a girl for another he loves far more, the spurned girl lures him back just for "a kiss or two," setting up the murderous rhyme of stabbing him "through and through," with a penknife. She dumps Henry Lee in a well, an act witnessed by a bird who threatens to "sing." A classic murder ballad, then, heading up a subgenre of the form in which men who couldn't keep it in their pants were schooled by women scorned: Dick Justice, indeed!

Jesus could do that," said the jury foreman to the judge, and then to the accused, "And you ain't Him.") but guilty of the lesser crimes of loose talk and hubris. The crowd erupted, the old mob mentality at play; the bleachers were overturned and the judge's robe set ablaze, the jury was chased around the small spit of land, and in the confusion the prisoners escaped, all three. They headed for the water, these shackled three. At the water's edge they all three paused, but Suss only for dramatic effect. Then he plunged forward, dragging the others along. He took one step, two, but was immediately brought down by the weight of his fellow prisoners, who did not share the gift or know the trick. They all three sank like stones and were drowned.

A Shining City Upon a Bluff

One does not appreciate the sight of earth until he has traveled through a flood.

—Mark Twain
Life on the Mississippi

For, lo, they are gone because of destruction:
Egypt shall gather them up, Memphis shall bury them …

—Hosea 9:6

1

One day out of Memphis, the pirates appeared. Well, called themselves pirates and had a ship of their own, originally the *Countrypolitan* but after its commandeering they renamed it the *Soul Queen*, in an attempt to curry favor with Memphis, capital of a new state formed out of West Tennessee from Jackson in, south to North Mississippi and down on through the whole of the Delta, and over to East Arkansas as far west as De Valls Bluff. This new state had not yet been named but had an official soul song ("Melting Pot," by Booker T. & the MG's), official sniper rifle (the Gibson semi-hollow body ES-355 electric guitar), and official religion (pulled pork shoulder).

A high-seas rout ensued. The pirates hung from masts. They swung from ropes. They capered about the decks. They flashed and twirled their swords, even tossed them in the air and tried to catch them. This accounted for the larger portion of the sword-inflicted injuries on this day. They were better with guns. For any goddamned fool can pull a trigger.

They cursed with impunity and immunity. They burned things. They lashed some prisoners to masts and made others walk the plank. They had seen enough pirate movies to know the score.

The country singers were the first to go. The politicians were next. No distinction was made as to hierarchy or chain of command. The governor followed Senior Counsel Bills down the plank, and preceded Commissioner of Correction Lynch. Bills took his time, walking the plank in a country mosey. He shrugged one shoulder, he did the trick knee thing, and when he was asked by one unimpressed pirate if he could hurry it the hell up, Bills said, "I might could," but did not, resuming his mosey.

Governor Trey Flattery, when his turn came, did not go easily unto his watery grave. He smooth-talked. He pulled rank, or tried to. He appealed to the pirates' sense of foul play—

"We're not so different, you and I." In the end, he begged to be lashed to the mast rather than made to walk the plank. He had nearly talked his way into that slow death when Bate, his old, best friend, intervened. With a whisper, Bate swayed them, and so it was that the governor, who could not swim, was shown the plank. Something bad finally had happened to Trey Flattery, and his best friend was behind it. Somehow he knew it would be like this.

Even so, he was Trey Flattery to the end. He fairly floated down and off the plank. He even plummeted with grace. It was only when he hit the water that he began to flail like a panicked child. He was sucked down almost at once.

Lynch walked stoically down the plank, seeming to realize the cruel irony of it all. This was not what he had in mind when he lobbied for more dying but less killing.

Captain Bull Chandler was not seen or heard, through all of this. It was wondered if he had slipped overboard, at the first sign of the danger, and made a swim for it, for his native Kentucky; perhaps he never existed.

Bate was lashed to the jackstaff of the *Soul Queen*, just below the pirate's flag; it fluttered and he drooped. Cruel punishment, he thought, but as long as he was alive he might outwit his captors, for he was a cunning and brilliant man and they were a band of drunken brutes who knew not the first thing about the point of balance for a sword and flung them in the air like majorettes with batons.

Freddie Davidson, the old sports writer, hung a press card from around his neck and began reporting. It was all he knew to do. He was somewhat out of his depth, not being a real news reporter, and this being his first pirate attack, so he just covered it like he would a sporting event. This, also, was all he knew to do. He just had to figure out who was winning and by how much. It seemed pretty clear, pretty quickly, the visiting pirates were whupping up on the home team. It was a rout, sure enough, reminded him of all those Vanderbilt football games he'd covered over the years.

A fortunate few escaped the steamer *Clementine*, huddling in the one room the marauding pirates did not bother in their mad search for plunder. The boy Meems led them there. He told them to be as stealthy as squirrels, and then began humming low an old Church of Christ hymn. He seemed an unlikely hero, and a little daft besides, but they followed him in. It was the room that lately had been the songwriters' lounge, dubbed the Tavernacle, and then was used as the ship's brig, but now was, again, a chapel. In the next few moments, after the empty bottles and ashtrays were cleared away, it became a place of much and fervent prayer, God's ear bent double and filled to overflowing.

Henry Lee the protest singer, Bascom Holcomb "Bud" Miller the banjo player, and the songwriters Leo Chance and Cig Murphy, left the room at once, taking their instruments and what bottles they could carry. Roaming about the Tennessee deck amid all the looting and cursing, they mistook the raid for a party, and were themselves mistaken for pirates, if shiftless ones. They were permitted to go about their way.

Along the way they came upon the famous piano player and his last sidemen. They all became a merry bunch, or at least a drunken one.

The pirates would burn the great steamer *Clementine*, but not before taking a smoke break. For looting was hard work, to say nothing of plunder. The songwriters and their new friends played a few songs, Henry Lee and Bascom Holcomb "Bud" Miller sharing lead vocals on "Big River" and "She's Got Jordan River in Her Hips," and a rockabilly version of the old

Blind Willie Johnson blues spiritual, "God Moves on the Water." They played what was by general agreement the best obscure soul song ever—"Everybody Knows (The River Song)," originally recorded by Memphis' own O.V. Wright, who was rather obscure himself, and unjustly so. Maybe, they all said, it was because his voice was too filled with anguish and his songs with sadness. "Everybody Knows" is about confusion and misery, about sitting by the Mississippi River and watching the fish swim by, about wanting to go to heaven but being afraid to fly. A song for these times, for all times. A song about the human condition, in three minutes and three seconds.

Sad as it was, though, it brought them all up, and they were able to carry on. The last sideman played lead guitar on a Gibson Les Paul Classic with a translucent cherry finish. He could make that thing sound like salvation at last call, like a half pint of penance, like nine miles of bad road, good booze, and gloriously dubious company. He played somber romps and spinning dirges, called to mind what one critic said about him once: that before he took up with the piano player, the sideman had a steady gig giving music lessons to trains.

There was no piano available, but it would not have mattered. The piano player did not deign to play, or to sing, even when the impromptu group dipped into his catalogue for a B-side obscurity called "That Old Slow Death Called Life." It was paid gigs only for the piano player.

It was a festive atmosphere, no matter. Jugs were passed around. Pirates reeled about and altogether forgot themselves. This enabled those huddled in the chapel to make their escape to the life boats on the port side of the steamer. They were led in this escape by the boy Meems, drawing on all the courage, pluck, and gumption God had given him, or that he had found, in himself. It was slow going, for the climb down to the life boat was fraught, and Dolores Blankenship, the state historian's wife, carried cargo more precious than any pirate plunder. As the last of the group was boarding the life boat, a stray pirate appeared.

It was only Meems and Blankenship left on board the *Clementine*, the others safely in the life boat, or nearly so.

"Tell my wife—" said Blankenship to Meems.

"I know," said Meems, who rather felt that he was in movie now, or an actual war, for it felt not at all real. "That you love her."

"No. Well, yes, of course." Blankenship nearly laughed, for he felt he had come alive in one of his beloved books. He had waited a lifetime for this to happen. "But tell her I'll be along directly. I have an idea."

He did not have an idea, per se. But he was a learned man, and the pirate was clearly stewed. No, not just stewed—peloothered. He could outwit him, surely, drawing from all he'd read and studied, all those old generals' tactics and gambits, from Jubal Early of the Confederate States of America to Robert Neyland of the Tennessee Vols. Would it be the sudden attack? The misdirection?

He took the measure of the pirate, who had a bottle in one hand and the other hand free. He dropped into a bit of a crouch—the pirate, that is. He reached for his sword for to slash the state historian to shreds and ribbons, but instead pulled from the sheath the bow from the fiddle that Western Swing great Bob Wills was said to have used in the recording of "Brain Cloudy Blues" and other such classics of the genre. He'd forgotten—he'd traded his own sword to another pirate, being a fan of the Texas Playboys generally and of Bob in particular.

A tense moment now, or anyway, a moment.

The pirate then looked at his bottle, saw that he had but a swig left. He took the swig, said *Ahh*, and grabbed the bottle by the scruff of its neck. He had a weapon, after all, and one which he could more familiarly wield.

The state historian thought of being cut where he stood, and he thought of dying where he fell. And he thought of his red-tressed Lo, so filled with life and spirit and twins.

He approached the pirate, who came out of his crouch and craned his head, curiously, as a dog would. He lowered the bottle but kept a good grip. He had expected the man to run, like a proper coward. It would have worked. Be damned if the pirate was going to chase anyone across the decks at this late stage. The ship would be fully ablaze soon enough.

So the state historian stood now before the pirate, a swarthy man of middle age, unshaven, rumpled, and smelling quite ripe. He took a step closer, against his better judgment. He reached in his back pocket—the pirate, in response, raised the bottle, just slightly—and pulled out his wallet. From his wallet he removed a picture of his wife, his beloved Lo. It was taken earlier that year, in the west of Ireland, on the Cliffs of Moher. It had been a cold day, with rain and wind, and you could barely see her face for the wild red tresses, which called to mind ocean waves, and the absent sun, and Maureen O'Hara in "The Quiet Man." You could only see her lips, a word leaving them and a smile just starting to form. It would be a wry smile, knowing, wise, in love, for the state historian, just before clicking the camera, had told her he could not see the mighty cliffs, for her beauty. He did not smile or laugh when he said it. "You silly, serious man," she said, and started to smile that smile. She smiled for the both of them. He clicked the camera. It was not so much that the winds there in the west of Ireland suddenly calmed or that the rain ceased to fall, in that moment, but that they ceased to be altogether, the wind and the rain, and those cliffs, too. That night or the next, before the fireplace in a thatched-roof cottage in Ballyvaughan, County Clare, the Blankenship twins were conceived.

The state historian held up the picture. "Lo," he said—his wife's name, and his own expression of wonder that he was hers and she was his.

The pirate dropped his hand, dropped the bottle. Dropped Bob Wills' bow, too. His knees seemed to buckle. Was it the power of love? The alcohol? All that plundering?

Whatever it was, one good breath would have toppled him, ass over scabbard.

The state historian punched him in the nose, just to be safe. And ran.

The pirates plundered well, if haphazardly. They rifled through Andrew Jackson's wallet, but finding it empty, tossed it. They likewise had no interest in a portrait of John Sevier, soldier and statesman who was the first governor of Tennessee, though it was painted by the famed Charles Willson Peale. But they snatched up a silver urn, a gift, in 1845, from the Whig Ladies of Tennessee to Henry Clay; the pirates thought it might contain the ashes of Davy Crockett, or Patsy Cline.

Mostly, they took what artifacts they could later barter or sell, and the clothes, of course, would come in handy, for Memphis was a big party town, and one needed a get-up to be noticed. Hank Snow's "Golden Rocket" Nudie suit was a particular favorite and was well fought over. Those Memphis gals did not go for a man in rags.

They kept most of the musical instruments. There was some thought to throwing all the steel guitars overboard, for the pirates, to a man, shared a certain chief of staff's disdain for that piercing, sad-sack whine. In the end, it was decided to keep them. They might come in handy, for torturing. And did, in fact. Soon, the sorrowful sound of the steel guitars, played poorly by drunken pirates, was joined by the anguished wail of Richard Franklin Bate, foiled genius, lashed to the jackstaff of the *Soul Queen*, and there left to die, of heat prostration, starvation, and real country music.

As for Old Smokey, the state's mothballed electric chair, they left it on the top deck of the *Clementine* to burn, considering it altogether too barbarous, even for pirates.

2

They made Memphis on a Saturday with a sky the color of bourbon-barrel char; the neon looked all the better against it.

They made the South Bluff, welcomed there by an old man in a stovepipe hat who said, "There is no hell. There is, however, a Memphis, and it's here the devil lives in relative pain and ease like any man."

"I don't give two damns about the devil," Cora said. "There any word of what's his name?"

"You got to be more specific, ma'am. Boss Crump? The Reverend Al Green? Ol' Chief Tishomingo of the Chickasaw Nation?" The man in the stovepipe hat smiled and tipped that hat, and from it a crow flew. He watched it climb the sky and then looked disappointedly into the dark of the hat, as to wonder why it was just the one crow.

"You know who I mean. Cheatham, they call him."

"Oh, him. Well, you know."

"Know what?"

But the man was deep in the task of fitting the stovepipe hat back upon his head. When he had it just so, he said again as he had said before, "There is no hell. There is, however, a Memphis ... "

She made for the gazebo, the band there. She took a bottle from the horn player and a swig from the bottle and then licked her cracked lips. She looked out upon the crowd of dancers on the dried-mud yard they called a dance floor, and began to sing. She sang murder ballads and gospel novelties about Jesus in an air-o-plane. She sang "Sweet to Mama" and "I Got a Gal." She dedicated songs to God and the devil and the chief of the Chickasaws, to the Rev. Green and the ghost of Furry Lewis and to her good man there in the crowd.

He watched from the wings, thinking, *And I married her. Me, whose history with wild things was fraught, disastrous.* She closed her eyes as she sang, threw her head back and shouted whispers. That's how it seemed to him, when she sang. And he was mesmerized, as ever. Maybe that's all it had ever been, he thought. Maybe she was right—it was not love, never had been. Maybe he collected her, the living ghost—or, more like, he thought, had been collected by her. Company for her better devils. *But my God, that voice.*

After, she asked the horn player, Tippo Jones, "I miss anything, Tip?"

"Never known you to miss a thing, Cora."

"You know what I mean."

"Oh, all that business with Cheatham. Well, funny thing."

"Funny how?"

"Well, people started seeing him everywhere, or said they did. He was over at Roxie's eating burgers and playing dominoes with that crowd, you know. He was driving Isaac Hayes' old gold-plated Cadillac, one with the fur-lined interior and refrigerated bar. He was throwing out the first pitch at Redbirds stadium, and playing center for the Grizzlies. Then the tales got tall. He was seen climbing the Sterrick Building like King Damn Kong. He was ten feet tall, then twenty, then a hundred. Then he caught a growth spurt! But he was sad and spent—everybody agreed on that. Some say he was mourning the loss of his own humanity. Others said it was remorse, for that murder they say he committed. Some expert from the university, professor of something or other, said Cheatham never was flesh and blood man, said he had no heart or soul, gizzard or shin. He was tall tale. Myth. He was a murder ballad walking. He was a story people told themselves. He was made-up, like in a book. He was a bogeyman."

"Poor Cheatham, I guess."

"Poor dead Cheatham. He went down to the river and laid himself down to die, what I heard," Tippo Jones the horn player said. "Head in Memphis and feet down in Vicksburg, Mi'sippi, they say. Displacing so much water along the way, they say, made the '27 flood look like a toddy."

Then he laughed; it was a deep and mellow tone, like you would expect from a horn player. That laugh was like silk had taught bourbon to sing. Then he was gone, off to play an after-hours gig at the mayor's house.

And Cora Flood, she went to find her good man, ready to tell him if he was ready to know, to ask. He was. She could tell by the way he stood waiting for her.

But he held her first, and they began to dance. It was their anniversary, after all. Well, more or less. Hard to know, for the days had become one. So they danced; some music would have been nice, and then it came: just fell from the sky.

The rain was song. It played mad piano rags on the tin roof of the gazebo, funeral marches on the dance-floor muck. They danced, no matter the rain. They danced and she sang it to him, the whole story, truth and all.

It's the one way she could tell him, the one way he could hear it.

3

God, the old, dying writer, and the author walked into a bar. It was a pirate-themed dive in Memphis, called the Cove. "Age before deity," said God at the door to the old, dying writer, who gave God the back of his hand, or part of it, anyway. The author paused behind, watched the bickering pair of them go, shook his head, and then followed them inside.

The bar itself ran the length of the long room, was shaped like a ship, with mast and sails. There were booths along the far wall, which was done up with pirate murals. There were tables in the center, and in the back a band was tuning up, a blues trio, old men, nattily dressed in dark, pinstriped suits, dapper hats worn at rakish angles.

There was a fair crowd for a Tuesday. God and the old, dying writer settled in at a booth. They sent the author for a round. It had been like this all day—the author had been valet and driver and toady just generally; now he was to fetch the drinks.

An old-fashioned for God, four fingers of Three Queens for the old, dying writer, a bottle of Ghost River for the author.

"Want to see the menu?" the author said, mockingly. "Some oysters, to start?" But he was ignored.

"You know your problem?" said the old, dying writer to God.

"Quality control?" God said.

The bickering again, or still. The author pulled a chair up to the booth, since neither God nor the old, dying writer would deign to scoot over and make space. God was facing the back of the room, the old, dying writer the front door.

"You're not ruthless enough," the old, dying writer said.

God smiled. Lifted His glass and tilted it just slightly at the old, dying writer. "The Old Testament?" he said.

"Ah, your early work," said the old, dying writer with a dismissive wave.

God shook His great head and began to say something back, but the band started up. They were three, but made enough noise for three times that. The guitar might have been strung with barbed wire, and the drums could have taught thunder a thing or two. The bass player stepped up to sing. There was a boom to his voice, as if it came from far off and long ago. There was deep river and road dust, soot and cigarettes and whiskey shots. It gave off feedback, that voice. It put words in the air you could practically see.

"Lay your burdens down, baby," the singer sang, "put 'em on the floor there with that dress."

It was the Tchula Three, just back from their co-headlining world tour with Mick and the boys.

4

And lo and behold, and many ticks south of there, the old seafarer Trimble steered the craft for deeper water. It was a fifty-five footer, a real beauty from the thirties, originally built as a staysail schooner but converted sometime later as a yawl, for racing. You expected to spy Bogart in the galley, looking for the scotch, saying to keep it down, for Bacall was asleep in the cabin. But it was empty, abandoned, as Trimble and Cheatham came upon it, some five miles into the Gulf, making do, or trying to, on Trimble's old flatboat. Perfect, Trimble proclaimed it, though in truth he might like to have stumbled upon Emmylou Harris, sleeping in the cabin, Bacall to his Bogart, in "To Have and Have Not," though admittedly he more resembled Walter Brennan's Eddie.

Trimble stood with his starboard lean, the old captain at his watch, looking out at all the water. There was more water than sky and a beautiful shade of blue it was. They were some miles into the Gulf now, and not long it would be time for decisions: west toward Sigsbee Deep and on toward Tampico or Veracruz, or southeast toward Cuba, or maybe on through the Yucatan Channel, South America suddenly in play.

The chickens scratched happily about the decks, as if to say the elegance of their new digs suited them fine. Cheatham was down below in a bunk, sleeping in. Sleeping it off, rather, for they'd hit the busthead hard the night before, and Cheatham's resistance had not yet built back up to its former prodigious state.

Trimble sipped coffee. He tried the crank radio, that pirate station out of Memphis, still coming in, if only faintly so. He sipped and listened. Traffic and weather and the news: the usual, plank walks and other pirate shenanigans, and then, *This just in*: a man resembling Trey Flattery and claiming to be the governor himself, walked up the bluff in Memphis and presented himself to authorities. Said he'd come to abdicate his office, but asked first to make one final proclamation, for the good of the former state and a dead man done wrong. He said posthumous justice was a poor substitute, but we do what we can. He talked with more of a twang than people ever remembered of the governor, but no matter. The request was so granted.

Cheatham appeared on deck a few minutes later. He stretched and yawned and cradled his aching head with those huge hands of his. "Lordy I hurt," he said, braving a smile. "I miss anything?"

Trimble laughed.

"It's a funny thing, but I don't know how you'll take it."

Cheatham sighed, remembered an old death-row joke, one of Shagbark Turner's.

"As the accused said to the accuser—try me."

"Well, they just came on the radio with the news. Seems like you got yourself a pardon, full and unconditional," Trimble said, scratching his chin for show. "Only it was—"

"Was what?"

Trimble just smiled and leaned toward Cheatham for a closer look. He craned his neck, viewing that mighty visage in way almost clinical. He said *tsk, tsk*, and *hmm*. He stepped back, took in the broad shoulders, which slumped just slightly on account of what might be called aftershocks from last night's drinking, not to say a rough few days since his liberation.

"Was what?" Cheatham said again.

"Ah, not to worry," Trimble said. "Some strong coffee and a few days of smooth sailing, we'll have you back from the dead before we hit La Désirade Passage."

Cheatham sat drinking coffee for the longest time, just watching the water, the waves, just listening to the almost-gentle, nearly-soothing sound of the engine, sounding like a hymn, next to the pounding in his head. Then the pounding stopped and it was only dull thuds now.

They were well out into international waters, and the radio began to twitch with strange sounds. Rhythm sticks, guitar spells, a woman's voice singing ghost notes in some fresh new, salty tongue.

"Posthumous, huh?"

"What they said on the radio there, yup."

Cheatham shifted his weight, made to stand but thought better of it. He smiled.

"So I don't exist anymore."

"Happened to me years ago. Kind of freeing, ain't it?"

"So wherever we go, I'm whoever the hell I say I am."

"Maybe give yourself a name other than Cheatham, would be my advice."

"Maybe."

The big man moved slowly, gingerly, toward the front of the boat, mindful as ever of his hangover. He took a seat beside the captain, sipped his coffee.

They sailed on. They were well south of South now. There was no sign of life whatsoever, just the occasional osprey or heron. The chickens would sometimes stop their pecking and look up at their crazy cousins of the sky. The crank radio played dance music out of Martinique, Antillean pop music, Trinidadian calypso, and something that sounded like Haitian carnival music gone dub. A singer sang of love, loss, and of Shango, the African deity. The station would fade and the Gulf waves would take up the song, or change the tune; the waves were, at any rate, altogether musical. Intoxicating, as well. Hair of the dog, then, Cheatham thought, as a tambura played, but gently now, in his head.

They didn't talk for an hour or more, and then:

"Hey Cheat, or whatever you're calling yourself these days?"

"Yeah, Trimble?"

"You think you'll miss America?"

Cheatham laughed. He thought of another old joke, couldn't remember whether he heard it on death row or somewhere else. "If I do," he said, "I'll just reload."

About the Author

David Wesley Williams, a native Kentuckian now living in Memphis, Tennessee, is the author of the novel *Long Gone Daddies*. His short fiction has been published by the *Oxford American*, *Kenyon Review Online*, and such literary journals as *The Common* and *The Pinch*. His stories have also appeared in Akashic Books' *Memphis Noir* and the Harper Perennial collection *Forty Stories*. He plays the musical saw in a cowpunk band called Citizen Cain't. All but the last is true.

Acknowledgments

Portions of this novel originally appeared in somewhat different form as the following:

"Her Better Devils" in Akashic Books' *Memphis Noir* (2015)

"Drinking Beer With Patsy Cline Up in Heaven" in *The Huffington Post* (March 5, 2013)

"Memphis Minnie's Ashes" in *Memphis* magazine (February 2003).

Scott Brown, Brittney Corrigan, Jessica Cuello, Barbara Cully, Suzanne Frischkorn, Victoria Garza, Reginald Gibbons, D.C. Gonzales-Prieto, Neil de la Flor, Caroline Goodwin, Jennifer Harris, Meagan Lehr, Brigitte Lewis, Jean McGarry, D.K. McCutchen, Jenny Magnus, Rita Mookerjee, Mamie Morgan, cin salach, Jo Salas, Maureen Seaton, Kristine Snodgrass, Cornelia Maude Spelman, Peter Stenson, Hugh Behm-Steinberg, Melissa Studdard, Megan Weiler, David Wesley Williams

jacklegpress.org

CPSIA information can be obtained
at www.ICGtesting.com
Printed in the USA
BVHW080834240123
656978BV00007B/559